DIRTY BUSINESS

EVIE HUNTER

First published in Great Britain in 2025 by Boldwood Books Ltd.

Cover Design by Colin Thomas

Cover Photography: Colin Thomas

A CIP catalogue record for this book is available from the British Library.

Paperback ISBN 978-1-83518-100-3

Large Print ISBN 978-1-83518-101-0

Hardback ISBN 978-1-83518-099-0

Ebook ISBN 978-1-83518-102-7

Kindle ISBN 978-1-83518-103-4

Audio CD ISBN 978-1-83518-094-5

MP3 CD ISBN 978-1-83518-095-2

Digital audio download ISBN 978-1-83518-097-6

This book is printed on certified sustainable paper. Boldwood Books is dedicated to putting sustainability at the heart of our business. For more information please visit https://www.boldwoodbooks.com/about-us/sustainability/

Boldwood Books Ltd, 23 Bowerdean Street, London, SW6 3TN

www.boldwoodbooks.com

1

'Still no word?'

Callie Renfrew aggressively stirred the straw in her dirty martini as though she bore it a grudge.

'Not a dickybird,' she replied.

Perched in her sumptuous office in the upmarket Frenchurch Falls Spa with a 360-degree view of the opulent atrium below her, courtesy of the floor-to-ceiling tinted glass, Callie frowned at nothing in particular. A frown was the mildest reaction anyone brave enough to mention her husband's abrupt disappearance from her life without so much as a by your leave was likely to provoke. Most people made a point of pussyfooting around the subject for fear of stirring up Callie's legendary anger. Only her best friends, Angela Dalton and Dawn Frobisher, who were helping her to demolish the martinis at that moment, had the courage to mention Gavin's name.

'It's been three months, Cal,' Angela pointed out unnecessarily. Callie knew to the hour, almost to the second, how long the waste of space had been gone, leaving her to fight off his creditors, assorted heavies, and those who wanted to muscle in on Gavin's turf. She was also having to deal with the increasingly intrusive enquiries from the old bill. It was open season on Gavin Renfrew's missus, no question. 'I know your Gav has always been one for going walkabout, but even he wouldn't scarper for this long without getting word to you. If he's in trouble, he'll need you to get him out of it.'

'Again!' Dawn added, rolling her eyes.

'Out with it, girls,' Callie said, taking a healthy swig of her drink and flicking a long, thick strand of expensively and meticulously styled, red hair over one shoulder. 'You think he's six feet under, or floating face down in the Solent somewhere. You might as well come right out and say it. Don't imagine the same thought hasn't occurred to me.' Callie glanced at the bank of screens that showed her what was happening in just about every corner of the spa, and in the Michelin-starred restaurant that had made the place famous. Both areas of the club were booked up for months in advance. A senior policeman was waiting to be seated. He glanced up at the camera and gave Callie an ironic little salute. 'Tosser!' she muttered.

'There is another possibility,' Angie said, 'and you know it. You just don't want to face up to it.'

Callie scowled at her friend, but Angie met her stony gaze without flinching. 'Yeah. He's run away from his problems and left me to sort them while he shacks up with some floozy in sunnier climes. Of course I know it's possible. Gavin's a creature of habit.' Callie leaned forward, tapping long, beautifully manicured fingertips against the tabletop. 'The thing is, he needs something to live on. His wealth is the reason why the little scrubbers are drawn to him like flies to you know what; he's always been in a position to flash the cash. But he hasn't touched any of his offshore accounts. I know because I have access to them and my phone'll ping if he even breathes on them.'

'Well, he's always known that,' Dawn pointed out. 'He gave you access in the first place in case he got his collar felt and needed you to move things about sharpish. But perhaps he has another stash you know nothing about. If he planned his departure, then it's the sort of thing he would have done.'

'Yeah well, it's possible. Either way, if he has the nerve to show his face here again, he'll wish he hadn't.'

'I thought you two were joined at the hip, despite his philandering,' Dawn remarked. 'I know you still love him, so you'll forgive him eventually. You always do, after you've made him squirm a bit.'

'Not this time. I do have *some* self-respect, you know.'

The three ladies watched a clutch of females in white towelling robes crossing the chequered marble floor two stories below them, chattering away.

'Business appears to be booming,' Dawn said.

'Appearances can be deceptive.' Callie sighed. 'Sure, we're booked out in the spa and the restaurant, but Gavin ran up debts you could only dream about. He's in deep with the sort of people who don't like to be kept waiting. I've bought myself some time, but they're not known for their patience.'

Angie raised an eyebrow as she shared a look with Dawn. 'And they say the age of chivalry is dead. Anyway, what are you going to do?'

'I have absolutely no idea. I sure as hell can't pay. Well... I could but I'm damned if I will. Gavin's dodgy dealings are nothing to do with me.'

'Except that he used this place to channel his ill-gotten gains,' Dawn reminded them all. 'That's no secret amongst the low lives he mixes with, so you won't get away with pleading poverty indefinitely.'

'Why don't you sell up?' Angie suggested. 'This place is a goldmine. You could clear the debts in question and ride off into the sunset. You're not too old to start again.'

'Ha! Forty-eight is getting on a bit.'

'Rubbish!' her friends said in unison.

'Forty is the new twenty or some such rubbish.' Dawn grinned. 'I believe that but then I would, wouldn't I?'

All three forty-something ladies laughed. It was true though in some respects, Callie thought. Times had changed since her mum's day. Women were no longer tied to the kitchen and eyebrows weren't raised if they continued to dress to impress after the dreaded forty milestone. Callie and her friends made full and excessive use of all the treatments available at the spa, battling against the ravages of time with every expensive means at their disposal.

Callie was a natural redhead, Dawn a stunning brunette and Angela's flowing blonde locks had been known to stop traffic. Their colour needed a bit of artificial help nowadays but so what? All three had taken care of their figures and were generally a great advert for the spa. Tired and fraught with anxiety, Callie still felt she was in her prime and far from ready to take up knitting.

'If you decide to cut and run, Cal, perhaps I'll come with you,' Angie said.

'You?' Dawn and Callie gaped at one another. 'I thought you and Paul were literally a marriage made in heaven. You've been together for more than twenty years. Longer than any other couple I know. Longer than you'd get for murder.'

'The honeymoon's over,' Angie admitted with a sad little shake of her head. 'Paul's changed since Gavin disappeared.

He's restless, edgy, snaps at me all the time. I hardly dare open my mouth for fear of upsetting him. I've given up trying to talk to him.' She sighed. 'We always used to talk about everything. No secrets. Well, perhaps the stuff he did with Gav in the early days he kept to himself, but everything else we shared.' She shook her head. 'Not any more.'

'You should have said,' Dawn responded, squeezing Angie's hand.

'He's missing Gavin,' Callie said. 'Well, someone has to, I guess. They were close friends and business associates, for want of a better word. Perhaps he was involved in whatever has driven Gavin away.'

'I've asked him, repeatedly, but he swears he doesn't know why Gavin went or where he is. He won't talk about it, or about their business affairs. Says it safer that way.' Angela let out a heavy sigh and allowed an elongated pause that neither of her friends felt the need to break. 'Okay,' she eventually said on a long breath, 'confession time. Talking of affairs, I think Paul's having one.'

'No!' Her friends both shook their heads decisively. 'He adores you.' Dawn tried to assure her friend.

'Not so you'd notice.' Angie curled her upper lip derisively. 'He hasn't touched me for weeks. He's lost the necessary momentum, so to speak.'

'That *does* sound suspect,' Dawn admitted, frowning.

'If he or George,' Callie said, referring to George Markham, Gavin's third partner in crime, quite literally, 'know anything about what made Gavin take off then you can be sure that Gav's creditors, for want of a better word, would have come on heavy. The fact that Paul and George still have all their limbs intact tells its own story.' Callie plucked at her lower lip and shook her head. 'No, I think Angie's right. If Paul's off in the bedroom department, then there's probably another woman involved.'

'Thanks for nothing.' Angie got up, went to the bar in the corner of the office and mixed fresh drinks for them all.

'Cheers, ladies!' Callie raised her refreshed drink in an ironic salute. 'All men are bastards!'

'I'll drink to that,' Angie said, taking too big a gulp and choking.

'Me too,' Dawn said, giving Angie's back a hefty pat.

'Well,' Callie said after a short, reflective pause during which all three ladies savoured their drinks. 'It seems to me that if we can't do anything to fix my problems then we can at least try and help Angie fix hers.'

Angie flexed a brow. 'How do you mean? You think Paul will tell you what ails him when he barely speaks to me?'

'Babe, you've been married for twenty odd years, have had four kids but are still off the scale when it comes to class, looks and sophistication. If he won't talk to you then he's protecting you from something or someone.'

'Or having an affair,' Angie said.

'Or that, but I still find it hard to believe. I've never known Paul to stray, and he's had more chances than enough. My Gav... Well, that's another story and he'll never change. I know he'll always come back but I'm fed up with being his doormat and was seriously considering getting out even before he did a runner.'

Dawn blinked at her. 'You never said.'

'Didn't get the chance. Gav took off before I finally made up my mind. Anyway, regarding Paul, I think he'll talk to me because he knows I'm juggling the dozen or so balls that Gav left behind. He'll probably be glad to get it off his chest.'

'I'm forty-five!' Angie wailed, still obviously convinced that

Paul's mood had to do with their personal relationship. 'My shelf life is coming to an end, and Paul will be looking to trade me in for a newer model.'

'I'll be after him with blunt scissors if he tries it,' Callie growled. 'He won't be any good to anyone else if he's minus his dangly bits.'

Callie's friends laughed, obviously thinking she was joking. She refrained from pointing out that she could use the practise because if or when Gavin ever tried to crawl back into her life, she would most definitely be castrating him.

'How are the kids?' Dawn asked.

Angie rolled her eyes. 'I've decided not to have any more.'

Callie laughed. 'Four is more than enough for anyone. I can't believe that you've kept your figure and still look like you're twenty.'

'I knew there was a reason why we're besties,' Angie replied, blowing Callie a kiss. 'But to answer your question, they're in danger of going off the rails, all four of them. I blame Paul. He granted their every monetary wish. They've never had to work for anything, so they've never learned the value of money in the true sense of the word. Always had the best of everything, the envy of their friends. As a result, Henry can't seem to stick at any work. Says it's bourgeois and that he doesn't agree with it. Paul used to think his attitude was funny, but he's now started laying down the law, insisting that Henry takes an active role in his car dealership, and it's causing ructions.'

'Is the car business doing well?' Dawn asked.

Angela shrugged. 'I have absolutely no idea. I assume so. It was Paul's first business, and he's kept it going all these years. It's also legit and I get the feeling that he wants to be sure that Henry stays on the straight and narrow. Not that he's ever involved him in any other aspects of his activities. That is one promise that he made early on. The kids wouldn't know how he made his dosh, and I have to say that Paul has always stuck by that promise. But Henry isn't daft, probably sees and hears more than he lets on and likely wants an in. Henry does like easy money.'

'Paul coming down heavy on Henry is something new?' Dawn asked. As a media mogul whom the camera loved, she had a nose for a story.

'He's always thought that Henry's lackadaisical attitude to life was amusing. True, Henry tags along with his dad sometimes to his legitimate business meetings but as far as I can make out, he doesn't actually do anything other than listen and learn. I prefer not to think about what's engraved in his DNA. Paul was a bit of a toerag when I met him and leopards and all that...'

'Where is Paul right now?' Callie asked.

'Away on business, or so he says. With *her,* more like.' Angie hugged her torso, slopping martini over one hand. 'He's been gone for a week. I have no idea when he'll be back, but I do know that I'm glad I took up the post here, Callie. I can never thank you enough for giving me the chance. Apart from anything else, having a career of my own keeps me sane. And away from the kids. Not that they need me any more, but still...'

'No thanks are necessary. You're a natural for the role and a great advert for this establishment.'

Ten years previously, when Gavin had acquired the spa and handed its running over to Callie, the need for a supervisor whom she could trust had made offering the position to Angie a no-brainer. She knew that her friend was bored with being a housewife and needed something to keep her brain occupied as well as lending her a modicum of independence. She hadn't once given Callie a reason to regret her decision. Angie ran the day-to-day side of the business, troubleshooting and keeping the members happy, like a military operation. Word had spread and there was now a waiting list for membership. Callie knew that her friend also kept her earnings tucked away for the inevitable rainy day. Callie hadn't said as much but she feared the mercury was about to take a rapid downturn. It had been on the decline ever since Gavin's disappearance. A disappearance that she was convinced Paul knew more about than he was willing to admit.

A disappearance she would force him to talk to her about.

Dawn asked, 'I assume he keeps in touch.'

'He's been gone for a week. He has always called regularly in the past but nowadays, the contact is spasmodic. He called yesterday, or was it the day before, and said he'd be home in a couple of days. But I'm not holding my breath.'

'Let me know when he turns up,' Callie said. 'I'll have a word with him.'

'Don't interfere, Callie. I know you mean well but I can handle my husband. I *will* talk to him myself. We can't go on this way. I feel a bit like a spare part. Henry's off the rails. The twins are eighteen and not much better. Mark's at uni but failing. He's a bright kid but he parties too much and doesn't study nearly enough. I think he's dabbling with drugs too. He'll be thrown out if he doesn't get his act together but there's no telling him. His dad's the only one he listens to, and Paul doesn't appear to give a shit.'

'Geez!' Callie scratched the back of her neck. 'Who'd have kids, eh? How's Ellie doing?' She asked referring to Mark's twin sister.

'She's supposed to be learning the beauty trade. She was doing well until she hitched up with Frazer Gibbons, one of

Paul's employees at the car lot. He's bad news but Paul seems to think the sun shines out of his backside. God alone knows what he does for Paul, but he's got his claws into our Ellie, and I don't like it one little bit. Paul says he's a good kid deep down and not to let it get to me. Easy for him to say. I barely see Ellie now. She seldom comes home and seems to have permanently shacked up with Frazer. She won't talk to me about it though and we used to be like sisters, discussing anything and everything.'

'You're dealing with this fallout on your own.' Dawn reached forward to squeeze Angela's hand. 'Except you're not on your own. You can always vent to us, and you know we'll do anything we can to help. You just have to say the word. I'm pretty good at knocking heads together, even though I say so myself.'

Angie smiled but Callie could see the tears welling. Their friend was suspiciously close to the edge. Callie recognised the signs because Angie's situation so closely reflected her own, but for the fact that she had an absent criminal husband who'd left her to deal with the fallout as opposed to a possibly cheating spouse and four unruly kids. It was hard for her to decide which situation was worse.

'Go on then,' Dawn said. 'What about Patrick, your baby?'

'Baby? Six foot two and full of attitude. Just finished his GCSEs and doesn't want to go on to do A levels. Doesn't seem to think that the rules apply to him, and he can do what the hell he likes. Well, there's no thinking about it. He *does* carve his own path. He's supposed to be enrolled in college, doing an IT course at the start of the new academic year but I wouldn't put money on his turning up. He's more interested in hanging out with his mates, none of whom I'd willingly give houseroom to.' Angela spread her hands. 'So, there you have it, ladies. My version of happy families. Is it any wonder that I feel like a failure?'

'The kids will come right. Or they won't,' Callie said without an ounce of sympathy in her tone. She wasn't emotionally involved, it was true, but as far as she was concerned, Angie had done a bang-up job with her offspring and had nothing to berate herself for. 'Let them get on with it and be there for them when they need you, is my advice. Not that it's worth much, given that I don't have any kids myself. It's always easier to have the answers to someone else's problem.'

'True,' Dawn agreed, 'but I think you're right. If Angie nags them, she'll only succeed in driving them away. Kids nowadays know it all and won't be told. Besides, they are adults in the eyes of the law, all except Patrick, that is. Let them make their own way, darling, and put yourself first for once.'

'I'm trying to,' Angie admitted, dabbing at her eyes with a tissue. 'What I mean is, I've decided to have it out with Paul. He's either my husband and we're a partnership or he's not. I've had enough of being shut in the dark like a mushroom left to wallow in the wreckage of my family life. He either tells me what's going on or I leave the lot of them to their own devices.'

'Wow!' Dawn said into the ensuing silence.

'You mean it, don't you?' Callie added.

'Yeah. I love Paul. I always have. I've never looked at another man twice since marrying him and God alone knows, I've had enough opportunities. But enough is enough. If he has problems, then he needs to share. I know he's trying to protect me but that ain't good enough. I'm a big girl. I can take whatever it is. It can't possibly be as bad as the scenarios that filter through my head at night when I can't sleep.' She sat a little straighter and discarded her scrunched-up tissue.

'Well then, ladies,' Dawn said, 'it looks as though we're on a mission. Between us, we need to find out what game Paul thinks he's playing and more to the point, what rock Gavin's crawled beneath.'

The three of them raised their glasses and clinked them together.

Callie smiled at her friends, feeling the love. Fresh determination to be proactive in her search for her missing husband coursed through her. Not because she wanted him back. He had shafted her once too often and she had her limits. She wanted to know where he was hiding, convinced that he wasn't dead, and she also wanted to know what he'd dragged Paul into. Paul was a big boy and had been up to his neck in Gavin's various dodgy deals for more than twenty years. So too had George Markham. If Gavin said jump, his two cohorts demanded to know how high.

'Let me know when Paul resurfaces,' Callie said casually.

'Okay.' Angie cocked her head to one side. 'Any particular reason?'

'Idle curiosity. I also want to know when you plan to confront him so I can have your back.'

'Sweet of you but there's no need. If I don't get answers then I'll pack my bags and move in here for a while, if that's okay. Just until I get myself sorted.'

'Blimey! That'll make him stop and think,' Dawn said, looking a little bemused. 'You've constantly been frustrated by him but never once hinted at leaving.'

'Yeah well, everyone has their limits,' she replied and fixed her friends with a determined smile.

2
___

Early the following day, with only a slight hangover to show for the excesses of the previous evening, Callie got stuck into the club's bookwork with renewed determination. Gavin had covered his tracks carefully and there were no obvious signs of where all the additional dosh that went through the books, coming out squeaky clean the other side, actually originated.

Callie had done an accountancy course... well, the first year of it, before meeting Gavin and being literally swept off her feet. But numbers still spoke to her, and she reckoned she knew her way around a spreadsheet better than a lot of the professionals. But she found it hard to concentrate because her mind kept drifting towards Angie's problems. Most marriages didn't stand the test of time, but Callie would have put good money on Angie and Paul's being solid.

She leaned back in her chair, needing to rest her eyes from constantly squinting at the screen as figures danced before them. She really would have to get over her vanity and have her eyes tested, she knew, but right now, her blurred vision hardly seemed important. Angie's security absolutely was, and Callie would do whatever she could to get to the bottom of things for her friend.

'There has got to be something I'm missing,' she muttered, returning her attention to the accounts and going through the receipts that Gavin had given her to cover influxes of cash and corresponding expenditure: refurbishment of the restaurant kitchen, upgrading the jacuzzi, landscaping. All legitimate insofar as *some* of the work had been carried out, but at a fraction of the cost recorded.

She had known all that before starting this re-examination of the books. What she didn't know is where Gavin had got the funds from in the first place. He ran a club called Phoenix on the outskirts of Brighton where the girls entertained some of the town's finest, including a number of high-ranking policemen who also came to her restaurant. Nothing illegal about that. Morals was another matter and not something that Callie was especially concerned about. She couldn't right all the world's wrongs. The girls were well paid and not coerced into doing anything they didn't want to. Callie's conscience was clear, even though she had absolutely nothing to do with the running of the club. Perhaps she should show her face there? She'd asked around when Gavin had first taken off and no one had admitted to knowing a thing. Time to rattle a few cages and get more proactive, she decided.

Callie got up to stretch and then fixed herself a strong coffee from the machine situated next to her private bar. She stood at the tinted glass, watching the flow of people moving about below her, secure in the knowledge that she herself couldn't be seen by them. Their facilities were bursting at the seams again that day, every beautician and masseuse booked solid, but the array of problems she faced precluded her from taking much satisfaction from the success she'd made of a business that Gavin had gifted to her as a hobby. A business that had been a means to an end from Gavin's perspective but which she personally had put her heart and soul into, determined to prove that she had what it took to be a businesswoman and garnering considerable satisfaction from making it so lucrative.

In some respects, she supposed, she had become a victim of her own success. If she hadn't made a go of the spa then Gavin wouldn't have made such free use of it for his own purposes, and she wouldn't now be warding off threats from questionable individuals. But Gavin's pride in her achievements hadn't prevented him from scarpering when things got too hot, leaving her to hold the fort.

Callie resumed her seat but sat upright when it occurred to her that bitterness had driven aside the love she'd always felt for her charismatic husband. Enough was enough. The business she'd worked so hard to establish could be snatched away from her if she didn't find a way to get Gavin's associates off her back.

Procrastinating, waiting for him to swagger through the door with a suggestive smile as though nothing happened and take control was no longer an option. It was time to drag her head out of the sand and fight for what was hers.

Callie drained her coffee mug and, with a sigh, returned to her study of the books.

She hadn't been at it for long before Darren, her PA, put his head round the door.

'Sorry to disturb you, boss, but there's a Philip Stafford here wanting a word.'

Callie let out a long breath. He was one of the questionable people that Gavin had dealings with and the last person she had any desire to see.

'Do you want me to get rid of him?' Darren asked, his handsome face marred by a frown.

'No. Best wheel him in and get it over with.' She closed her accounts screen and sat back in her chair. 'It won't improve his mood if I blank him.'

Darren looked set to argue the point. He was a brilliant employee, more of a friend nowadays, who'd been with Callie for five years. A great gatekeeper, efficient and organised. He kept Callie's diary, filtered her mail both electronic and the old-fashioned variety, protected her from unwanted callers *and* took charge of organising security for the spa and restaurant.

At first, Callie had been reluctant to take on a man in what she looked upon as a female role, but Gavin had persuaded her to give Darren a chance. Gavin had known Darren's farther and owed him a favour, apparently. Tall, tough and ruggedly good looking as well as fifteen years Callie's junior, Darren had never given her reason to regret her decision.

'You sure?' he asked, looking concerned.

Callie often reckoned that Darren knew more about Gavin's other activities than she herself did and that Gavin had put him in her office to keep an eye on her. But over the past couple of years and especially since Gavin had disappeared, Darren had shown unswerving loyalty towards Callie, and she knew that he'd always have her back. Darren had become one of the few stable influences in her life since she'd been left to dig her way out of the mire, and she depended upon him perhaps more than was wise.

'I don't have a lot of choice.'

Callie straightened and flicked her hair over her shoulders as she waited for Philip Stafford to join her. The wait was a short one. A stocky individual with hair in full retreat and belly protruding over his waistband walked into her office with a swagger. The smell of cigarette smoke that clung to his expensive clothing competed with the aroma of equally expensive cologne. She stood to shake his hand, topping his diminutive height by a good two inches.

'Callie. You look delicious,' he said, smacking his lips together and looking at her as though he wanted to eat her whole. His attitude made her skin crawl, and she removed her hand from his grasp with a speed that caused him to frown.

'Hello, Philip.'

She indicated the arrangement of chairs in front of the glass that she and her friends had occupied the previous evening, pointedly taking a single-occupancy seat herself to avoid being pressed up against Stafford on a sofa.

'No sign of the old man then?' he asked.

'Nope. He's gone to ground for reasons that he failed to share with me,' she replied, opting for honesty that clearly surprised Stafford.

'Nice set-up you have here,' he said, making it sound as though he'd never been in the room before. 'Business looks good.'

'We get by.' Callie sat forward, determined not to appear cowed by the man's menacing appearance, albeit disguised behind mohair, handmade shirts and pseudo sophistication. 'Anyway, to what do I owe the pleasure?'

'Gavin still on the missing list, is he?'

Callie tilted her head, thinking they'd already covered that one but unsurprised that Stafford wanted to labour the point. 'The smart money's on his being shacked up with some tart somewhere,' she replied casually.

'The man's an idiot!' Stafford snorted before fixing Callie with a narrow-eyed look of suspicion. 'You sure you don't know where he is?'

'I wish people would stop asking me that.' Callie rolled her eyes. 'If I did know where he's been all this time then I'd have run him to ground before now and he'd be missing a few body parts.'

Stafford roared with laughter. 'That's what I like about you, Callie. You've got balls. Not many people would dare to speak to me with disrespect.'

'No disrespect intended. It's just that when someone asks me a stupid question, I tend to get a bit antsy.'

Stafford's expression darkened. 'Careful!' he warned.

'I take it this isn't a social call but, as you're well aware, I have nothing to do with Gavin's business activities so I don't see how I can help you.'

'I need you to put a few invoices through your books for me, darlin'. Gavin said he'd do it but... well, he ain't here and you are.'

'Your arrangement is with Gavin, not with me. I don't break the law.'

Stafford guffawed. 'Keep telling yourself that.'

'Look, since Gavin had it away on his toes, it's been open season on me. The filth that enjoy the services of this place for free are all over me, wanting to know where Gavin is. God knows why.'

'I can keep them off your back if you do me this little favour.'

'I don't need anyone's help.' Callie folded her hands in her lap. 'Sorry, Philip, you're going to have to find Gavin and get him to do your dirty work because I don't wanna know.'

Stafford leaned forward, getting into Callie's face. His breath was fetid but she didn't flinch. Show the slightest sign of weakness and she knew he'd pounce all over her. She'd learned at least that much during the course of her marriage to a sophisticated villain. 'Think carefully before you turn me down. A lot of bad things happen in the world nowadays, especially to woman who live alone.'

'This isn't the dark ages, Philip. Threaten me and I'll defend myself.' She stood to make it clear that their conversation had come to an end, hoping he wouldn't notice that her hands were trembling. 'Now, if you don't mind, I have work to do.'

'Think about it, Callie. I'll be back. Do the sensible thing and I'll protect you.'

'I don't need protecting, thanks all the same.'

Stafford made an ugly scoffing sound. 'Darling, you're way out of your depth and you know it. Gavin's deserted the sinking ship and left you to try and keep it afloat, but you don't stand an earthly. Those that want to muscle in on Gavin's turf are already gathering and when they decide to swoop, you'll be collateral damage. Never doubt it.'

Callie knew he was right but said nothing. Instead, she pressed a button and Darren appeared almost immediately to show Stafford out.

'How's your dad?' Stafford asked him as he walked through the open door. 'Is he out on licence yet?'

As soon as the door closed, the trembling started in earnest. Callie was sorely tempted to take a shot of brandy to steady her nerves, but it was only eleven in the morning. Besides, she wouldn't give Stafford the satisfaction of knowing that he'd gotten to her, even though he wasn't there to see her reaction. He would know what he'd done, though. Thugs like him used intimidation like a badge of honour.

'What did he want?'

Darren returned to the office so quietly that Callie didn't hear his approach and started violently.

'Don't do that!' She placed a hand over her heart. 'You trying to finish me off?'

'Sorry.' Darren sat in the chair beside hers. 'He's a nasty piece of work and, just so you know, he doesn't make idle threats.'

Callie fixed Darren with a prolonged look. Throughout their five-year working relationship, Callie had remained friendly but professional. Not once had she asked Darren personal questions, aware that he'd been installed in her office originally because Gavin wanted him there. Now Callie couldn't imagine managing without him. But they had never crossed that professional line before. Darren hadn't asked after her business, and she hadn't considered involving him.

'Your father is in prison?' she asked, buying herself some time by answering his question with one of her own.

Darren nodded. 'Manslaughter,' he replied. 'He was banged up over six years ago now. Won't be out for a while yet.'

'I see.' Callie asked no further questions about his crime. She didn't want to know. 'I'm glad you haven't followed in his footsteps.'

'It was a close-run thing, I won't lie. Flirting with the law was all I knew.' Darren ran a hand through his wavy hair. It fell beautifully back into place again, skimming with his eyebrows. 'Having the police knocking on a regular basis was something we got used to in our house and it would have been too easy to take the... well, the easy way out.'

'Why didn't you?'

Darren chuckled. 'I'm claustrophobic. Can't stand enclosed spaces.'

Callie laughed too. 'Ah. A good enough reason.'

'I did some office work, bookkeeping and stuff, jumping from job to job. Then Dad got convicted and Gavin offered me a place here. I've found my niche and not looked back, thanks to you.'

Callie thought that was a little too simplistic. She trusted Darren, as much as she trusted anyone, but her suspicions were still on high alert. 'Why are you telling me this now?' she asked.

'Because men like Stafford don't piss about, Callie. If you don't give him what he wants, then he'll crush you. Never doubt it.'

'And if I do, he'll never let me off the hook.'

'One step at a time.'

'He wants me to put some dodgy cash through the books.'

Darren nodded. 'I thought that would be the case.' He fixed Callie with a speculative look. 'You did it for Gavin.'

'Gavin's my husband and he set me up in this business. I knew what I was getting into.'

'Well, when Gavin comes back—'

'We've got beyond that point.' Callie stood and restlessly paced the length of the office. 'It seems to me that I have two choices,' she said, opting for transparency. She needed a sounding board and Darren had proved his worth. And, she thought, inhaling sharply, she was flattered by his attentions. She had fifteen years on him, but she could tell by the way he looked at her that he liked what he saw. Was she really so starved of affection that she could be so easily influenced? What did that say about her neediness? 'I can either sell up and ride off into the sunset, or I can try to find out where Gavin is and why he scarpered.'

'Sell up and start again,' Darren said without hesitation. 'You're in over your head here.'

'Really?' She turned on her heel and glowered at him. 'What do you know that you're not telling me?'

'Nothing.' He pushed his hands towards her, palms first. 'Straight up. I have no idea what Gavin was in to, but I did grow up in a criminal household. My father and Gavin were involved in... well, something.'

'The person your father killed.' Callie's insides roiled. 'You think Gavin was involved in some way?' She widened her eyes. 'You think he killed him on Gavin's orders?'

'I have absolutely no idea, but it would explain why he suddenly took an interest in me, wouldn't it? If Dad took the fall for Gavin, then he's not saying. But I do know that my mum and my siblings have been well looked after while Dad's been inside, and I got this opportunity. Criminals take care of their own. It's an unwritten code.' He waved an apology. 'Sorry if that sounds harsh, calling Gavin a criminal, I mean.'

'No need to apologise. We both know you're not lying.'

'I wouldn't have said anything, but I recognised Stafford from when my dad was still in the game. And he's bad news, Callie. A hard man, heavily into drug dealing, who always gets his way, no matter what he has to do to make it happen. I'm reckoning he had some arrangement with Gavin and probably wants to muscle in on his territory now that he's gone to ground and shown no signs of returning.'

Callie sighed. 'By forcing me to launder money through the books.'

'The course of least resistance?'

'Frenchurch Falls is not a laundromat. I'm proud of what I've achieved here, leaving aside the dirty money, and I want it to be successful in its own right. I won't have others muscling in. I'd rather pack it in.'

'Well, I can understand that, but you've got a problem in Stafford. He won't take no for an answer, you can't sell up overnight and he won't ask quite so politely the next time.'

'I'm aware of that,' Callie snapped.

'Yeah, I guess you are.'

Callie paused to consider her options, such as they were, grateful to Darren when he left her to her cogitations. 'What do you actually know about Gavin's whereabouts?' she asked, turning on her heel to watch his reaction as she posed the question.

'Nothing, and that's the God's honest truth. I was as surprised as you when he legged it and I have no idea where he is.'

'You must have heard whispers.'

'Because my dad's banged up?' There was an edge to his voice and Callie wondered if she'd offended him. But then again, he was the one who'd opened up about his father's situation and so she bit back the apology that sprang to her lips.

'Because you come from that world,' she replied unflinchingly. 'There are always rumours and I don't believe you haven't listened to them.'

'Word is he had a run in with some hard people and needed to lay low. Never thought he'd be gone for this long, though.'

'What hard people?'

Darren shook his head. 'I don't know but I can ask around.'

'Do that.' Callie paused. 'I'm thinking he's taken a prolonged holiday with female company. That's his usual method when he needs to keep a low profile.'

'Well, if that's the case then he hasn't shown his face anywhere in Brighton.' Darren grinned. 'I've been putting out feelers and no one's seen hide nor hair of him.'

'Right.'

Darren's emphatic response depressed Callie. The fact that he'd been trying to trace Gavin worried her. What was his angle? Could she really trust him? Perhaps Gavin really was dead. Perhaps it would be as well if he was. It would make her life easier, she thought, ruthlessly shoving aside her emotional reaction, but only if she could produce a body. That was the only way she'd ever get the Staffords of this world off her back, and perhaps not even then.

'Okay. It was just a thought.'

'You could use the detectives that Gavin had in his pocket to get rid of Stafford.'

Callie shook her head before Darren stopped speaking. 'Grass, you mean? I'm not suicidal.'

'Yeah, forget it. That was a stupid idea.'

'Not necessarily, but if I get desperate, it could be a last resort.' Callie threw back her head, struggling to ward off a headache. 'For now, I need you to try and find Gavin for me. Try really hard please, Darren. It's the only way I can see out of this mess.'

'Consider it done.'

She resumed her chair and smiled at the guy. 'Thank you,' she said softly. 'I can trust you, can't I?'

'100 per cent. I'm firmly on the side of the angels.'

Callie laughed. 'That lets me out then.' Her expression sobered. 'Since you appear to have connections I knew nothing about, perhaps you can try and track down Paul Dalton for me while you're at it. My friend has misplaced her husband, and I need to talk to him.'

Darren flashed a smile and pushed himself to his feet. 'I'm all over it,' he said. 'Oh, and don't forget there's the charity auction tonight. You said you'd be there. Who are you taking? You can't go alone.'

She smiled at the younger man. 'Do you have a tux?' she asked.

3

Darren left her, smiling broadly and assuring Callie that he knew how to dress to impress. She just bet he did! Gavin had always seemed envious of Darren's ability to attract women based on nothing other than his looks, comparative youth and natural charm.

Callie had never discussed her PA's private life with him. She wondered idly if he had anyone permanent in his life or if he was still playing the field.

'Get a grip!' she muttered, wondering why she was dwelling upon something so inconsequential when she had far greater concerns to struggle with.

She transferred her thoughts instead to Darren's sudden urge to probe into her private affairs. Why now? Had she done the right thing by letting him get a foot in the door? She was ordinarily so careful, but he'd caught her at a low ebb. Besides, he would have known who Stafford was. He was vulnerable too, she realised, since Stafford would be aware of his family background. She needed to know more about Darren's siblings. Were they on the straight and narrow or had they followed in their father's footsteps? Perhaps Stafford had used them to get Darren to do his dirty work for him.

'Be careful!' she told herself, feeling better for speaking aloud to the empty room whilst simultaneously wondering if she's lost the plot.

Of course, it was always possible that Darren was in secret contact with Gavin and spying on his behalf. She shook her head, chasing the thought away before it could take hold. She and Gavin hadn't parted on bad terms. If he *was* Gavin's eyes and ears, he was more likely to be charged with finding out how Callie had dealt with all the shit that had come her way since her cowardly excuse for a husband had left her in the lurch.

From Callie's perspective, Philip Stafford's unwelcome visit had forced her to abandon the blinkers. She had been marking time, going through the motions, just like she always did when Gavin did a runner. She'd kept things ticking over as she waited for him to come swanning back into her life and resume control. Several guys who claimed Gavin was in debt to them had paid her a visit since he'd legged it, but she'd been able to fend them off. Stafford, she knew, would not go as easily.

'Pathetic!' she cried in exasperation as she forced herself to take an impersonal look at the way her life had turned out and not much liking the view. She wondered why she had permitted herself to become such a pathetic doormat. She was a strong, independent woman who'd made a success out of her business. She could do anything she set her mind to, and that did not include being a patsy in her husband's complex web of deceit.

She worked steadily through the books for the rest of the day, going right back to the start, making notes, a plan forming in the periphery of her subconscious. Someone was pulling

Gavin's strings, that much was given. Someone powerful enough to make him scarper, which worried Callie because beneath all that superficial charm, Gavin was as hard as nails and didn't scare easily. That being the case, Frenchurch Falls had to have been the brainchild of someone he looked up to. Someone who'd been pouring money in and out of the place since day one.

Someone who Gavin had crossed.

Callie threw her pen aside and leaned back, tired, dispirited and temporarily defeated. She could find dozens of questionable transactions but had absolutely no idea where they'd originated from. Going through the receipts filed online, looking for clues, was the obvious way to go. People got sloppy, made mistakes. The problem was, there were hundreds of them, and it would take forever.

Unless...

Unless she took a chance and put her trust in Darren. He was a whizz with paperwork and if there was anything to be found, he'd find it. Even so, her mind went full circle. Could she trust him? Whose side was he actually on? She was too long in the tooth to be seduced by a pretty face and a dose of unfiltered flattery. She *was* flattered by his concern for her, but she'd seen it all during her nearly thirty-year marriage and knew better than to take anyone at face value.

But still, she reasoned, set a thief to catch a thief and all that. If she opened up to Darren and asked him to scour the receipts for clues about the origins of Gavin's ill-gotten gains, and if he was reporting back to her no-longer-quite-so-beloved husband then Gavin would know she was on his case. And he also knew her well enough to realise that when pushed too far, she had a tendency to push back.

Hard and ruthlessly.

'Beware the female of the species when she's pissed off,' she muttered aloud.

Decision made, she'd talk it over with Darren during the charity auction, gauge his reaction and trust her instincts. God alone knew, she had precious little else to go on and Philip Stafford would not hold back for long.

* * *

Angie was a lightweight when it came to alcohol and had definitely gone way past her limits with the girls the previous night. But sometimes, it was necessary to numb the pain for a few brief hours in an effort to forget about the mess and worry her life had become. She was glad in retrospect that she'd opened up to them about Paul and the kids. The relief of a burden shared and all that. She should have done it long before. Not that Callie or Dawn could do anything to sort her dysfunctional family but at least they would be there for her, unjudgmental and squarely in her corner, willing to let her vent and offering useful advice. Callie, with all her connections, might even be able to figure out what game Paul was playing. Angie had sensed her keenness to get involved; perhaps because it would divert her mind from her own myriad of problems.

Yeah, the booze had hit the spot right enough, and loosened her tongue, but she knew the moment she opened her eyes that she would be paying the price for the rest of the day. She sat up in bed and groaned as she reached for a pint glass of water and downed half of it in one long, inelegant swallow. She glanced at the clock and swore. Bugger, it was past nine. She needed to get the kids sorted and off to school.

She pushed back the covers but then remembered that she

had no kids to organise. Even if any of them had been at home, they were beyond the age of needing anything from her. That was part of her problem, she supposed: empty nest syndrome. She fell back on the pillows again as the pain of realisation competed with her hangover and gave it a run for its money. She swung her legs sideways, expecting her feet to bump against the comforting presence of Paul's body, just starting to run to fat around his midriff.

Nothing.

'Where the fuck are you?' she asked aloud, angry now rather than worried. Perhaps airing her dirty linen had woken her up to the fact that she'd become too dependent on a man who she'd thought would love her unconditionally for the rest of her days. 'Stupid!' she muttered, aware that the majority of men were incapable of monogamy and often, when they reached Paul's age, suffered a mid-life crisis that required putting it about a bit to prove... well, something.

She didn't have to work today and so wondered what to do with herself. The hours hung heavily on her hands and the temptation to crawl back beneath the duvet and sleep for a month was compelling. With renewed determination, Angie sat up and this time did push the covers aside. She was through with hiding. A long shower would set her to rights and then she'd get her act together.

Angie had just finished drying her hair when the doorbell sounded. She abandoned the straighteners and answered it.

'Oh, it's you.'

She turned away from Tom Travis, Paul's manager at the car showroom. She detested the way that he always looked at her like he was imagining her naked and briefly considered closing the door in his face. But he might conceivably have come with a message from Paul, who didn't always trust phones for his more sensitive communications, so she turned away from Tom and left the door swinging open. He stepped into the hall behind her and closed it after him.

'I could have hoped for a warmer welcome.'

'Born optimist, are you?'

'How you been, Angie?' he asked, seemingly undeterred by her hostile tone.

'What do you want?' She glanced at the admittedly attractive younger man as she spoke, wondering if he had a permanent someone in his life. What a weird speculation to have had at that precise moment, she thought dispassionately. She knew absolutely nothing about his private life and was perfectly content for it to remain that way. Besides, Angie would bet the farm that he wasn't the monogamous type and felt a brief moment's pity for any female who hoped he'd settle down to her alone. Paul, for all his faults, had always put her first. Well, until recently anyway.

'A coffee would hit the spot.'

'There's a Starbucks down the road. I'm about to go out so whatever you've come for, make it quick. Paul isn't here.'

'He's not back yet then?' Tom sauntered round Angie's lounge, hands shoved casually into the front pockets of his jeans. 'Have you heard from him? A few people are getting a bit lairy and he's needed at the showroom.'

Angie finally looked at him and could sense the worry beneath the casual veneer. 'You don't actually know where he is either, do you?'

'Wouldn't be here if I did, darling.' He winked at her. 'Well, I would if I thought you'd be pleased to see me. And if I could be sure that Paul wouldn't find out. I don't have a death wish.'

'Cut it out, Tom.' Angie sighed. 'I don't know where Paul is but I'm guessing he's doing a bit of business somewhere, or else hanging out with some female. He'll turn up.'

'You realise that Henry's on the missing list too.'

'Henry? My Henry?' Angie stopped dead in her tracks and gaped at him. Tom had her complete attention now. 'No, he's around.'

'When did you last see him?'

'I expect he's with Sonia. He hangs out at hers a lot.'

'Try calling him.'

Angie turned on her heel, ready to tell Tom to take a hike, but something held her back. She *hadn't* seen Henry for over a week, now she came to think about it. That wasn't unusual but he did usually ring her once every few days. An angry oldest child who wanted to be like his dad but felt protective towards his mother; loyalties divided. He probably knew a lot more about Paul's activities than she herself did. Paul had promised that none of their kids would become involved with any of his dealings that were even slightly suspect. She'd believed him at the time, but now she didn't know what to think.

'Okay.'

Angie nodded distractedly, her mind in overdrive as she picked up her mobile and hit Henry's number. It went straight to voice mail. She left a message asking him to ring her.

'What does this mean?' she asked, cutting the call and looking directly at Tom.

She wandered into her massive kitchen, all granite surfaces and stainless-steel appliances, and made Tom the coffee he'd said he wanted. He nodded his thanks, sat on a stool at the island and sipped at it.

'That I don't know, but what I can tell you is that some unpleasant people have been at the showroom asking for Paul.'

'Who?'

'Philip Stafford for one and him, I will not mess with.'

'I know the name.' Angie sat opposite Tom, leaned her elbow on the island and her chin on her fisted hand. 'I think he's someone that Gavin knows. I've seen him around the Falls a few times. Nasty piece of work who radiates hostility.'

'You got that right, darling, and I don't scare easily.'

'You imagine he'll come here, assuming I know where Paul is.' Angie disliked the fact that her voice wobbled.

'I wouldn't discount the possibility. You might be better staying at the spa until Paul resurfaces.'

Angie briefly considered that option but as quickly discarded it. 'I won't be driven from my own home. I have an alarm, and cameras. And Mace. Besides, Paul's associates will know that he doesn't discuss his business with me so why would they bother coming here?'

'Because they think you know where he is.'

'But I don't!' she wailed.

'You and I both know that, but I'm betting you have some idea, if you think hard enough.'

'Don't patronise me!'

'Sorry.' Tom held up a hand by way of apology. 'Just have a care.'

'What's he got himself involved with?' Angie surprised herself by asking. Although perhaps it wasn't so surprising, given that she was desperate to find Paul, to say nothing of her son, and that Tom was the best person to help her.

'I honestly don't know, love. I'm no boy scout, I'll be the first to admit it. I fetch and carry for Paul and knock heads together when necessary, but I'm way down the food chain and know not to ask questions.'

'But you see and hear stuff. He runs his business out of the showroom.'

'Only sometimes. I think he and Gavin Renfrew have got themselves into something they can't handle.'

'What?'

Tom held up a hand. 'I have absolutely no idea. It's just a gut feeling. Besides, Paul and Gavin going on the missing list at the same time is one coincidence too many, don't you think?'

'I don't know what to think.' Angie absently tugged her hair over one shoulder, pulling at the ends hard enough to make her scalp tingle. 'Paul never disappears without at least letting me know when to expect him back, even if he doesn't tell me where he'll be. But it's different this time.' She fixed Tom with a penetrating look. 'Not to put too fine a point on it, I'm worried.'

'I know. Me too and I'll make no bones about it.'

Angie took a moment to mull the situation over. Tom left her to cogitate, obviously comfortable with the heavy silence and not attempting to tell her what she ought to do. She was grateful for that, even though any advice at that moment would have been welcome.

'Look,' she said, coming to a decision. 'Callie has offered to put out feelers and try to figure out where Paul has gone. To say nothing of why. You might know stuff that will help her. Can you come to Frenchurch Falls at about five tomorrow?'

'I could be there,' Tom said cautiously.

'I don't want to make you feel uncomfortable but it's in all our best interests to get to the bottom of this mess before the Philip Staffords of this world muscle their way in.'

He drained his coffee and stood. 'Okay, darling, take my mobile number.' He reeled it off and Angie programmed it into her phone. 'Call me day or night if you have any concerns. I can be here fast.'

'Why are you so concerned about me?' she asked as she walked with him towards the front door.

'You shouldn't have been left in the dark like this. It ain't right.'

His explanation didn't ring true. There had to be more to it than that but now wasn't the time to probe. 'Well, thanks anyway.'

'Besides, it's nice not to have you giving me the cold shoulder.'

He winked at her and disappeared through the door. She waited until he turned a corner at the end of the road and there was nothing left to see before slowly closing and bolting the door. Tom had spooked her so it was better to be safe than sorry.

Seated back at the kitchen island, Angie admitted to herself that it felt good not to be on her own any more, even if she didn't entirely trust Tom. He had reasons for wanting to find Paul that didn't match her own, of that much she was sure, but that didn't really matter. Any port in a storm and all that. Besides, the goalposts had changed. Her eldest child was on the missing list and finding Henry was now her priority.

Angie folded her arms on the island and lowered her head onto them, physically and emotionally exhausted. She couldn't take much more of this. There was nothing to tie her to this gilded cage any more, she realised, glancing dispassionately around her luxury kitchen. The kids didn't need her, nor did they listen to her. And now Paul didn't seem bothered about her wellbeing either.

She'd find Henry, make sure he was okay, and then it would be time to put herself first.

4

Callie eschewed the 'safe' black and defiantly pulled on a shiny, red sheath that skimmed her body and made all those hours of sweating away in the gym and watching her diet worthwhile.

'I've still got what it takes,' she said aloud, examining her reflection from all angles and feeling as though she didn't have anything to apologise for. Callie didn't obsess about her weight, but she did remain active and was a slave to yoga. *Never drive if you can walk. Take the stairs, not the lift*, had always been her mantras.

She had been hiding herself away since Gavin's latest disappearance, she realised with a jolt. She always did. She got tired of being asked where he was and seeing the knowing looks exchanged between the cattier of her female friends. Gavin was an attractive guy so it followed he must have a bit on the side somewhere because Callie could no longer satisfy his needs.

Perhaps that was true, but she wasn't about to apologise for her husband's inability to keep it in his pants. She still had a lot to offer, she reminded herself, thinking of the success she'd made of the spa. She was through with keeping a low profile and tonight, she'd pull out all the stops. She and Gavin had donated a meal for four at Spartacus, Frenchurch Falls successful restaurant which was booked up months in advance, to the charity auction. Gavin loved these events. They gave him an opportunity to put it about and to come across as the big benefactor, thumbing his nose to the police who attended, some of whom were in his pocket, many of whom wanted to be.

It occurred to Callie now that Stafford was the first of many who would close in on her, thinking she was an easy touch, because Gavin had been on the missing list for longer than usual. Gavin had been planning something big; that much she did know. He'd made obscure comments about an upcoming turf war. She hadn't taken much notice, aware that he wouldn't tell her anything she didn't need to know. Now, she wished she'd pressed him for details. Stafford was one of his main competitors for control of the various rackets they both worked in the area, but for the fact that Gavin didn't have anything to do with drugs. Well, as far as Callie knew, he didn't. She felt as though she no longer understood the man she'd married. Gavin and Stafford maintained a civilized attitude when social-ising, but Callie knew that either one would cheerfully cut the other's throat without breaking a sweat.

She figured Stafford must have done something to make Gavin take off, but hell if she knew what that something might be. Her thoughts turned to Darren, who definitely knew more than he was letting on. If only she could find out if something out of the ordinary had got the two of them at one another's throats then she would be able to decide if discretion was indeed the better part of valour.

In other words, sell up or front it out.

Callie returned her attention to her make-up and knew she looked as good as she ever would. Her hair had been freshly coloured that week with blonde highlights threading through the red. She'd had it blow-dried into a tumble of curls at the spa that afternoon. Her nails were freshly manicured, and diamonds sparkled on her fingers, at her neck, and dangled from her ears.

'You'll do,' she said, blowing herself a kiss in the mirror as she slid her feet into four-inch stilettos. She'd probably lose all feeling in her toes before the night was out, but it would be worth it, just to make a statement. *Hey world, I'm not finished with you yet!*

She'd just sprayed herself with her favourite perfume when the doorbell rang.

'Right on time,' she muttered, her confidence already taking a downturn as she went to let Darren in.

Doubts about her date's loyalties resurfaced but it was too late to back out. Besides, it would do her ego no harm whatsoever to be seen on Darren's arm, even if she had to endure snide remarks about cradle snatching. It was unfair, she thought, that men could date women twenty or thirty years younger than them and it was accepted as the norm, but if it happened the other way around, she'd be branded as a cougar, or worse. Not that Darren would be anything other than her guest, she reminded herself. She wasn't looking for a fling, or a sympathy shag, but still, their appearance together would definitely set tongues wagging.

'Wow!' Darren stood back when she opened the door, subjected her person to a prolonged scrutiny and expressed his approval in that one word.

'Thanks,' she replied, opening the door wider and letting him in. 'You don't scrub up so bad yourself.'

That, she thought, was the understatement of the century. In his tux, with dark hair flopping across his brow and an irreverent smile playing about his lips, he looked like he'd stepped straight from the pages of a gent's magazine.

'Drink?' she asked.

'Why not.'

He took the chilled bottle of champagne from her hands, expertly popped the cork and filled two crystal flutes without spilling a drop.

'What shall we drink to?' he asked as he handed a glass to her.

'Prosperity,' she replied, taking a grip of herself. It was a business engagement, no more than that, and she'd been around too long to be seduced by a wicked smile on the face of a man almost young enough to be her son.

Hold that thought!

'Prosperity it is then,' he said, clinking his glass against hers.

They drank in silence for a moment or two. Darren glanced around the large and Callie hoped tastefully furnished room and through the folding glass doors to the bar and indoor swimming pool beyond.

'Nice,' he said.

'Yeah.' Had Gavin never brought him here before? she wondered. Presumably not. 'Gavin bought the plot, fought with the council to get planning consent and we designed the house ourselves. That was twenty years ago, when we still hoped to fill it with raucous kids, but it didn't happen.' She sighed. 'Perhaps in retrospect, that's just as well. Angie reckons her four are all out of control.'

'Kids are a big responsibility.'

'How many siblings do you have?'

'Three. All younger. Two brothers and a sister. My sister's

married and has three brats but I think if she had her time over then she'd reconsider the procreation bit.'

'What about your brothers?'

'They're into this and that,' Darren replied vaguely. 'I don't see much of them, but we all keep in touch with Mum.'

'As you should. Hopefully, Angie's lot will realise what their mother has done for them in the fulness of time. What about a significant other? Are you thinking of following your sister's example?'

He shrugged the question aside. 'I'm too insecure to settle down. I wouldn't wish myself on anyone.'

'In other words, mind my own business.'

Darren laughed. 'I guess I just haven't met the right woman yet.'

'Why tie yourself down to one when you can play the field.'

Darren shuffled his feet, looking uncomfortable. 'Something like that. Anyway, I took it upon myself to increase the security levels at the spa,' he told her, making it clear the subject of his romantic conquests was off-limits. 'I hope you don't mind. Given Stafford's threats, I thought it was sensible to ensure the guys are aware of a possible problem and remain alert.'

Callie opened her mouth to protest but then closed it again without speaking. Of course he'd done the right thing. She ought to have thought of it herself. 'The restaurant kitchen too?' she asked. 'It seems to me that tampering with the food and giving our customers gip would be a good way to make his point.'

'On it,' he assured her. 'Don't worry. No one who isn't supposed to be in that kitchen will gain access. All deliveries are being left in the scullery and checked by François personally before being used.'

Francois was the French chef whose reputation had helped to enhance the spa's popularity. He was a stickler for detail and didn't leave anything to chance. Callie breathed a little more freely, knowing that Darren had covered all the necessary bases.

'Thank you.'

'Just doing my job, boss.'

Callie took a swig of her champagne. The bubbles went up her nose and made her sneeze.

'I guess we'd best get going,' she said, putting her glass aside.

'Eric's waiting outside,' Darren told her, referring to her chauffeur.

'Okay then. Golf club here we come.'

Darren helped her with her coat, then opened the door to let her pass through it ahead of him, the ultimate gentleman. Perhaps a little too polished.

Eric nodded when they appeared. 'Evening, Mrs R.'

He opened the rear door to the Mercedes E Class that he drove for Gavin. Callie had swallowed her pride when Gavin had taken off and had quizzed Eric as to his whereabouts. If anyone knew where he'd got to then she'd assumed it would be Eric, but he genuinely seemed to be as much in the dark as Callie herself. Anything he did know about Gavin's life away from the marital home he was keeping to himself, and Callie had too much pride to push him on the point.

'I've just completed the purchase of that extra land adjacent to the spa in the hope of turning it into a golf course,' she remarked as the car purred smoothly along the quiet back roads. She had not involved Darren in the acquisition process. 'I know there are a lot of golf clubs in the area, but I've done some research, and they all seem to be oversubscribed. That being the case, I'm taking a chance of there being room for another. I can't see anyone objecting since the land is unsuitable for building.'

'Golf never goes out of style. You'll need to get planning permission, as well you know. I'll put out a few feelers if you like.'

'Thanks. Do that. But quietly. I don't want the world to know about our plans. Gavin didn't think it was worth the effort, but Gavin ain't here and it's me making the decisions now.' *If I decide to keep the spa*, she thought but did not actually say. The stronger her empire became, she reasoned, the harder it would be for Philip Stafford *et al* to bully her.

Callie sat a little straighter. It felt good to exert herself. She knew Gavin hadn't been keen on the idea simply because the spa was a means to an end, a glorified laundromat from his perspective. It hadn't been part of the plan for Callie to put it on the map quite so comprehensively. She was a victim of her own success in many respects and wondered now if that success had been the reason why Gavin had taken off. The Staffords of this world had the spa in their sights. Was there some kind of turf war? She shook her head, wishing her brain would switch off, just for a few hours so that she could enjoy her evening.

'What is it?' Darren asked.

She was acutely aware of his close proximity within the confines of the luxurious car. She could smell the earthiness of his cologne and feel his breath on the side of her neck as he leaned in a little closer.

'It's nothing.' She waved his concerns aside. 'Anyway, we're here.'

Eric pulled the car to a halt at the front steps to the club and then got out and opened the door for Callie. She thanked him as she slid from the vehicle and straightened her dress.

'Ready?' Darren asked, offering her his arm.

Callie hesitated and then placed her hand on it, appreciating the old-fashioned gesture. Darren could probably sense her nerves and was doing everything he could to put her at her ease. An instinctive gentleman or was he trying to gain her trust?

'Good evening, madam.'

Callie smiled at the woman who stepped forward to take her coat, and then walked into the reception at Darren's side. Several heads turned in their direction.

'They are going to think that I haven't wasted any time replacing Gavin,' she said with a nervous little laugh.

'Do you care what they think?'

Callie smiled up at him. 'Actually no,' she replied, accepting a glass of champagne from a waiter's tray and realising that it was true. She really didn't care. 'If they're talking about me then I guess it gives someone else a rest.'

'That's the spirit!'

Darren seemed totally relaxed and completely at home amongst some of Brighton's finest. If he noticed the quizzical and admiring glances sent his way by several women, then he made a good fist of ignoring them. She thought about the snippets he'd let slip about his family connections and couldn't help admiring the way that he'd put his past behind him, opting for the path of the straight and narrow. Well, as far as anyone connected to Gavin could be regarded as legit, she reasoned, herself included. She didn't indulge in criminal activity and Gavin went out of his way to exclude her from that side of his life. Even so, she knew it went on and allowed her business to be used for money laundering. That made her complicit, didn't it?

'Callie!'

Callie inwardly groaned as she turned to greet Superintendent Fallow.

'No sign of that wicked husband of yours yet?'

'He has some business to attend to,' Callie replied, aware that Fallow had been one of the first detectives that Gavin had cultivated, back when the man had still been a sergeant. He'd been in Gavin's pocket ever since, but Callie knew he'd be worried about Gavin's absence and thinking about his own hide if their connection came to light.

'Well, I hope it won't take too long. He and I have unfinished business.'

'You'll have to take that up with him. He doesn't involve me in his dealings with you.'

'Ah, but my dear, I can't if he isn't here. You, on the other hand...'

'I don't know what it is that you want or expect from me,' she said, taking him to one side and talking in an exaggerated whisper, her voice hard and uncompromising. *Let them know you're no pushover*, she thought. 'Whatever it is, I can't help you. Just hold tight. Gavin will return when he's had his fun. He always does.' She moved back to stand beside Darren, who'd watched the exchange but hadn't tried to involve himself in it. 'Excuse us,' she said. 'There's someone I need to talk to.'

'He's worried,' Darren remarked. 'A lot of other greedy bastards with a lot to lose will be as well. Gavin's disappearance has given them all a case of the jitters.'

'He should be worried. He's had a fortune from Gavin over the years. He won't want that coming out.'

'Gavin's not here to squeal on him.'

Callie flashed a brief smile. 'But I am.'

'You?'

'I learned early on to protect my back.' Why did she feel the need to tell Darren about her safety net? 'I've kept details of payments I shouldn't know anything about: dates, times, favours granted. I can wreck a lot of careers if those involved get heavy.'

Darren chuckled. 'Clever!'

'Nope. More a case of survival. If I've learned nothing else during the course of a thirty-year marriage to a man of Gavin's persuasion, I at least know that it's every woman for herself.'

'All well and good when it comes to someone like Fallow, who's a public servant and could be jailed if it's proven that he's taken handouts, but that won't work with Stafford. Sorry if this frightens you, but you could easily disappear without trace if you cross him.'

'You think I'm not aware of that!' she snapped.

'Sorry, but I need to be sure you know what you're dealing with.' Darren paused. 'Speaking of whom, he's across the room. No, don't look. He's seen us but there's no reason for you to talk to him.'

'Hey, are we late?'

Callie was pleased when Dawn, looking sensational in sparkly, figure-hugging white dress, ran up to her. The ladies embraced.

'Right on time,' Callie assured her.

'Who's this?' Dawn sent Darren a simmering smile.

'Behave yourself!'

'Hey, Darren,' she said, standing on her toes to kiss his cheek. 'I really didn't recognise you for a moment. You know John Shelton, my cameraman. John, my friend, Callie Renfrew and this is Darren Bishop.'

Callie was surprised that Dawn was with John and not her editor boss, with whom she had a love/hate relationship.

John shook hands with Darren and kissed Callie. 'Quite a turnout,' he remarked.

'The good and the great like to show their philanthropic side,' Callie replied. 'To say nothing of dressing up and rubber-nosing.'

'Are you going to cover the event on the local news channel?' Darren asked.

Dawn waggled a hand from side to side. 'We have a junior reporter here, but we won't give it much coverage. Unless there's a scandal,' she added, her eyes sparkling with mischief.

'And if there isn't one, something can always be created.' Callie laughed as she linked her arm through Dawn's. 'You're incorrigible.'

'Is Angie coming?' Dawn asked.

'No. I couldn't persuade her. She's worried about Paul and says she wouldn't be good company.'

'Bloody men! I knew there was a good reason why I've never tied the knot.'

Callie smiled as they made their way to their table, the men sauntering behind them.

'Can you come over tomorrow morning about eleven?' Callie asked. 'Just you. And Angie. I'm going on the offensive. Since Gavin hasn't come back or been in touch, I need to make some decisions. I can't just assume that he'll turn up. It's been too long. I need your suggestions and support.'

'I'll be there,' Dawn said without hesitation. 'Anyway, what made you trot Darren out? Not that I'm complaining, mind. He's very easy on the eye. You should have done it ages ago.'

'I'm married, in case you've forgotten.'

'Darling, it's not me that needs to be reminded of that fact.'

'Yeah okay, point taken.' Callie inhaled sharply. 'I'm fed up with hiding away, Dawn. I've done nothing wrong, but now I have a ton of grief heading my way,' she added, inclining her head towards Stafford, 'and that leaves me with two choices.'

'Fight or flight.'

'Right, and I'm not the flighty type. As to Darren... Well, I have to trust someone and if he is in touch with Gavin then word will get back to my not-so-nearest-and-dearest that I've had enough.'

'Gavin wouldn't want you to sell up. He makes use of the club.'

'Right again, but Gavin isn't here and I'm the one taking the flack. Anyway, this is us.'

There were several people at their table whom Gavin had dealings with, all of whom asked after him with varying degrees of genuine concern. Without exception, all the men scowled at Darren, but their disdain appeared to bounce harmlessly off his tough hide. The ladies on the other hand, fell over themselves to talk to him.

The wine flowed and the conversations got louder, raunchier. Callie played her part on autopilot, conscious of Darren seated beside her and backing her up, not always with words but with the reassuring solidity of his presence. She ignored the spiteful asides that she had known would come and that she was probably supposed to hear about cradle snatching, toy boys and more.

Eat your hearts out, ladies.

An enthusiastic compère started the auction and there was a flurry of bids for fairly mundane prizes: a day at the races as an owner, a spa day at a facility way inferior to Callie's, a case of fine wine.

Then the table for four at Spartacus came up. The

auctioneer built it up, and rightly so. It was by far the best prize on offer.

'Come along, ladies and gentlemen,' the man chided. 'The restaurant is booked up six months in advance. You'll never get a better opportunity.'

The bids rose exponentially, finishing at five grand. Callie groaned. Stafford had placed the winning bid, and Callie was obliged to go up and present him with his voucher.

'What point is he trying to make?' she asked Darren in a quiet aside as she stood up.

'Don't let him get to you. You've got this.'

Applause rang out as Callie joined Stafford on the dais and handed him his voucher. He made a big show out of kissing her cheek. Callie quelled the desire to wipe her face clean and instead smiled for the cameras.

'Don't forget our arrangement,' he said as he placed a beefy arm around her shoulders.

'What arrangement?' She left him standing where he was, his arm hugging thin air, and returned to her table.

'Let's get out of here,' she said to Darren the moment the dancing started.

5

Callie had not been looking forward to showing her face at the auction but against all the odds, she'd enjoyed the raised eyebrows and speculative looks directed her way, thanks in no small part to having Darren as her escort. The spiteful comments failed to bother her. She didn't have the strength to care about what people thought of her. She wondered if news of her outing would reach Gavin's ears and what he would make of it, always assuming that Darren hadn't given him advance warning. She hadn't lost sight of that very real possibility.

Gavin had put it about a lot during the course of their marriage. There was always a swagger in his step whenever he'd got a new conquest, but in his eyes, the same rules didn't apply to her. Not that she'd ever strayed, but Gavin had made it clear to her that he didn't like sharing what he considered to be his property, just in case she was tempted to play him at his own game. He had a vicious temper when roused to jealousy and Callie wondered if her public appearance with Darren, which he would look upon either as a betrayal or as a statement of intent, would draw him out from his hiding place. Either way, it felt good to be proactive.

All actions had consequences though, and she wondered now what affect their night out would have on her working relationship with Darren. Her immediate reaction was to push him away again. It would be dangerous to let him get too close. If whoever was after Gavin thought that Darren had taken his place, then her young assistant would be in the direct firing line. For that reason and others besides, she decided to treat him the same way she always had – friendly but professional. She reminded herself that it wasn't safe to put her trust in anyone, and yet the relief of a burden shared had been palpable at the time of unloading.

It still was.

Darren had been with her for five years and seemed to be entirely loyal to Gavin. It seemed unlikely that his allegiances lay elsewhere and even if they did, since Callie had little idea about Gavin's nefarious activities, there was nothing to be gained from cosying up to her and pumping her for information.

With that thought to cheer her, she was in her office early the following morning, beating Darren to it. She used the time to call Angie.

'Hey,' she said when her friend answered, her voice groggy. 'Hope I didn't wake you. I know it's your day off.'

'What's up?'

'A call to arms is what's up. Stuff has happened and I need to decide what I'm gonna do. I'm through with waiting for Gavin to ride back and save the day. The time's come to fight my corner and I need you and Dawn to help me. Like I say, I know it's your day off, but this is important, so if you don't have plans...'

'I'll be there. It's funny but I'd kinda reached the same decision over Paul. I've talked it through with someone.'

Callie was about to question the wisdom in that, then remembered she'd done more or less the same thing.

'Okay, does this someone have a name?'

'Tom Travis.'

Callie leaned back in her chair, phone on speaker. 'The guy who runs Paul's car place? The guy who has an eye for you? The guy who gives you the creeps?'

'He's not so bad when he's not posturing. Besides, I had to talk to someone; he just happened to knock at my door, and he knows Paul better than anyone.'

'Yeah well, I can't say much. I said stuff to Darren last night that I hadn't intended to.'

'How did it go?' Callie could hear the smile in Angie's voice. 'Not before time that you got a life of your own and I sure as hell wouldn't kick Darren out of bed.'

'Angie!' Callie laughed in spite of herself. 'He's young enough to be my son. Well... almost.'

'Who cares?'

'Get over here and I'll tell you more. About what I said to him and his reaction. There's nothing else to tell, in case you were wondering, and I know that you were.' She paused. 'Bring Tom if you feel you can trust him. I have no choice but to involve Darren. Dawn's coming too.'

'Tom's getting some pressure at the showroom, I think. He didn't actually say in what respect or who from but that's what brought him to my door, wanting to know if I could shed any light on Paul's whereabouts. So, what I'm saying is that I can trust him as much as I trust anyone.' She sounded dubious. 'Well, I think I can. Besides, it's not a question of trust. Paul's gone on the missing list, and I need to find him. End of.'

'Right. I hear you.'

Callie did hear her friend and wished that her situation was as straightforward. Although she hadn't actually committed any crimes in real time, she *did* knowingly launder her husband's ill-gotten gains through her club's books. The fact that Gavin had bought the club and put it in her name for that very reason was beside the point. She knew very well that in the eyes of the law, she would still be considered culpable and probably banged up if the truth came out.

'See you in a bit then.'

Darren arrived just as Callie hung up.

'You're early,' he said, putting his head round her door. 'Anything I can get you?'

'No, I'm good, thanks. But there is something you can do for me.'

'Name it.' Darren replied as he entered the office and sat down opposite her.

Callie was glad that he'd got his business head on too and didn't presume that their night out changed the dynamics of their business relationship. Paradoxically, she was peeved when he didn't even refer to it. Pushing aside her oscillating feelings, she explained about the receipts and her need to find out where the laundered funds had originated.

'It's a long shot,' she said with an apologetic shrug, 'and a laborious slog, but instinct tells me that Gavin's done something here at the club that got away from him. Perhaps he misappropriated someone else's funds.' She threw up her hands. 'I have no way of knowing, but it would explain his abrupt disappearance; if he has heavies after him, I mean.'

'It would explain Stafford's threats, to say nothing of Superintendent Fallow's jitters. Fallow will have his ear to the ground and know what's going on. Gavin's probably isn't the only payroll he's on.'

'Gavin would have to have a death wish to cross Stafford. My husband is many things, but stupid doesn't form part of his DNA, so I think... I hope, Stafford is using his absence to chance his arm.'

Darren waggled a hand from side to side. 'It's possible.'

'I can't explain the feeling I have but I'm convinced something's about to go down.' Callie tapped her fingers on the surface of her desk. 'Or was, until a fallout amongst thieves put the cat amongst the proverbial. Anyway, the answer could well be buried amongst those receipts, and I need to know what it is.'

'I'm on it.' Darren stood. 'Leave it with me.'

'Thanks,' she said. 'Keep this between us.'

'Of course.'

He looked slightly offended, and she regretted calling his loyalty into question. She wanted to say something personal to get things back on kilter but held back. One night out as friends did not make them joined at the hip. Besides, if they got up close and personal and Gavin reappeared, which Callie was still convinced that he eventually would, then Gavin would not take kindly to Darren muscling in on his territory. Callie had no intention of bringing Gavin's wrath down on Darren's head when he was only trying to help her.

Wasn't he?

'I've come to a decision,' she said.

'Oh yeah, what's that then?'

'I need to ring fence my interests and get people like Stafford off my back and the only way to do that is to go on the offensive.'

'Be careful,' Darren advised, frowning. 'The Staffords of

this world don't play by the rules. He's a tough bastard and your gender won't stop him from getting heavy if you don't do what he wants.'

'I'm well aware of that,' she snapped, more sharply than had been her intention. 'Sorry.' She held up a hand in apology when he flinched at her tone. 'It's occurred to me that I've been doing what I always do when Gavin takes off, and that's burying my head, asking no questions, getting on with running this place and obediently waiting for him to come back.'

'I know.'

'It hasn't mattered before because he's never been gone this long but, like I say, the sharks are circling, and self-interest is now my first, my only, priority.'

'Which is why you need to know whose dosh he's been putting through the books.' Darren nodded. 'I hear you. But here's the thing: what help will it be if you find out? That person, perhaps Stafford, will expect service as usual and isn't the type to accept a polite refusal.'

'I realise that but I can't decide how to play it until I know what I'm dealing with.'

'Fair enough.'

'Angie and Dawn are coming over in a bit for a conflab. I'd like you to join us.'

Darren looked surprised but a slight smile graced his lips as he nodded. 'Sure.'

'If we can find Paul, I'm pretty sure he'll know where Gavin's holed up.' Callie went on to explain about Tom, causing Darren to frown.

'I know Tom. A cocky bastard and very loyal to Paul.'

'You're loyal to Gav,' Callie pointed out. 'But I hope you're well and truly on my side in this.'

'Never doubt it.' Darren headed for the door. 'I'll get started on the receipts until they arrive.'

'Thanks.'

Callie didn't move after the door closed behind Darren. She closed her eyes, feeling tired and unsettled, and fighting a headache. She wondered if she should simply put the club on the market and start afresh somewhere else. Business was booming and she'd get more than enough from it to keep her in style for the rest of her life. Her problem was that the books wouldn't stand up to close scrutiny. That truth hadn't occurred to her before, and she'd been holding on to the option of selling up as though it was a life preserver. Now she felt boxed in and thoroughly depressed.

A deep audit would, she knew, throw up all the anomalies Gavin hadn't tried *that* hard to hide. The person who did their books was paid well enough to look the other way and sign them off. So far, the revenue hadn't asked any questions. The police that Gavin had on the payroll managed to prevent the law from raiding the place on some flimsy warrant and putting their own forensic accountants on their books, but with Gavin in the wind, it could only be a matter of time.

'Face it,' she said aloud, 'rocks and hard places don't come into it.'

'Hey, girlfriend!'

Callie's eyes flew open again and she jerked back to full consciousness as Angie breezed through the door.

'Sorry. Didn't mean to startle you. Darren said to come straight on through.'

Callie smiled as she got up to hug her friend. 'No offence, but you look awful. Have you been sleeping enough? Stupid question, of course you haven't. Bastard men! They put us through it.'

'Amen!'

Callie made coffees for them both and they sat on the comfortable seats opposite one another. 'I actually hadn't realised that Henry's on the missing list too,' Angie said, reiterating what she'd already told Callie on the phone. 'What sort of mother does that make me?'

'Henry's a big boy and doesn't live at home any more. Why would you know he'd gone? Besides, he's likely with his dad. It's too much of a coincidence to think they'd both take off at the same time for different reasons. Anyway, you can bollock them both when they deign to return.'

'I don't know…'

'Don't know what, darling?'

'I don't know if I want Paul back. Him taking off without a by your leave has given me time to assess my life and what I want from it. The kids don't need me any more and Paul obviously has another life I know nothing about. But what do I have?'

'A successful career here,' Callie replied without hesitation. 'You don't need that barn of a show house that Paul insisted upon and can quite easily start again with your share, if it comes to that. Not that I think it will.'

'Says a woman who sticks by her philandering husband no matter what he does.' Angie covered her mouth with her hand. 'Sorry, I didn't mean that the way it sounded.'

'You're only telling it like it is.' Callie sighed. 'My problem is, there's no easy out for me, even if he's dead.' Callie went on to explain about the money laundering. 'I don't think Gavin's dead, but I do think he's into something he can't handle, so he's taken the coward's way out and scarpered until the dust settles.'

'Sell up.'

Callie explained why that wasn't an option.

'That's why I want us to put our heads together today,' she finished by saying. 'If we can figure out what we're up against, perhaps we can think of a way round it, and find our husbands into the bargain. Not that I want Gavin back. He's gone too far this time, and I've had enough. But I do want him to buy me out of this place so I can start again without having to look over my shoulder.'

Dawn breezed through the door. 'What did I miss?' she asked, hugging them both.

Callie waved a coffee cup at Dawn as she reiterated what had already been said.

'Finding Paul is probably going to be easier than finding Gavin, who's well and truly gone to ground, the cowardly bastard!' Dawn exclaimed. 'Once we get our hands on him, we can apply the thumb screws until he tells us what's going on and who we need to kill. By use of the media, obviously,' she added, grinning, when Angie looked startled. 'That's almost as effective and we wouldn't have to do time.'

Callie laughed. 'Don't tempt me.'

'Or me,' Angie added.

'So,' Callie said, smiling at Dawn and turning her attention to Angie. 'We need to know all about your night of passion with dishy Tom.'

'What's all this?' Dawn demanded to know. 'What have I missed? Come on, Angie, we need details.'

Angie briefly explained.

'That guy has always wanted to get into your knickers,' Dawn said, once Angie had given them an account of Tom's surprise call.

'You can see why she does so well with the media, Angie,' Callie said, laughing. 'She has such a way with words.'

'Sometimes, you have to say it like it is,' Dawn replied, shrugging.

'Well, Tom's worried, that much I do know, and he's not the type to scare easily. Some heavy people have been round the showroom, looking for Paul. They don't believe Tom doesn't know where he is. And to cap it all, Henry's on the missing list too.'

'Sorry, babe.' Dawn squeezed Angie's hand. 'Bad enough misplacing your husband, but Paul's a big boy. He can take care of himself. Henry, though.' Callie sent Dawn a warning look. 'Sorry. Me and my big mouth.'

'It's okay. Really.'

Darren put his head round the door. 'Tom's here. You ready for us, ladies?'

'Darling, I've been ready for you all my life,' Dawn said, blowing Darren a kiss and making them all smile, lightening the mood.

'Come in, gentlemen,' Callie said. 'Don't mind my friend.'

Tom sauntered into the room ahead of Darren, hands in the front pockets of his jeans, looking confident as he nodded at Callie and Dawn. He was a good-looking guy, Callie conceded, but lacking on the sophistication front. Perhaps that wasn't such a bad thing. Gavin, despite his lowly origins and lack of education, oozed sophistication and look where that had gotten him.

Tom's gaze landed on Angie and was slow to move away again. It was obvious that he cared for her and Callie sensed a glimmer of answering interest on Angie's part. Perhaps, like her, she needed a broad shoulder to lean on right now. It didn't mean anything more than that.

This situation was harder for Angie on a personal level, Callie realised, because Paul had never strayed before, as far as she was aware. But Gavin... Well, what was there to say? Callie was used to his wandering eye and honestly didn't care any more. What did that say about the state of a marriage that had become more of a partnership: a business arrangement?

'Okay,' Callie said once they were all settled, with Tom sharing a sofa with Angie. 'I think you're all aware that I've been left high and dry by Gavin. I have absolutely no idea where he's gone, and I haven't heard a word from him in almost three months. He takes off regularly but never for this long without getting in touch. That said, I don't think he's dead.' She flapped a hand. 'Don't ask me how I can be so sure. It's just a feeling.'

'Don't mean to sound heartless, but if one of his associates had done for him,' Tom said, 'then a body would have been found. They'd be making a point by ensuring that it was.'

'Do you know something we don't?' Darren asked.

'Nope.' Tom spread his hands. 'On my life, I only know what Paul wants me to know, which is that he and Gavin are becoming increasingly legit, but there's an increasing amount of friction between them. Paul resents being second fiddle, is the impression I get.'

'Perhaps someone doesn't want them to be legit,' Callie said, nodding. 'Anyway, working on the basis that Gavin's still breathing, at least until he shows his face here again and then all bets are off, then where the hell is he? Suggestions would be appreciated, and don't spare my feelings. I'm well aware that he puts it about.'

Callie felt bitterness coursing through her veins at having to admit that her husband was a class-A shit. But then, she figured she wasn't telling the guys anything they didn't already know. Besides, if she spoke openly then hopefully they'd return the favour. The time to protect her wounded pride was long past; the blinkers had come off and she was now out for number one.

'The club is the obvious place to ask questions,' Darren said into the ensuing silence. 'Phoenix, I mean.'

'I've never set foot in the place,' Callie said. She glanced at her girlfriends, who both shook their heads.

'They don't encourage female clientele, if you get my drift,' Tom said, but he was no longer smiling. 'Gavin and his partners run some high-class hookers out of the place, and I know Gavin had his eye on one of them. Melody. A Croatian girl. Relatively new on the scene.'

'Is she still around or has she disappeared too?' Callie asked, keeping all emotion out of her voice.

'No idea,' Tom replied. 'I don't frequent the place, but I can find out.'

'Do that, please,' Callie said.

'What about Paul?' Angie asked, clearing her throat. 'He's a partner in the place too. Does he have a favourite girl?'

'If he has then I've never heard anything,' Tom said, smiling at her. 'He makes a point of not mixing business with pleasure.' He fixed her with a prolonged look, causing Angie's cheeks to flood with colour. 'Besides, why would he feel the need?'

'Unlike Gavin,' Callie said, unable to keep a note of bitterness out of her voice. She noticed Darren in the periphery of her vision sending her a sympathetic look. Fuck! She wasn't in the sympathy game and needed to keep this professional. 'Anyway, do you think Melody might be able to help us?' She directed the question to Tom. 'It's the only possibility we have right now.'

'I'm not sure,' he said. 'And even if she could, I doubt whether she'd talk out of turn to me.'

'But she would me,' Callie said, straightening her shoulders. 'Woman to woman. I'd make it worth her while.'

Tom and Darren both shook their heads. 'Have you met Lucy Denton? She runs the club.'

'I know the name,' Callie replied, 'but I don't think our paths have ever crossed.'

'She's more likely than anyone to know what Gavin and Paul are up to. Nothing gets past her. And if she thinks Melody might know something, she'd get her to talk to you.'

Callie tapped her fingers as she considered the situation. 'She must be in the same boat as me, if Paul and Gavin are both off her radar. Open for someone else muscling in, I mean. What security does she have, Tom?'

'The usual. Discreet muscle on the door but nothing more has ever been necessary. The girls are there because they want to work out of the club. The punters pay a lot for their services and know better than to get rough.'

'There is security in the bar area, just in case fights break out, but it's a private club and membership is censored, so there isn't usually much trouble.' Darren shrugged. 'Don't look at me like that. I've been there. Gavin's asked me to help out once or twice.'

'You could do worse than to ring Lucy,' Tom said. 'Have a heart-to-heart with her. Not sure if she's into sharing but there's only one way to find out.'

'No.' Callie thought about it for a moment and then shook her head. 'I don't want to give her the chance to shut me out, which she will if we talk on the phone or if I try to arrange to see her. Better I turn up unannounced. Does she live over the premises?'

Tom and Darren both nodded. 'Yeah. There's a private door at the side.'

'Then that's what I'll do. If she won't talk to me then I'll need one of you to twist her arm but let me try it my way first.'

Darren didn't look happy but nodded. 'You're the boss.'

'Right.' Callie turned her attention to Tom. 'Angie tells me you have people coming at you, trying to find Paul. People you'd prefer not to piss off. Do these people have names?'

'They didn't say, and I knew better than to ask. I've seen them around, though. I think they're part of the O'Keefe mob.'

'Wonderful!' Callie rolled her eyes. 'Stafford and the O'Keefes hate each other but Gavin managed to keep both onside.'

'O'Keefe is, if anything, harder than Stafford, which is saying something,' Darren remarked.

'You wouldn't think Brighton was big enough for all these villains,' Dawn said.

'It isn't really, which seems to be part of the problem,' Callie replied. 'Okay, thanks guys.' She indicated Tom and Darren, who both stood up.

'Get in touch if you need anything else,' Tom said.

'Just let us know if you hear from Paul, or any word on the street,' Callie replied. 'Thanks for stopping by.'

Left alone with Angie and Dawn, no one spoke for a prolonged moment.

'We appear to have a turf war going on,' Dawn said, breaking the silence.

'Yep, I thought that might be the case and if Stafford and O'Keefe are the two main players, perhaps there's an opportunity to play them off against one another.' Callie's voice, filled with bravado, probably failed to hide her jitters. These people were out and out thugs. She'd be playing with fire if she took them on.

'Whoa!' Angie held up both hands, palms outward. 'Just

remember our husbands appear to be running scared. And if they're scared what hope is there for us?'

6

With a hiatus in the conversation, the question of O'Keefe and Stafford hanging in the air, Angie sensed her two friends zeroing their interest in on her.

'What?' she demanded to know.

'You tell us,' Dawn replied, waggling her brows.

'Stop it!' But Angie laughed. 'He's worried about his own backside, which is why he's trying to help me find Paul.'

'Keep telling yourself that,' Callie advised.

'Careful, or I might get right back at you and demand details about Darren. But still, as we're no longer teenagers...'

'What's going on, Cal?' Dawn asked, her expression sobering. 'My journalistic nose is twitching. Potentially one of the biggest news stories in the area for decades and I can't report on it out of loyalty to you.' She pouted. 'Life's *so* not fair.'

Callie smiled. 'Sorry, babe, but your time will come. Like you pointed out earlier in a roundabout sort of way, us feeble females don't need muscle power to go up against the men. Anyway, as to what's going on, I'm guessing here but the mention of the O'Keefes has got me thinking. They and

Stafford are both into loan sharking, amongst other things. Stafford has diversified into drugs. O'Keefe does dodgy property deals, cramming loads of desperate people into inadequate housing. They've coexisted in the area for a while now without treading on one another's toes, but I do know there's not much love lost between the two organisations.'

'You think one is trying to expand by taking over the other's patch?' Angie frowned. 'But what has that got to do with our husbands?'

'I have absolutely no idea, but I reckon that Gavin got involved somehow.'

'He wouldn't need to launder their loan-sharking funds because they weren't obtained illegally. Well, they were if you think about the extortionate rates of interest they charge.'

'Wherever the funds came from, they haven't been run past His Majesty's tax inspectors, which is why they need laundering.' Callie sighed. 'Drugs are easy money, and we know Stafford's name is all over them.'

'Paul wouldn't have anything to do with drugs, no matter how tenuously,' Angie said with more conviction than she actually felt given that she was no longer sure she knew her husband at all. 'We agreed early on in our marriage that we hated the destructive and addictive nature of narcotics and wanted to keep the kids away from them. He would never renege on that agreement.'

'Hopefully not,' Callie said, squeezing her friend's hand, 'but we can't afford to ignore the possibility. He may have got himself dragged into something despite his principles, which is why he's laying low, waiting for the dust to settle.'

'The movement of drugs,' Dawn suggested, looking pensive as she tapped a long talon against her teeth. 'Perhaps Paul's cars are being used, with or without his prior consent, to move drugs around the country.'

'Now you're really scaring me,' Angie said, conscious of the colour draining from her face and ice trickling through her veins.

'It's possible,' Callie agreed, sending Angie an apologetic smile. 'Bear in mind that Gavin's a junior partner in the business and he might have had a hand in getting the drugs moved, willingly or otherwise.'

'It's harder to get them in through the usual ports of entry nowadays,' Dawn said. 'We did a piece about it on the channel. Intelligence is better, and the authorities know where to look as well as who to suspect. So the smugglers have had to get more ingenious.'

'I imagine that private vehicles, or new cars being moved from one place to another for example, won't show up on Customs' radar,' Callie suggested, tag-teaming Dawn's speculations.

'But why?' Angie spread her hands, anxious and on the verge of tears. 'Why would either of them get involved in such a cut-throat and destructive business when they know that Stafford has the local market cornered and wouldn't take kindly to competition? It's not as though they need the money.'

'How much is enough, babe?' Dawn asked. 'I've seen it more times than I care to recall. People comfortably off, living the life and gaining reputations as hard men, decide that they want to up their game, be treated like a real player who's both feared and respected. It's all to do with ego, I often think. Someone they know has got more dosh, more respect, and they want to go one better.'

'Not Paul.' Angie shook her head as she narrowed her eyes

at Callie. 'I don't hear you denying the possibility of Gavin getting involved.'

'Because I wouldn't put it past him.' Callie's expression closed down. 'Dawn's right. He used to have standards: limits he wouldn't cross. Then he started mixing with the great and the good in Brighton, fancied himself as an entrepreneur and well... That sort of thing costs money. But it's more than just money. It's... Well, swagger for want of a better description.'

'Always assuming we're on the right track, do you think they're just doing the logistics or are they trying to get into the distribution game themselves?' Dawn asked.

'Well, I don't think they'd be running scared if they were simply supplying a service,' Callie replied, 'but I still find it hard to believe that Gavin would be stupid enough to go up against Stafford.' She shook her head. 'The idiot!'

'Sorry.' Callie reached across to squeeze Angie's hand. 'What was I thinking? Running my mouth that way. Nothing Gavin does would surprise me, but your Paul has standards.'

'It's not Paul I'm worried about.'

Callie and Dawn shared a glance. 'Henry,' they said together.

'Henry,' Angie agreed, nodding and impatiently dashing at a tear that slid down her cheek. Now was not the time to fall apart. 'What the hell has Paul got him involved with? I'll kill him with my bare hands when I get hold of him.'

'So, if we've got this right then Gavin saw the profits pouring in from drugs because he put some of it through our books and decided he wanted some for himself.' Callie shook her head, glaring at the array of screens showing activity in all parts of the club but probably not actually clocking what was going on. Like Angie herself, Callie was trying to make sense of a senseless situation and scaring herself with the scenarios they'd invented. 'Sorry, but I just don't buy it.' She impatiently tapped her toe against the rug. 'Even if Gavin had pressing money problems that I know nothing about, he was still street-wise enough not to go up against hard men like Stafford and expect to keep all his body parts in the right places. No, we must be missing something.'

'We don't even know that it *is* drugs,' Angie pointed out, an edge to her voice.

'Nope, we don't, but there's someone who might be able to enlighten me.'

'Lucy Denton at Phoenix,' Dawn said.

'Right.'

'Damn.' Dawn looked frustrated. 'I wish I could come with you and hear what she has to say.'

'I doubt if she'll say much to me,' Callie replied, 'but she sure as hell won't talk to a reporter.'

'We're nice people,' Dawn protested. 'Why do we get such bad... well, press?'

Callie grinned. 'Beats the hell out of me.'

'Well,' Angie said, 'if you're going to see Lucy then I'm tagging along.'

'I'm not sure, babe. The chances are that Lucy won't talk to me alone. If we go in mobhanded, it's even less likely that she'll open up.'

'In our husbands' absence, presumably we have some sway,' Angie replied assertively.

'True, I guess, and I know you're worried about Henry. You deserve some answers, so let's do this. If Lucy knows anything, we'll get her to talk. I haven't been married to Gavin for all these years without learning a trick or two of my own and I'm not about to be fobbed off with platitudes and vague denials.'

'That's more like it!' Angie said, looking starkly determined.

'Okay.' Callie glanced at the clock. 'By the time we get there, it ought to be close to midday. I'm guessing that Lucy works nights, but she ought just about be out of bed by then.'

'I have to run along anyway,' Dawn said, looking torn. 'Good luck, ladies. Let me know how it goes and if there's anything I can do to help.'

'We will.'

Dawn embraced them both, then picked up her bag and headed for the door, waving over her shoulder. 'Play nice without me, ladies.'

Callie and Angie glanced at one another and a long silence evolved.

'Are you sure you really want to do this?' Callie eventually asked.

'I've never been surer of anything,' Angie replied without hesitation, glad that Callie had agreed to let her tag along. She'd imagined that her friend might pull rank and try to stop her. She could be that way sometimes. 'Let's do this.'

'Okay. But we might not like what we find out.'

'Anything will be better than not knowing,' Angie replied. 'All the wild scenarios that have been playing out inside my head are driving me mental.'

'I hear you.'

'We're off to track Lucy Denton down at Phoenix to see if she can shed any light,' Callie told Darren as they walked out into his domain.

Darren looked highly dubious but refrained from comment. 'I'll give Eric a bell,' he said instead. 'Have him bring the car round.'

The club was on the outskirts of Brighton, close to the coast. If anyone was watching the place for signs of Gavin, then the ladies would be seen arriving. Angie consoled herself with the thought that anyone wanting to find Gavin badly enough would already have paid Callie a visit. Even so, Angie was glad that Eric would be there to have their backs.

'It's probably odd for Eric to be driving us ladies to what could be quaintly referred to as a house of disrepute,' she said in a quiet aside to Callie, giggling as she slid onto the soft leather of the car's back seat.

'Right. But it will be good to have him with us all the same. He doesn't take shit from anyone. He's not just a driver but muscle too.'

Angie glanced at Eric's very broad shoulders and burly physique and nodded in agreement.

The journey took half an hour and passed mostly in silence. Angie glanced out the window at the passing scenery, thinking that Brighton looked overcrowded, drab and run down. She was glad they didn't live in the city but then chided herself not to think about her luxurious living standards in the leafy suburbs on the borders of Frenchurch village. If Paul really had involved himself with the drug trade, or taken up with another woman, then Angie wouldn't hang around and her comfortable lifestyle would be a thing of the past. Better that and still maintaining her self-respect, she thought, glancing at Callie and wondering how she had put up with Gavin's philandering all these years and held on to her pride. Some women didn't put a lot of stock by fidelity, she knew, but Angie wasn't one of them.

'Not too close, Eric. Stop round the corner,' Callie said, her voice snapping Angie back to reality.

'Best drive in,' he replied, indicating tall, wrought-iron gates that were firmly closed, presumably to deter unwanted visitors or the plain curious. 'No one arrives here on foot.'

Without waiting for a response, Eric lowered his window,

punched in a four-digit code and the gates swung smoothly open.

'You've been here before, Eric,' Angie said with a nervous little laugh. 'I can tell.'

'Brought the boss here once or twice.' Eric drove in and the gates swung silently closed behind the car. 'You sure you don't want me to come in with you?'

'Quite sure. Wait for us here.'

Eric pulled the car around the side of a detached, three-storey house set in extensive grounds, parking up where it wouldn't be seen from the road. Then he got out and opened the door for the ladies.

'Use that staircase there,' he said, pointing to a metal spiral on the outside of the building. 'Lucy's private apartment is on the top floor.'

'Okay,' Angie replied dubiously, breathing in the smell of the sea that she could hear crashing against the cliffs a short distance away.

'It looks so *ordinary*,' Angie said.

'That's the point, I'm guessing. Anything goes in Brighton, but a knocking shop in suburbia that actually advertises its trade. Uh-huh.' Callie waggled a finger from side to side. 'Might frighten the horses.'

'I don't know what I expected but... Well, I guess it's the oldest profession for a reason. Supply and demand and all that.'

'Not all the girls are doped up to the eyeballs. Gavin told me that a growing number of them have business heads on their shoulders. They know their self-worth and understand that they have a limited shelf life. Do this at the high end of the game for a decade, squirrel away the earnings and you're set for life. Some of them have financial advisors, business plans and career moves lined up when they pack it in, apparently.'

'That makes me feel a bit better about what they have to do. I think.'

'None of them at this establishment are forced into the life, Angie. Gavin was at pains to point that out to me when I raised similar objections to yours.'

'Yeah, I know. But still…'

'Come on. Let's see if we can make it up these stairs without breaking our necks.'

Their heels clacked against the metal which moved slightly beneath their weight, but they reached the top without mishap. A stout door barred their way. Callie pressed the bell. They heard it echoing through the flat but there was no response other than the yapping of a dog. Glancing at Angie, Callie placed her thumb on the bell for a second time and left it there.

'There's no one in,' Angie said in frustration. 'We'll have to come back during business hours.'

'There's someone in,' Callie replied, keeping her thumb where it was. The barking increased in intensity and eventually, they heard footsteps clacking against a wooden floor just before bolts were shot back and the door swung open. A woman of a similar age to them stood on the threshold wearing a dressing gown and a frown. Her eyes were puffy from sleep and a tangle of blonde hair fell across her eyes.

'Yes,' she snapped.

'Lucy? I'm Callie Renfrew and this is Angie Dalton. Sorry to wake you but we need to talk to you, and it can't wait. Can we come in?'

Without waiting for a response, Callie pushed past the woman and Angie followed swiftly in her wake. The dog, a small pug, had now gone into a frenzy of barking but Callie simply bent to stroke its head, and the noise immediately stopped.

Lucy opened her mouth, presumably to protest. Then she clocked the determined set to Callie's features and had a change of heart.

'In here,' she said, opening the door to a meticulously tidy lounge. 'Sit down.' She waited for Callie and Angie to take chairs and then sat opposite them. 'I know why you're here, but I can't help you. I have no idea where they are either and I have people asking me. Unpleasant people. Believe me, I'd tell them if I knew.'

'Tell us what you do know,' Callie replied. 'When did you last see Gavin?'

'He was here about three months ago, I suppose. Not seen hide nor hair of him since. Paul was around a bit more recently.' She sent an uncertain glance Angie's way. 'He... Well, he had a thing about... Well, about one of the girls.'

'Name,' Callie snapped.

'Melody.'

Callie glanced at Angie.

'Is she still here?'

'Oh yes. He didn't take her with him, if that's what you mean. Besides...'

'Besides what?' Angie asked, feeling her blood run cold when Lucy's gaze rested upon her.

'Melody and Paul are good friends.'

'Friends?' Callie sent the woman a quizzical look.

'I run the house, not their lives,' Lucy snapped.

'What about Henry?' Angie asked.

'Henry?' Lucy stared blankly at Angie.

'My son. He's on the missing list too.'

Lucy shook her head. 'Don't think I've ever laid eyes on the lad. Do you have a picture?'

Angie reached in her bag for her phone and pulled up a picture of her eldest child.

'Ah yes, I have seen him with Paul once or twice, but he didn't partake of the services here, if that's what you're so worried about. I got the impression that he acted as a gofer for his dad, but I didn't ask. You learn not to ask questions in this business.'

'What's going on, Lucy?' Callie asked, her voice firm, demanding. 'You might not ask questions but I'm betting you don't miss much. Gavin and Paul have got in over their heads with something and now they're running scared. If it's anything to do with this place, even tenuously, then Gavin's tame policemen won't be able to protect you indefinitely so you might as well work with us and try to get to the bottom of things.'

'On my life, I don't know.' She held up her hands. 'Not for sure. But I have my suspicions. Gavin and I had a barny just before he went on the missing list. Technically, I'm his employee but it's my neck on the line if we get busted. Of course, a lot of the old bill are regular clients, so we're protected to a degree but, like you say, there are some things that are beyond protection. For that reason, I made it clear to Gavin before he did a runner that I wouldn't tolerate drugs on the premises and that if any found their way here, I'd be on the phone to the local nick.' She sat a little straighter. 'I'd have done it too. Drugs are bad news. There's nothing glamorous about them. They ruin lives and I don't want my girls anywhere near them. End of.'

'We thought it might be drugs.' Callie closed her eyes and sighed. 'Stafford deals and frequents this place. Gavin has got something going with him,' she added, presumably thinking of his demand to use the spa to launder funds. 'But we don't know what.'

'If he's involved with drugs then he doesn't discuss his business here, Mrs Renfrew. I have an investment in this place and manage it too. It's highly lucrative but Gavin and Paul both knew that if I quit, I'll set up elsewhere alone and take the majority of the girls with me. I have their trust, you see, and they respect me because I put their interests first and foremost. I was in the business myself once, which is how I know what they need, how to treat them and most importantly, to keep them off drugs.'

'Okay.' Callie leaned forward. 'First off, call me Callie. I'm thinking we all have the same problem. It's safe to assume that Gavin, and perhaps Paul too, have severely pissed off either Stafford or O'Keefe. I've already had Stafford in my office and dare say I can look forward to a visit from O'Keefe too in the not-too-distant future.'

'Then there's the question of my son's whereabouts,' Angie added. 'How has he got mixed up in whatever's happening?'

'O'Keefe's been here asking questions about Gavin but there was nothing I could tell him. Stafford too.'

Angie tapped her fingers on her thigh. 'Can I speak to Melody, please? Alone.'

Angie thought at first that Lucy would create problems but instead, she nodded once, got up and put a call through on the in-house system.

'Go down to the front door,' she said. 'She'll let you in and talk to you now.'

'Thank you.'

Angie retraced her steps but before she could ring the front doorbell, it opened and a tall, stunningly beautiful woman with a waterfall of dark hair hanging to her waist ushered Angie inside.

'You are Mrs Dalton,' she said in slightly accented English. 'It is a pleasure to meet you.' She offered a slender hand which Angie shook. She hadn't had time to wonder how she would feel about meeting the woman who was screwing her husband and so was surprised to find herself already predisposed to like her. Paul might be besotted but for Melody, presumably, it was simply a business arrangement.

She led Angie into a large, tastefully appointed lounge with a small bar in one corner and artfully arranged soft furnishings. Even in broad daylight, the ambiance gave off a vibe of relaxation and something more fundamental. Angie almost laughed aloud as that thought struck home. There was clearly more to this business than met the eye.

'How can I help you?' Melody asked, crossing one shapely and impossibly long leg over its twin.

'Paul has gone missing, but I expect you already know that. What you may not know is that my son is missing too and he's only twenty-one. It's Henry I'm more concerned about.'

'Of course you must be going out of your mind and I'm sorry. I wish I could help you. Paul spoke of his son with great pride, but I have never met him. He did not come here, as far as I am aware.'

'I think he must be with his father and that they are running from something.' Angie swallowed. 'I hope you will be able to tell me something, anything, that will help me to find Henry.'

'I am very sorry. If I could then I would but I know nothing. It's safer that way.'

Angie hardened her expression. 'You know nothing, or you are not prepared to tell me what you do know?'

'The first. Paul spoke to me only about his guilt.'

'His *guilt?*'

'Yes, for being with me. Be assured I did nothing to tempt him. It was what he wanted and what I do for a living. There is no emotion on my side. It's purely a business arrangement but men, sometimes they get too involved and then pour their hearts out afterwards because they feel they have been unfaithful.'

'There's no *feel* about it. Paul *was* unfaithful to me. Just because you are a professional sex worker, that doesn't mitigate the betrayal in my eyes. Not that I blame you, but still...'

Melody met her gaze, her expression devoid of all emotion. 'I understand,' she said.

'Mrs Renfrew and I think that Gavin and Paul have got involved with something that got too big for them. Drugs perhaps.' She studied Melody closely as she voiced the suggestion. 'What can you tell us about that?'

'Nothing.' Melody stood and no longer seemed quite so poised. 'I'm sorry, Mrs Dalton. I spoke to you because Paul is a friend, a client, and I want him to be found safe and well. But there is absolutely nothing I can tell you about anything else. And so now, if you don't mind...' She waved towards the front door.

Angie thanked her for her time but left feeling more disgruntled than ever, absolutely convinced that Melody was hiding something.

7

Callie felt awkward being left alone with Lucy, who didn't feel the need to make conversation. She seemed amused by Callie's discomfort, as evidenced by the wry little smile that played about her lips. Why Callie felt so unsettled by the woman's poise was hard for her to decide. She wasn't a prude, far from it, and didn't much care what went on in this house behind closed doors between consenting adults. Nor was she in the blame game. Lucy had a living to make, just like everyone else.

Restless, Callie stood up and strolled towards the window, taking in the view of the leafy suburbs. Angie was taking her sweet time. She wondered what she'd found to talk about to the woman who her supposedly devoted husband had been screwing and half thought about riding to her rescue. Before that idea could take root, Angie emerged two floors below.

'Okay,' Callie said, trying to keep the relief out of her voice. There was just something about this place that made her feel uncomfortable. 'Looks like we can get out of your hair now. Thanks for your time.' She handed Lucy a card containing her personal contact details. 'Keep me posted with developments.

Any news or rumours about Gavin and Paul, I'd appreciate hearing them.'

'I'll do that, but don't come back here, Mrs Renfrew,' Lucy replied. 'I know where to find you if there's anything to tell.'

Callie narrowed her eyes at Lucy, refusing to be intimidated. 'Any particular reason why you'd prefer me to stay away?' she asked in a pleasant tone. 'I'm thinking, you see, that with Gavin in the wind then it's down to me to keep an eye on his investment.'

'Use the sense you were born with!' Lucy finally lost her composure. Not many people, Callie suspected, stood up to her and the woman clearly didn't like being confronted. 'The people who are getting heavy with you are doing the same thing here. Don't imagine your visit will have gone unnoticed. They will assume that you and I know something and that can only lead to trouble for us both.'

Callie resisted the urge to gesture towards the quiet, leafy road beyond the gates and ask who could possibly have seen her arrive.

'If they think we're colluding...' Callie nodded and left without another word, allowing Lucy to think she was calling the shots. If another visit to Phoenix proved necessary, nothing and no one would prevent Callie from making it.

She descended the outside staircase carefully, wondering why Lucy hadn't let her out through the house by more conventional means. An act of petty one-upmanship, she supposed, glancing over her shoulder to see Lucy standing outside the door at the top of the steps watching Callie's precarious progress.

'She's gorgeous!' were the first words to leave Angie's lips when Callie joined her in the grounds.

'So what?' Callie felt disgruntled and spoke more sharply

than had been her intention. 'She wouldn't last long in an up-class establishment if she wasn't. Sorry,' she added belatedly when Angie's face fell. 'Take no notice of me. I got out of bed on the wrong side. Take comfort from the fact that no matter how gorgeous Melody is, she's still reduced to making her living on her back.'

'She reckons she's doing what she does because she wants to, and because it pays so well. But... oh, I don't know.' Angie screwed up her eyes, pausing before they walked back to the car, presumably to gather her thoughts. 'I think I felt sorry for her. She has absolutely no feelings, no emotion, nothing. She's kinda robotic in a glamorous sort of way.'

'I guess she would have to keep emotion out of it.' Callie paused. 'Detach her mind from her body. It wouldn't do for her to get emotionally attached to one of her punters. Sorry!' Callie added hastily when Angie's face flushed. 'Anyway, did she have anything worthwhile to say?'

'Only that she's never met Henry, which is all I really wanted to know. I don't think I care that Paul apparently talked to her about me.' Angie frowned. 'That makes it worse in a way. That he would talk to her about personal stuff, I mean, rather than just screw her and scarper.' Angie looked angry and upset. 'He felt guilty, apparently, for partaking of her services.'

'He probably did. Paul loves you. He's just having a mid-life crisis.'

'Most men buy motorbikes to get over that particular hurdle,' Angie snapped.

'Yeah, good point.'

'Anyway, she says she has no idea where either of our husbands have taken themselves off to.'

'Did you believe her?'

Angie waggled a hand from side to side. 'Perhaps. Probably.

At least insofar as their whereabouts is concerned. But I do think there's something going on at this place and she knows more about it than she let on.'

'Sex workers are like priests. Their clients tell them all sorts of stuff, but they know better than to repeat what they hear.'

'Melody seemed nervous, on edge. She says it's safer to keep her head down and see and hear nothing, which kinda supports your theory.'

'Well then, I don't see there's much more we can do.' Callie let out a frustrated breath. 'We can't have the place watched and even if we did, we'd be no further forward, what with all the comings and goings. We need someone on the inside.'

'That's not going to happen.'

'No, you're right. It would never work and Lucy sure as hell won't play ball. That one thinks only of herself so we'll have to see what other ideas we can come up with.'

Eric got out the car as they approached and opened the door for them. 'All okay?' he asked.

'Hunky-dory.' If Eric picked up on Callie's sarcasm, he gave no sign. 'Take Mrs Dalton home first please, Eric, and then me back to the club.'

'No, I'll come back with you. My car's there.'

'Right-ho,' Eric said, starting the engine.

The gates swung open as he approached them; no keycode necessary for departing punters. Callie had a good look around as they left and didn't see anyone lurking in the undergrowth with a long-lens camera, but then she figured that she wasn't supposed to. Even so, she had a feeling that her visit would not have gone unnoticed – Lucy had got that much right. Perhaps it would spook someone, maybe even Gavin, into taking action. Anything was possible.

'I'm gonna hit the shops,' Angie said, when they got back to the spa. 'Nothing like a little retail therapy to take a girl's mind off her troubles.'

'That's the spirit!' Callie embraced her friend. 'Let's touch base later.'

'Sure thing.'

Callie, as always, had a ton of work waiting for her and made her way straight to her office.

'Any luck?' Darren asked, lifting his head from whatever he'd been studying on his computer screen.

Callie told him what had occurred. 'It's only served to increase my suspicions,' she finished by saying. 'Lucy was cagey, Angie says that Melody was downright scared and although I didn't see anyone loitering, I'm pretty sure our visit was clocked.'

'Almost certainly, but that may not be a bad thing. Anyway, what now?'

'I have absolutely no idea. Suggestions would be welcome. All I know for sure as things stand is that whatever put the wind up Gavin and Paul started at that house.' She threw back her head, closed her eyes and growled with frustration. 'We need an in.'

'Have you considered making use of Fallow?' Darren asked, breaking the ensuing silence.

Callie's head abruptly jerked forward again, and her eyes flew open. 'What do you mean?' she asked.

'He'll be running scared, what with Gavin in the wind. He's been on the take for years and so his career's on the line.'

'If Gavin's collar's felt then he might spill the beans to help himself, I take it you mean.' Callie nodded. 'Yes, I think he is worried, but it doesn't follow that he knows where Gavin is, or why he scarpered.'

'But he will be thinking about his own skin, so he has as big a motive to find Gavin and make sure he keeps his mouth shut if he's running scared.'

'Yeah, I see where you're going with this.' Callie frowned. 'I think.'

'Fallow is a regular at the brothel.'

'How do you know that?'

Darren smiled. 'I just know. Ask Eric if you doubt it. He's spent a lot of time outside that place waiting for Gavin and he doesn't miss much.'

Callie took a moment to consider Darren's comment. 'You're suggesting that I ask a senior policeman if he knows what scam's going down at the brothel?' Callie shook her head. 'Surely if he knew then he'd have a duty to do something about it.'

Darren's responding laugh owed little to humour. 'An honest plod would feel that need.'

'Of course.' Callie flapped a hand. 'Sorry, my mind's all over the place.'

'No worries. My point is, if Fallow wants to keep his name out of Gavin's nefarious activities, then he can do worse than to pass information to us. To you. After all, he's still on the payroll.' Darren grinned. 'Perhaps you could entice him with the offer of a pay rise. My guess is that he knows the game's up and so he's probably saving up to make a quick exit to sunnier climes as and when.'

'I don't think I can trust him,' Callie said after a prolonged pause as she mulled the suggestion over. 'But I also think it won't do much harm to have him in here and test the waters, so to speak.'

'Be careful, Callie. He might be bent but that makes him dangerous and unpredictable. We already know that he'll do whatever it takes to cover his own back. Besides, he still has a lot of power within the sphere of law and order. I happen to know that he's got previous when it comes to planting evidence.'

'He can't do that to me,' Callie replied with more conviction than she actually felt. 'I didn't come down in the last shower and I've been keeping private records for years about how much has been handed out by Gavin, and to whom.'

'Christ!' Darren ran a hand through his hair. 'You never cease to amaze me. Monies paid into bank accounts that the revenue knows nothing about, I assume you mean.'

'I do.'

'Blimey. Does Gavin know about your records?'

'I don't tell him everything.' Callie smiled at Darren's shocked expression. 'When I realised just how much use he was making of this place for financial dodgy dealings, I decided to protect myself. After all, if Gavin gets collared then I'd go down with him. I decided that wasn't going to happen.'

'Smart lady!'

Callie felt ridiculously pleased to see the admiration reflected in Darren's eyes.

'Yeah, well,' she said, 'when the shit finally hits the fan, I always knew that I'd be on my own. I didn't sign up for this, but I *did* know how Gavin made a living when I first met him, so I can't pretend to be an innocent pawn.'

'Best not let Fallow know you've kept records,' Darren said, frowning.

'Nope, probably not, but I do have to shake a few trees if I want to find out what's got Gavin running scared, and if I want to get Stafford and co off my back.' She let out a long breath. 'As things stand, I'm stuck between a rock and the proverbial hard place. I can't sell up and I won't launder their dirty money, which I guess makes me expendable, so my only option is to fight fire with fire. That might mean coercing Fallow by implying that records do exist, that Gavin kept them and they're in a safe place.'

Darren shook his head. 'I don't like it.'

'I'm not over the moon myself but unless you can think of a better idea...'

Darren sighed. 'Not off the top of my head.'

'Well then, I'll ring Fallow.'

'Have him come here then and leave the intercom open so I can hear what's said.'

Callie eyed her PA for a prolonged moment before responding. 'Why are you so keen to have my back?' she asked. 'This isn't your fight.'

'Speaking openly, I don't like the way that Gavin has scarpered and left you to deal with all this shit. It isn't right.'

She smiled. 'Ah, so chivalry isn't dead.'

'Nah, I don't deserve that. I'd feel the same way if he left a male partner in the lurch. But don't forget too, in my family, I'm the boy scout who chose the path of the straight and narrow, which didn't make me popular. I could so easily have gone the other way, been dragged into Dad's way of life, which is what I see happening to you. If that's what you want then go for it, but I'm pretty sure it isn't.'

'You're right,' she conceded. 'And going up against these people will be tough. The men who are pressuring me will dismiss me as an irrelevance because I'm a woman, but there's more than one way to fight back, and it doesn't necessarily involve brute force. Women are recognised as the more deadly species for a reason.'

Darren chuckled. 'Remind me never to get on your wrong side.'

'Joking aside, Darren, this could get ugly.' Callie said

nothing more, hoping the silence would work in her favour. She now had to decide whether she could trust Darren absolutely. Hedging her bets was no longer an option.

'I've told you about my background and what I've had to fight against to get recognition,' Darren said, meeting her gaze and holding it. 'I've never committed a crime in my life but the same can't be said for my father, and my brothers. Mud sticks. And I don't think that you realised how it would be for you once you married Gavin.' Darren's expression closed down. 'He used you the way he uses everyone and treats them well while he needs them. But when they've outlived that usefulness...' He spread his hands and left the words hanging.

Realisation dawned at that moment. Gavin had done something to harm Darren, or someone close to him. He wanted revenge upon Gavin, which either sealed the question of his loyalty towards her, or else made her collateral damage. A means to an end. She was tempted to push the issue, but decided against it. Darren had been with her for five years, she reminded herself, so if he *was* out for revenge then he was a very patient man. There had to be more to it than that but now was not the time to press him.

'I'm going to message Fallow,' she said, grabbing her phone and pulling up his mobile number. He was on her list of contacts because Gavin liked to socialise with the people whom he had in his pocket from time to time, presumably so that he could remind them in a not-so-subtle way of the hold he had over them. Callie punched out a text, asking him to come and see her that afternoon. She didn't say why.

'And now we wait,' she said, putting her phone back on the desk. 'What's on the agenda this afternoon, Darren?'

They spent the next half-hour talking business.

'Any progress with the invoices I asked you to check?' Callie asked when they'd covered everything else. 'I know it hasn't been long, but...'

'I'm working on it. I've set up a spreadsheet and the system's running it. It will pick up invoices from the same origins. I've set up another using banking codes, in case funds are going into the same account from different sources.'

'Wow! You have hidden talents.'

He flashed a sexy smile and winked at her. 'You have *no* idea!'

Callie was still laughing when he returned to his own desk.

She got down to paperwork after he'd left her, but her concentration was shot, and she found herself going over the same ground several times. She was glad of the interruption when Darren buzzed her.

'Superintendent Fallow is here, Callie,' he said.

'Send him in,' she replied, leaving the intercom open.

'Where's the fire?' Fallow asked, walking into the room and scowling.

'Nice to see you too,' she replied, not bothering to offer her hand.

'I do have work to do, you know.'

'When you take the devil's shilling, you have more than one paymaster, Barry,' she replied briskly, indicating the chair in front of her desk, glad of the solid barrier between them. The way the man looked at her had always made her skin crawl.

'No sign of Gavin, I take it.'

'That's what I need to talk to you about.'

'Don't look at me. I have absolutely no idea where he's got to. Or why. Probably got too big for his boots and crossed someone it would be unwise to upset.' That possibility appeared to cheer Fallow up.

'I'd have thought it would have been in your best interests

to find and protect him,' Callie replied in an even tone. 'He might be in trouble and need bailing out.'

Fallow grunted. 'I'm not the fucking AA.'

'No, but your income will take a hit if we don't find him.'

'Not my problem.' Fallow looked pleased with himself. 'All good things must come to an end.'

'Do you really think Gavin's daft enough to give you hand-outs and not keep records?'

Fallow half rose from his chair, his face crimson. 'Now just a minute! Don't involve yourself in matters that don't concern you. It's not healthy.'

Callie sat back in her chair, her pose relaxed as she flashed a smug smile designed to annoy the man. 'Neither is issuing crude threats, Barry. Those records are in a safe place and if anything happens to me then they *will* find their way into the hands of your superiors.' She paused, watching a gamut of emotions flicker across Fallow's unattractive features. 'You'd likely get a lengthy custodial sentence if that happened and I hear bent coppers, especially the senior variety, don't do too well inside.'

'What do you want?' he asked ungraciously.

'That's better.' She sent him a withering smile. 'I need your help to find my husband. Not because I want him back but because I want all his associates off my back. I'm sure that's what you want too, so it makes sense for us to work together.'

'Better just to let him fester wherever he's got to. I can't imagine why you want him back here, muddying the waters with his outlandish plans.'

'Plans... what plans? Anyway, why I need to find him is my business, and yours too.' She paused. 'The brothel near the marina that Gavin and Paul both have an interest in.'

Fallow snorted. 'An interest? Is that what they're calling it this week?'

'Keep it professional, Barry. I don't care where Gavin dips his wick. I'm not the vindictive type. Nor do I waste energy on jealousy. I just need to get my life back. And whatever's got Gavin and Paul running scared has to do with Phoenix. Since you're a regular, I need you to find out what it is for me.'

He laughed in her face. 'What do you think we do in that place? Discuss the latest share price?'

'You're a senior policeman, Barry. I'm sure you can figure something out. And don't take too long about it. I'm under pressure, which means you are too. I called there today and spoke with Lucy but if she knows what's going on then she's not saying.'

'You did what?!' Fallow's bushy eyebrows shot up his forehead.

'I've transferred a little bonus to your account, so earn it. Get back to me as soon as.' She stood to make it clear that the interview was over, wondering why her visit to Phoenix had bothered him quite so much. 'Keep in touch.'

'Well,' Darren said, entering her office once he'd shown Fallow out. 'That went well. You frightened the hell out of me and your threats weren't directed my way.'

'What made you think they were threats?'

Callie glanced at the clock. The afternoon had gotten away from her, and she knew she wouldn't achieve anything else that day.

'I'm off home,' she said. 'A bath and an early night beckon.'

'Good idea,' Darren said. 'See you tomorrow.'

The bath helped her to relax but the early night wasn't to be. She'd only just drifted off to sleep when her phone rang. It was the police.

'A woman has been taken into intensive care,' she was told. 'She's been badly beaten. There was no identity about her person other than a card. Your card.'

Callie's blood ran cold. There was only one person she'd given her card to that day who could conceivably be the victim.

Lucy.

8

Callie gathered her wits as best she could whilst her mind whirled with increasingly unpalatable possibilities.

'I give my card to a lot of people,' she said, surprised that her voice sounded so calm, so detached. 'Is the poor woman badly hurt?'

'Her injuries aren't life-threatening.' The policeman spoke with the minimum of civility. He probably knew who she was, Callie supposed, and police who weren't on the take were constantly frustrated by their inability to pin any crimes on Gavin.

'I'm pleased to hear it.' Callie sat up in bed and pushed the hair away from her eyes. 'How can I help you? If the lady's conscious, presumably she'll be able to tell you who she is, so why the call to me?'

'She's in an induced coma. There's swelling on her brain, and she has a couple of fractured ribs amongst other injuries. She was probably kicked in the head.'

'Ouch! Hardly non-life-threatening then. I hope she recovers. Was it a mugging, do you suppose?'

'We are not in a position to speculate. No one is permitted to see her at the moment, but we wondered if you'd be prepared to come down to the hospital tomorrow and let us know who she is?'

'I can certainly do that, if I recall meeting her. Presumably though someone will report her missing before then.'

'We are checking the missing persons reports, obviously.'

'Well, all right, Constable...?'

'Pearson, madam.'

'Okay, Constable Pearson. Have someone call me tomorrow if you still don't have an identity. Where did the attack take place as a matter of interest?'

'She was found by a dog walker in the early hours on the cliffs at Rottingdean. A good job too, otherwise she'd have been out there all night.'

Damn! That was close to the club's location, making it even more likely that the victim was Lucy.

'I see. Well, thank you, Constable.'

Pearson offered grudging thanks in return and Callie cut the connection. She fell back on her pillows, unnerved, and thought about this alarming development. Her visit to Lucy and this vicious attack *had* to be connected. A warning, perhaps. Callie was sorry that Lucy had been so brutally attacked but hadn't taken a liking to the woman and so refused to feel culpable. Gavin wouldn't have been involved. For all his faults, he had old-fashioned ethics and would never physically attack a woman. Besides, she was his partner in a lucrative business and so why would he feel the need to punish her just because Callie had been to see her?

Callie tossed and turned for the rest of the night, having triple-checked that the house was locked up tight and that the CCTV system was in full working order. She woke early with a slight headache and no clear answers to her problems. She considered calling Angie and telling her what had occurred but decided against it. Her friend was on edge as it was, concerned more about her son than her husband, and Callie didn't see the need to burden her with this latest development.

At least, not yet.

She stood in the shower for a long time, allowing the hot water to pound down on her head as she slowly regained full consciousness. Having towelled herself dry and brushed out her hair, she slid her arms into a cosy dressing gown and headed for the kitchen. Coffee was the first order of the day. She couldn't think coherently until she'd been caffeinated.

Despite her need to protect her friend, Angie would have to know, she decided, as she sat at the island with a steaming mug and toying with a slice of buttered toast that she didn't really want. If Lucy had been targeted, it implied that her attacker had either wanted to know what she'd discussed with Callie or was issuing some sort of obscure warning. That being the case, the chances were that she or Angie would be next on that person's list. Callie made a mental note to ensure that she still had a can of Mace in her bag. She'd put another in her coat pocket, just in case.

Fallow was the only person outside of her small circle whom she'd actually told about her visit but surely even he wouldn't go so far as to have Lucy attacked. Or would he? It was impossible for Callie to know what lengths an increasingly desperate man would go to in order to protect his own hide. Had she made an error in pulling him in yesterday? A man with his swagger and degree of arrogance would resent having a woman calling the tune, she belatedly realised, having long since labelled him as a condescending misogynist.

Sighing, Callie abandoned her uneaten toast, drained the

coffee mug and then returned to her bedroom. She dried and styled her hair and then dressed casually but with care. Appearances mattered, especially in her current circumstances. People would be less likely to underestimate her if she was well turned out. Gavin had taught her at least that much. He'd always been a smart dresser and told her that people looked upon him as a man to be taken seriously if he didn't show himself unshaven, wearing ripped jeans and sporting an armful of tattoos.

Callie finished applying her make-up, squirted herself with her favourite perfume and decided that she didn't look too bad. No one would know that she'd spent a largely sleepless night worrying about the disturbing turn events had taken. She still had absolutely no idea why Lucy had been attacked but she had no intention of keeping a low profile. Now was the time to exert herself so that people would think twice before setting their sights on her.

Still early, she drove directly to the local hospital. Even before eight, the car park was almost full, and she struggled to find a space. She then made her way to A&E and asked after the mugging victim brought in the previous night.

'Are you a relative?'

'I don't think so.' Callie was very good at winning people over and smiled ingratiatingly at the young nurse. 'The police called me. The lady had my card on her and they thought I might be able to help identify her. That is, if you haven't found out who she is yet.'

The nurse – her name badge identified her as Sally – looked confused. 'Well, I don't suppose there's any harm in your having a quick peep. Everyone deserves to have a name, don't they? Besides, if we know who she is then we can access her medical records. Come this way.'

'Is she still in a coma?'

'Yes. The doctors will see her later and might bring her out of it, but we shall have to wait and see.'

'Right.'

'Here we are.'

They stopped outside of a window to a private room. For some reason, Callie hesitated to peer through the glass. Only when she sensed the nurse watching her with open curiosity did she force herself to do so.

And gasped.

Poor Lucy, who was still just about recognisable, had a battered, swollen face and one wrist was in a cast. She was breathing on her own but so shallowly that Callie could barely see her chest moving.

'Do you know her?' the nurse asked.

'I'm... I'm not sure.' Callie swallowed. 'It's almost impossible to see her features. I give my card to a lot of people. She could be a client at my spa.'

Callie's survival instincts had kicked in. She absolutely didn't want to be dragged into the identification process. Perhaps that was the point of this vicious attack – to get her directly involved.

'You look upset.' Sally, full of compassion, touched Callie's arm. 'Sit down for a while. I'll get you some tea.'

'No. No, I'm fine, thank you. It's just so awful. I suppose you see stuff like this all the time and get immune, but I'm not good around injury.'

Callie knew she was over-explaining and abruptly shut her mouth.

'You never get immune, but you have to be professional, otherwise you'd be no help to anyone.'

'Of course. Well, I'm sorry I couldn't identify the poor woman. I won't hold you up any longer. I know you're busy.'

Callie almost ran back to her car. The first thing she did was to call Fallow on his mobile.

'What now?' he barked.

Callie briefly explained. 'It is Lucy,' she said, 'but I don't want to get involved. Get your constable off my back.'

'How am I supposed to do that?'

'You're the boss. You can do anything you like. But be assured, if Constable Pearson doesn't back off then I might just have to let drop that you know the victim too.' She paused. 'And how.'

'God, you're a bitch! I'll see what I can do.'

'I thought you'd see things my way.'

Feeling a little better to have got the last word with Fallow, Callie drove to work. Angie was already there, chatting with Darren.

'Ah, I'm glad you're both here. Come into my office. There have been developments.'

'Sounds ominous.'

Wordlessly, Darren made for the coffee machine and produced brews for all three of them.

'Go ahead, boss,' he said, once they had their beverages in front of them.

Callie explained about her late-night call from Constable Pearson.

'Bloody hell!' Darren looked shocked. 'Didn't see that one coming.'

'Is it Lucy?' Angie asked.

Callie nodded. 'Yes. I just went to the hospital. Her face is battered and swollen but it's her. No question. I pretended not to know her, though.'

'Sensible.' Darren nodded his approval.

'You don't want to be dragged into an enquiry?' Angie asked.

'Right. I called Fallow and told him to get his constable off my back.'

Angie looked dubious. 'Will he do it?'

'He can't afford not to,' Darren replied before Callie could. 'He knows that Callie has a hold over him.'

'Unless, of course, he was responsible for Lucy's attack. He's the only person outside of this room who knew that we went there, Angie. That's assuming we weren't noticed by someone else...'

Angie looked pale, and worried. 'I don't understand any of this,' she said.

'Join the club, darling.' Callie forced herself to remain impassive. 'All I do know is that we've shaken the right tree just by going to the Phoenix, even if we weren't aware that we'd stirred things up. Not that we intended for anyone to get hurt, but I'm convinced Lucy must know what's going down in her club. She manages that place more efficiently than a sergeant major putting his troops through a survival course and nothing gets past her. Gavin mentioned more than once that he admired her for her attention to detail.'

'So, what will happen to the club now?' Darren asked. 'Who will run the show, I mean?'

'A very good question.' Callie rubbed the back of her neck. 'Presumably there's a second in command.'

'My advice is to close up until Lucy's better,' Darren said.

'Why?' Angie asked.

'To disrupt whatever's going on there,' Callie answered for him. 'And that's not a bad suggestion, Darren. As Gavin's wife, presumably I have the power to make those sorts of decisions.'

'Yeah, but how do you go about it?' Angie asked.

'I know the man who runs security there. Gavin put him in place. You know him too, Callie.'

Callie blinked. 'I do?'

'Sure. Peter Bersted. He used to work for you. You were upset when he left.'

'Gavin told me he'd got a better offer!' Callie cried indignantly.

'He did, it seems,' Angie remarked, a cynical edge to her voice. 'From your husband.'

'I couldn't tell you when you asked,' Darren said apologetically. 'It was not long after I came to work here; Gavin had given me the job and I had to prove my loyalty.'

'I understand,' Callie said, waving aside his apology. 'The question is, will Pete do as I ask?'

'I'm sure he will. I have a number for him. Do you want me to call him?'

'Let's think this through first.' Callie paused. 'We have no idea how long Lucy will be out of action, but I can't see her being fit again for at least a couple of weeks. The girls will lose a lot of income. Perhaps they'll even leave and set up shop elsewhere.'

'With good luck, Melody will lead the deserting rats,' Angie said with feeling.

'I doubt it.' Darren spoke with authority. 'But you will have to go back and explain to them why they need to take an enforced holiday. Take charge, sell it to them right and they'll toe the line.'

'Especially if any of them are involved with whatever's got our husbands chasing their tails,' Angie added, an edge to her voice.

'Whoever attacked Lucy will be watching to see what we do

next,' Callie said pensively. 'And they won't expect us to be proactive.' A slow smile illuminated her features. 'I like the idea of showing them who they've taken on. We'll go over later this morning. Give the girls a chance to wake up first.'

'Okay, so what do we do in the meantime, boss?' Darren asked.

'Any luck with your spreadsheets?' Callie felt weary, worried and every second of her age. 'We're down to that, I'm afraid.'

'Actually, there is something.'

'What?' Callie and Angie asked together.

'I've identified invoices from three different sources.' He paused and grinned at them. 'All with the same bank details.'

Callie offered her assistant a high five. 'A break!' she cried.

'Hopefully.'

'Okay, so don't keep us in suspense,' Angie said. 'Whose account do the bank details belong to?'

'A company name. Ever heard of Porchester Holdings, Porchester Investments and Porchester Estates?'

'Not much imagination,' Angie said as she shared a look with Callie. Both shook their heads.

'It's obviously the same organisation using an umbrella name,' Callie said, tapping her fingers restlessly.

'Yeah, and Porchester Holdings is the one that appears the most frequently.'

'Are there any directors named?' Callie asked.

'Nah, it doesn't work that way with bank transfers. I only just came up with this. My next point of call will be Companies House, but I bet there'll be a solicitor named as custodian. And I also bet that solicitor won't tell us diddly squat about who owns the company. That's the whole point of hiding behind the legal profession.'

'Even so,' Callie said, attempting to hide her disappointment. 'It's a start.'

'Okay.' Darren stood. 'If there's nothing else, I'll put a call in to Pete now and get a visit to Phoenix arranged for this afternoon.'

'Thanks, Darren.' Callie smiled absently at her PA as he left the room.

'You want me to come with you this afternoon?' Angie asked.

'No, I think I'd best do this one alone.'

'Well, at least take Darren with you. You don't know what you're getting yourself into, Callie. It's no joking matter. Think of what happened to Lucy, just for talking to us.'

Callie's expression sobered. 'Yeah, I hear you, but now is the time to show strength. Gavin's the owner and major shareholder in Phoenix and in his absence, I'm taking over. But yes, I will take Darren, so don't worry. If you want to help, you could do worse than show your face at the car showroom. Same applies there in your case as it does for me at the club.'

'Ah, I see what you mean. I'm stepping in for Paul.'

'Exactly. Take a look at the books and generally poke your nose in, ask awkward questions. Make your presence felt and see who gets nervous. Oh, and ask Tom if Porchester Holdings rings any bells with him. You never know.'

'Yeah, okay.'

'Cheer up.' Callie rounded her desk and gave her friend a hug. 'I know you're going out of your mind with worry about Henry and so the best thing you can do is to be proactive. Keep yourself busy.'

'I know.' Angie let out a long breath. 'I have to believe that Henry is with Paul and when I get my hands on the bastard, I'll rip him to shreds for putting me through this. That's before I pack his bags and throw him out. Paul crossed a line when he got together with Melody *and* involved Henry in his nefarious activities. He swore blind that he'd never do that.' She threw back her head, sending blonde hair cascading over her shoulders. 'It's not too late to start again, I've decided. Either that or live alone. I'll get a dog for company, or something, but I can't take being trampled over any more.'

'I've never seen you this way.'

'I've never been shafted by the man who I thought loved me unconditionally, that's why. Even if he begs, my pride won't allow me to take him back.' Angie sat a little straighter, her expression thunderous. 'Time to put myself first.'

'Go, girl!'

'What about you, Cal? Will you take Gavin back yet again?'

'Probably not. That's why I want to get his cohorts off my back. If I can get this place straight, the books clean, then I can sell up and move on. We're neither of us getting any younger, Angie, but we aren't in our dotage either. It's time for me to enjoy myself without constantly looking over my shoulder.'

'Okay,' Angie said, gathering up her bag. 'I'm off to stir them up at the showroom. Let's touch base later.'

9

Angie felt as though she'd taken back control of her life as she drove with renewed determination towards the showroom. She wondered now if Paul really had been faithful all these years, or whether he'd simply hidden his transgressions from her. She'd been wrapped up first with the kids and then with her job and had trusted him, so perhaps she hadn't seen the signs.

Be that as it may, she was seeing them now with twenty-twenty clarity and didn't much like the view. Callie might not hold much stock with fidelity, but Angie was old-fashioned in that respect and had always abided by her marriage vows. Taking a fresh look at the manner in which she had simply trusted Paul and assumed he shared her values made her realise just how naïve she'd actually been.

'No more!' she shouted, her voice ringing out in the confines of her car and temporarily drowning out the oldies station that her radio was permanently tuned to. The time really had come to put herself first and as soon as she'd made sure her son was safe, that was precisely what she'd do.

She arrived at the car lot and parked in Paul's regular spot. A couple were looking at a BMW on the forecourt and one of Paul's salesmen was giving them the spiel. He glanced at Angie as she got out of her car but quickly looked away again. Angie recognised the guy. Paul had his employees round to theirs for a barbeque every summer, which was about the only time she saw any of them, other than Tom. She gave a little wave to... Simon, that was his name, and headed straight for the showroom.

'Hey.' Tom was sat behind a desk, doing something on a computer. He looked up when she entered, and a broad smile illuminated his features. 'What brings you to these parts?' he asked, standing.

'Well, since Paul's on the missing list, I thought I should show my face and let the troops know it's business as usual.'

'Glad you did.'

Angie thought he looked sincere.

'Any news of Henry?'

She liked him a little more for asking. 'Nothing yet.' She shook her head. 'It's wearing on my nerves.'

'I can imagine. I won't tell you not to worry because... well, because of course you're worried. Anyway, coffee?'

'No thanks.' She smiled at him, her confidence boosted by the approval she saw in his expression. 'I'm gonna run an eye over the books in a mo, just to see if I can spot any anomalies, but can we talk first?'

'Sure.' He led her into Paul's office and closed the door. 'What gives?'

Deciding to trust him because she had to trust someone and because her instincts told her he was on her side, she explained about their visit to Phoenix and Lucy's subsequent attack. He would hear about it anyway, she figured, and might even have some idea who carried it out. And why.

'Fucking hell!' Tom scratched his head. 'You obviously poked the bear.'

'Yeah, that's what we thought but we have absolutely no idea who we upset.' Angie shuddered. 'Someone must have seen us arrive, but we didn't notice anything out of the ordinary. It's all a bit spooky.'

'And then some. Will she be all right, Lucy, that is?'

'Apparently so, but Callie says she a right mess. They've kept her in an induced coma because of swelling on the brain.' Angie scowled. 'Who'd go to such extremes?'

'You don't mix in that world, darlin', but I can tell you there's some right hard geezers involved in the drugs trade, always assuming that's what you've stumbled on.'

'Well anyway, Callie's going over there this afternoon to shut the place down for a couple of weeks. Can't run it without Lucy to keep control is what she's thinking.'

'She's likely right about that and clearly wants the girls to know who's in charge, a bit like you're doing here.' He nodded. 'Makes sense.'

'Yeah, we're groping in the dark while we try to get a handle on things. Talking of which, does Porchester Holdings ring any bells with you?'

'Nope. Can't say that it does,' he replied without hesitation. 'Why do you ask?'

Angie explained.

'Sounds suspicious. Let's hope Darren can find out a bit more. Could be Stafford or the O'Keefes.'

Angie nodded. 'You think Gavin might be behind the Porchester set-up?'

Darren waggled a hand from side to side. 'The possibility occurred to me.'

'We'll just have to see what pops. But as I say, in the meantime, I'm here to show my face. Can you log me into the accounts, please?'

'Sure.'

Angie was sitting in Paul's chair, blocking images of his handsome face and the enticing smile he'd fixed on her on the last occasion when she'd visited the showroom and found him sitting right where she was now. Paul's good looks and compelling charm no longer held the ability to affect her, she reminded herself, feeling her stomach lurch and her spirits plummet.

Tom moved behind her, leaned over her shoulder and pressed the appropriate keys to bring up the business's accounts. He smelled of citrus soap and arresting masculinity.

Whoa! Down, girl!

'There you go,' he said, smiling like he knew what the close proximity of his body to hers had done to her. But, in her own defence, it had been a while since any man had shown an interest in her. Including Paul. Especially him. She wondered why it had taken her so long to realise he'd neglected her. Familiarity, she supposed. Married couples generally got into a rut and took one another for granted.

Well, not any more.

'Thanks. You can leave me to it. I'll give you a shout when I'm done.'

Angie was in her element when it came to accounts. It was what she enjoyed doing, and she was good at it, even if marriage to Paul had prevented her from finishing her accountancy course and qualifying. She and Callie had that course in common. It was how they'd met and started mixing in the same circles. It seemed like a lifetime ago now. Numbers still made sense to Angie though in the way that other people had a natural talent for singing or whatever. She scanned the pages, looking for anything that jumped out at her. Especially alert for signs of Porchester Holdings, or Porchester anything.

Nada.

After an hour, she admitted defeat. She knew that the books couldn't be as perfect as they appeared to be, but any transgressions had been too well disguised for her to make any sense of them during this first, brief examination. She sat up and stretched backwards, attempting to get rid of the kinks that had accumulated in the small of her back.

'Thought you could do with some tea.'

Beccy, Paul's pretty office girl who'd been with him for quite a while, put her head round the door, bearing a steaming mug and a plate of biscuits.

'Nice to see you here, Mrs Dalton,' she added, placing the refreshments on the desk. 'Is there anything else I can get you?'

Angie resisted the urge to ask Beccy if she knew where Paul and Henry were. She had no intention of actually telling the girl that she'd misplaced her husband and son. She wondered instead if Paul had got up close and personal with Beccy. Now that she knew he'd strayed once, she found it hard to believe it had been the first and only time. He was just better at covering his tracks than Gavin had ever been.

'No, I'm good, thanks.' She summoned up a smile and helped herself to a biscuit. 'How's business?'

'We're doing well at present. A lot of people decide to change their cars at this time of year. Convertibles are always in demand.'

'Okay, thanks. I'll let you get on.'

Angie watched Beccy as she left the office, slim hips

swaying as she closed the door quietly behind her. She had never taken to the woman, even though she could not have said why. It seemed odd that she hadn't asked where Paul was and when he was likely to be back. He didn't spend much of his working life at the showroom, it was true, leaving the day-to-day running of it to Tom. Even so, he made a point of at least showing his face every day or two. So it followed that Beccy either knew where he was hiding or thought it wiser not to ask questions.

She was still mulling over the complexities of the part of her husband's life she knew little about when her phone rang. The number was withheld but she answered it anyway.

'Mum, is that you?'

'Henry. Oh my God, Henry!' Angie felt her heart thumping against her ribcage. She felt faint with relief. 'Are you okay? Where are you?'

A sob echoed down the line, turning Angie's blood to ice. 'Come and get me, Mum,' he pleaded, sounding like the little boy that he hadn't been for a very long time.

* * *

'All set?' Darren asked, putting his head round Callie's door. 'Pete's ready to meet us at Phoenix.'

'Good. Does he know why?'

'Well, he knows Lucy's gone AWOL but I didn't enlighten him further. I figured you'd want to tell him yourself. I just told him to wake the girls up and have them assembled for when we get there.'

'Okay.' Callie stood, grabbed her jacket and picked up her bag.

'Do you want me to drive us?' Darren asked.

'No, have Eric do the honours. We need to create the impression that we won't be messed with.'

Callie felt a gamut of emotions trickle through her as she made the same journey in two days, albeit for differing reasons. For the same underlying reason. Find Gavin and kill him if he's not already dead. Find out why he took off for so long and get his criminal cronies off her back.

How hard could it be?

'You okay?' Darren asked. 'You're muttering to yourself.'

'Just trying to decide what to do to Gavin when I find him, and in what order,' she quipped.

Darren briefly squeezed her hand. 'You must have considered the possibility that he's dead.'

'Of course I have, but I don't buy it. If he is then either Stafford or O'Keefe would have done the deed. They are the only two serious heavies he has connections to, as far as I'm aware. And if one of them had done it, the other would know.'

Darren nodded. 'Good point. Stafford wouldn't have asked you quite so nicely to step up if he knew Gavin was already dead. He would simply assume that he could intimidate you into doing whatever he wants, what with you being a feeble woman and all that.'

'There is nothing feeble about me!' Callie protested.

Darren laughed. 'I know that, and Stafford has now made the same discovery for himself. I reckon he thought you'd be a pushover, but your reaction knocked the wind out of his sails.'

'I guess we never know what we're capable of until we're backed into a corner. Gavin's way of doing things must have rubbed off on me over the years without me realising it. He doesn't like being pushed around, and it seems I'm disinclined to give in to bullies as well.'

'It's a dangerous game, Callie.' He again squeezed her hand,

and this time was slow to let it go. Callie closed her eyes for an expressive moment, unwilling to admit even to herself that the simple contact boosted both her determination and her ego.

'What choice do I have? I fully intend to fight for what's mine but not necessarily by using brute force. Anyway, my instincts tell me that Gavin's still breathing. He ran off when things got hot and left me to take the flack, just like always.'

'Why have you put up with it for so long?'

'Good question.' Callie sighed. 'I suppose it's never been this bad before. I've been preoccupied making a go of the spa. I either hadn't realised or else chose not to notice before now that it was being used quite so comprehensively by Gavin for other purposes. Anyway, I can't bury my head any longer, so in some respects Gavin taking off has done me a favour.' She straightened her spine. 'Enough is enough.'

'It's sometimes simpler to take the easy way out. I could have done that, but I just couldn't have followed in my father's footsteps. I saw the futility of a criminal life and wanted no part of it. He's never forgiven me for that and all but disowned me.' Darren chuckled. 'Some role model, eh?'

'Yeah, I can't go against my conscience either, but that doesn't mean that I intend to be a pushover. I didn't start any of this, nor did I ask to get involved, but I *am* involved, and I will do whatever it takes to extricate myself from Gavin's criminal connections. Anyway,' Callie sat a little straighter as Eric slowed the car at the now familiar gates and pressed in the code, 'it's show time.'

'Right.'

Callie thanked Eric when he opened the door for her, and she slid elegantly from the car. Aware that they were likely being watched from the house, she straightened her shoulders and walked towards the front door with purpose, Darren faithfully at her side. She would never admit how glad she was to have him and Eric in her corner. The chauffeur had not asked if he was needed but simply followed along behind them, solid and reliable.

A man that Callie vaguely recognised met them on the front porch.

'Pete,' Darren said. 'You remember Mrs Renfrew.'

'Nice to see you again,' Pete said, offering Callie his hand.

'Thanks,' she replied, shaking it. 'Are all the girls inside?'

'Yep, all six of them, moaning and wanting to know what's going on.'

That saved Callie one question since she'd be wondering how many pissed-off females she'd be confronted with.

'Lucy's been attacked, Pete,' she said. 'She's in a bad way and will be out of action for a while.'

'I'm sorry to hear that,' Pete replied.

'Anyway, I need to let the girls know. I'm going to close the place down for a couple of weeks. Lucy needs to be here to run it.'

'Yeah, I can see that, but the girls won't like it.'

'Then they don't have to stay. Anyway, let's do it. Stay here please, Eric. We don't want to go in mobhanded. I'll shout if you're needed.'

Eric nodded and silently stationed himself at the door.

The sound of muted female voices abruptly halted when Pete opened the door to the large lounge that Angie had described to her. The statuesque beauty of the women occupying it, briefly made Callie feel inadequate. And very old. She squared her shoulders, reminded herself why she was there and that she was the one in control as she walked across the room to lean against the bar. A shot of brandy to steady her nerves would hit the spot but, of course, that was out of the question.

She would have to do this stone-cold sober and somehow convince this bevy of beauties that she had everything under control, without activating a max exodos. Would she care if they all left, and the place had to close down? She had no idea how much of Gavin's income came from the brothel and anyway, that wasn't her problem. If the girls wanted to walk, let them, she thought defiantly.

'Sorry to have dragged you out of bed,' she said to the ladies. 'In case you don't know who I am, I'm Callie Renfrew, Gavin's wife. Gavin, for reasons best known to him, has gone on the missing list so I'm taking over in his absence.'

A rumbling of discontent was not the response she'd hoped for, even if it wasn't unexpected.

'Where's Lucy?' one of the girls asked.

'You are?'

'Melody.'

Callie nodded, having thought as much. She was head and shoulders above the others when it came to looks and style. No wonder Angie was so pissed off. It was easy to see why Paul would have been tempted but less obvious why such a stunner would feel the need to revert to the oldest profession.

'Lucy's been attacked.'

'Attacked?' several of the girls said, glancing at one another.

'Is she okay?'

'What happened?'

The questions came thick and fast, but Callie held up a hand to stem the tide. 'I don't know, is the answer to all of those questions. She's in an induced coma but her injuries aren't life-threatening, apparently. But still, the bottom line is that she'll be out of action, at least for a few weeks.'

'We can manage without her,' one of the girls said.

'I don't doubt it, but you won't have to. I'm closing this place down for two weeks.'

This time, the protests were loud and incensed.

'I won't have you put in danger, any of you. Until we know who attacked Lucy and why, it isn't safe to carry on with business as usual.' Callie's voice rose above the protests, effectively silencing them. 'Take a couple of weeks off. You can stay here or go elsewhere. That's up to you. Your jobs will still be here when you get back, if you want them. And,' she added, 'I'll pay you all a decent wage for doing nothing.' She named a figure that immediately stemmed the latest round of protests. 'Any questions?'

There were none. Melody stood apart from the others, holding Callie in a death glare, but even she said nothing.

'Right, that's it. Thanks, ladies. See you in a fortnight.'

'That was a generous offer,' Darren said, watching the ladies as they left the room, talking amongst themselves.

'None of this is their fault, as far as I'm aware, so they don't deserve to lose out. Besides, I'm told this is a safer place than most for them to work. I don't want them having to go anywhere else.'

'Are you sure you've thought this through? If Gavin doesn't come back, do you really want a brothel?'

Callie laughed. 'I haven't got that far. One hurdle at a time.'

'Fair enough.'

'Come on. Let's get back to the spa. I'll leave you to sort out payment of the bonus I offered them all. I take it they have bank accounts.'

Darren laughed. 'Half of them take credit cards.'

'Blimey, I am out of date.' She chuckled. 'Not that I've ever been up to speed on the preferred methods of payments to sex workers, but you know what I mean.'

They had just got back into the car when Callie's phone rang.

'It's Angie,' she said, taking the call. 'What is it? What? Slow down, you're not making any sense.' She listened for a moment. 'Where is he? Right, we're not far away. We'll meet you there.'

Callie cut the call. 'Eric, go to the cliffs, please. That first bus stop past Roedean. Henry's turned up.'

10

Angie was shaking so much from a combination of relief and anxiety that there was no way she'd be able to drive to her son's rescue. Tom, who had overheard her conversation, took charge.

'Come on,' he said. 'I'll take you to pick him up.'

'I must let Callie know.'

Angie walked beside Tom with her phone pressed to her ear. She conducted a short conversation with Callie, barely aware of what she said as her mind went into overdrive. Where had Henry been? Why was he calling from a strange number? Why did he sound so afraid?

Tom led her to a Jaguar and opened the passenger door for her.

'Did Henry sound okay?' he asked, as he pulled out of the car lot, indicated left and headed for central Brighton.

'He sounded scared, like a little boy again. I couldn't get much sense out of him.' Angie's knees jiggled. 'Put your foot down, Tom, for goodness' sake! You're driving like an old woman. I need to reach my son.'

'I'm doing the best I can, darling, in this heavy traffic. Don't worry, we'll get to him and hopefully also get some answers about Paul's whereabouts.'

Angie huffed. 'I don't give a shit about him. I just need to see Henry with my own eyes and make sure he's okay.'

'I know.'

Angie bounced on the edge of her seat. 'Sorry. I didn't mean to take it out on you. I know you want to help.'

'It's okay.' He flashed a smile. 'My shoulders are broad.'

They eventually got clear of the habitual, bumper-to-bumper traffic in Brighton and Tom was able to speed up for the last bit of the journey.

'I wonder whose phone he used to call me,' Angie said. 'It wasn't his own.'

'He'll be able to tell us at least that much.'

'Oh God, this is so awful!'

Angie's iron control over her emotions gave way to a flood of tears. Tom glanced at her, reached into his pocket and produced an old-fashioned handkerchief, which he passed to her. The gesture caused her tears to dry up and for a brief smile to play about her lips. She didn't think men carried pocket handkerchiefs nowadays and certainly hadn't imagined that Tom would buck that trend. He was full of surprises.

'Thanks,' she said, mopping her eyes. 'Sorry.'

'Don't apologise. You've been through a lot.'

Tom screeched to a halt at the bus stop Henry was waiting at, but a Mercedes had beaten them to it.

'That will be Eric,' Tom said.

Angie barely heard him. She was out of the car before it came to a halt and ran towards Callie, who was sitting in the bus shelter beside a dishevelled but very much alive Henry. She held out her arms and for the first time in almost ten years, Henry fell into them, allowing his mother to hug him. She ignored the unpleasant aroma that rose up from his clothing and unwashed body. As far as she was concerned, he had never been more fragrant, more wholesome, more comprehensively hers. She would never take him, or any of her children, for granted ever again, she vowed.

Only wearing a thin t-shirt that was grubby and ripped in places, Henry was trembling. Darren took off his jacket and draped it round his shoulders.

'What happened to you?' Angie asked. 'I've been going out of my mind.'

'You don't know?' Henry looked at her properly for the first time and appeared shocked. She noticed grazes beneath the stubble on his chin and what appeared to be a fading black eye. Renewed anger coursed through her at the thought of anyone beating her son.

'Not here,' Darren advised gently. 'We don't know who may be watching.'

'Take him back to the spa, Angie,' Callie said. 'It will be safer there.'

'Oh, but I...'

'Go with Callie,' Tom said. 'Give me your key and I'll pop in and pick up some fresh clothes for Henry. You still have a room there?' Tom addressed the question to Henry, who didn't appear to hear it.

'He does,' Angie replied for him. 'Second on the left upstairs.' She fished in her bag for a key. 'Thanks.'

'No worries. Glad to see you safe, bud,' he added to Henry.

Henry mumbled something incomprehensible. He looked worryingly subdued, and his hands were shaking. Angie shared a concerned look with Callie as she ushered Henry towards Eric's car. Darren got into the passenger seat, leaving the rear free for the ladies and Henry, who sat between them, still in a near-catatonic state.

Angie was itching to ask Henry questions but knew now wasn't the time. Instead, she linked her fingers through his and gave his hand a gentle squeeze.

'You're safe now, Henry,' Callie said softly.

Henry stared straight ahead as though he hadn't heard her speak.

Eric arrived at the spa but drove round to the side of the building so that they could enter the office area through a side door, lessening the possibility of Henry being seen. Angie wasn't too sure why it would matter if he was. Presumably, whoever had been holding him had let him go because he'd served his purpose – whatever that might have been. The state he was in proved that he must have been held by someone, for some purpose, against his will. So many questions needed answers.

This was all Paul's fault. She would never forgive him. If she harboured any doubts about the death of her marriage then one look at the state of her beloved son and they were swept aside.

Once inside, Darren took over.

'Come on, bud,' he said. 'Let's get you showered.'

Henry went with Darren, as docile as a lamb.

'Oh God, Callie!' Angie fell into a chair in Callie's office. Wordlessly, Callie went to the bar and poured generous measures of brandy for them both. Angie took her glass from Callie's hand and downed half of its contents so quickly that she choked.

'Easy!' Callie said, taking a more modest sip of her own. 'At least we've got Henry back.' She picked up her internal phone and ordered a light snack for the boy. 'He'll feel better once he's clean and has had something to eat. Then he should be able to tell us where he's been and why.'

'Yeah.' Angie finished the rest of her drink and felt the colour slowly return to her face. 'How did it go at Phoenix?' she asked.

'The girls weren't happy, but I've left Pete in charge. He's changed the code on the gates so that anyone who knows it won't be able to get in. Any punters who press the bell will be told that they're closed.'

Angie found it hard to sit still and so got up and paced around the room, fury slowly replacing the crippling fear for Henry's wellbeing that had gripped her ever since she'd realised he was missing. Whoever had traumatised her son would now have her to deal with, and since it was all Paul's fault, he would be the first in line.

'You okay?' Callie asked gently.

'Never better.' She threw back her head and growled. 'Come on, Henry, get a wiggle on. I want to know where you've been and what part my useless husband played in your disappearance.'

As though summoned by the power of Angie's anxiety, Henry appeared wearing one of the spa's tracksuits. He had obviously towel-dried his hair, which stood up in haphazard clumps around his head. Mercifully, he now smelled of citrus body wash. Some colour had returned to his face too and when sandwiches and coffee was delivered, he tucked in with gusto. Angie was grateful for the resilience of youth.

'How do you feel?' Angie asked, sitting close beside him on a sofa.

'I'm okay, Mum. There's no need to fuss.'

'Can you tell us what happened?' Darren asked. 'Where you've been? Your mum has been going out of her mind.'

'I don't know where I was. In a flat somewhere. I was locked in a room for... for however long I've been gone.'

Angie opened her mouth to tell him it has just been a couple of days but then closed it again without speaking. To her shame, she had no idea how long he'd actually been on the missing list.

'Start at the beginning, mate,' Tom said. 'Where were you when you were taken? Who were you with? What's the last thing you can remember?'

'You don't already know?' Henry blinked at his mother. 'Where's Dad? He could have told you.'

'I'll explain but you first,' Angie said, feeling like the worst mother in the world as she gripped Henry's hand.

'It was a Wednesday,' Henry said hesitantly, Sending Angie another searching look. 'Yeah, definitely a Wednesday because I always have a drink with Dad on a Wednesday.'

'Over a week ago then,' Callie muttered.

'Your dad was involved in this?' Angie thought she'd burst with anger, even though she already knew that he must have been. Suspecting was one thing. Having it confirmed entirely another. At a signal from Callie, she managed to hold back everything else she'd intended to say. Callie was right to imply that Henry was on edge, traumatised. He was also very close to his father, and nothing would be achieved by criticising Paul in his presence. He would know soon enough that Paul hadn't reported him missing and was himself in the wind.

'Go on,' Tom encouraged.

'We were having a drink at... at...' He glanced at his mother, blushed scarlet and stopped speaking.

'At the Phoenix, I'm guessing,' Angie said, her calm tone at direct odds to the swirling anger churning inside of her like a washing machine stuck on the spin cycle.

'Yeah, there.'

'Did Paul often take you the place?' Callie asked.

'Now and again, if he had business. He liked to have meetings there in the private rooms.'

'I'll just bet he did!' Angie couldn't help muttering. Henry sent her an odd look and she somehow managed to refrain from letting rip with the tirade Paul so richly deserved. What self-respecting father took his child to a brothel? Not that Henry was still a child, she conceded, not in the eyes of the law or in his own mind. But he was not nearly so worldly as he imagined and being aware what his father got up to in his "private meetings" was not fair on the kid.

'What do you do?' Darren asked. 'While your dad's in his meetings?'

'I chat to the girls in the lounge if they don't have customers.'

'Any one of them in particular that you got along with?' Callie asked casually.

'Melody,' Henry replied without hesitation, blushing again. 'She had a hard time of it back in Kosovo and was lucky to get out unscathed. She said the experience had changed her, but she didn't go into details.' Henry narrowed his eyes. 'Anyway, what has Melody got to do with anything?'

Angie caught Callie's eye. They were both aware that Melody had denied ever setting eyes on Henry, much less giving him her life story. What the hell was that all about? And why lie about it?

'Probably nothing,' Callie said easily. 'Just trying to build up a picture of what was happening when you were taken.'

'Okay,' Darren said. 'So you were chatting with the girls while your dad had his business meeting. How did you get from there to being held captive?'

'Not too sure. All the girls were busy, and Lucy didn't like me being there. She made no bones about it and never spared me the time of day, so I was on my own in the lounge, wondering if Melody would be free to chat before Dad said we had to leave. Anyway, because it was so quiet, I could hear raised voices coming from the room where Dad had gone with a couple of men.'

'Did you recognise them?' Callie asked.

Henry shook his head. 'I only caught a glimpse of them but I'm pretty sure I'd never seen either of them before.'

'Then what happened?' Tom asked.

'The men left and Dad said we had to go. I wanted to stay but could see he was in no mood to listen to me. You know how he can get when he's wound up, Mum.'

'All too well,' Angie replied, giving Henry's fingers a reassuring squeeze.

'Well anyway, Dad and I left the club. The motion-detector light didn't come on in the car park for some reason, so it was pretty dark. And then...' Henry's breathing became laboured. 'Someone grabbed me from behind. It happened so fast that I didn't have time to react. I was bundled into the back of a van, and it drove off at speed. I heard Dad calling out my name, but he was never going to catch up.'

'Terrifying,' Angie said, resisting the urge to hug her son. She could tell that the shock had worn off and he no longer felt the need to cling to her. It had been nice while it lasted, despite the fact that the need for his mother's comfort had sprung from such a horrendous experience. Henry, she sensed, was now rather enjoying relating the details of his ordeal, especially the part about the brothel and his friendship with the girls. He'd definitely sat a little taller when he talked about them.

'Where did they take you?' Tom asked.

'A flat somewhere. We went up in a lift, but they blind-folded me, so I have no real idea where it was. They kept me in a small room with a mattress on the floor and a bucket to piss in. A blind was pulled down and permanently nailed to the window frame so I had no daylight and but for my watch, wouldn't have known if it was day or night. They delivered junk food twice a day, but I never saw any faces.' Henry paused. 'I did hear a man and a woman talking in the next room, though. I don't know how long they held me. I consoled myself with the thought that the police would be looking for me and that Dad would know which direction to point them in.'

Guilt swept through Angie since she hadn't once considered reporting her son's disappearance to the police. Well, that wasn't strictly true. She'd thought about it endlessly but knew Paul had to be somehow involved in Henry's abduction. Ergo, the hard men he mixed with must be behind it, using Henry to coerce Paul into doing something for them that he obviously didn't want to do. Henry's account bore out that supposition. If the police had come knocking, Henry's life expectancy would have been zero. Dead men tell no tales, and Angie simply wasn't prepared to risk Henry being found face down in a ditch somewhere.

Angie knew that Henry was lucky to be alive. She had yet to decide why he had been released unharmed.

'I didn't even have Helen's number,' Angie said, referring to Henry's latest girlfriend, 'so couldn't get in touch with her to see if you were with her. Besides, I thought you two had broken up.'

'We made up,' Henry replied shortly.

'The police didn't find you,' Darren said, breaking the uneasy silence that ensued, 'so why did they let you go?'

'I can't say for sure. All I know is that the woman kept

banging on about not being able to hold me for much longer. She seemed to be in charge. The man said to hold fire. That Dad would deliver and all would be well. I don't know what he was supposed to deliver. Anyway, today they blindfolded me again, put me back in that van and dropped me on the cliffs. They threw my phone and wallet at me and sped away. I couldn't even get the van's registration number.' Henry sounded disgusted with himself. All Angie could think was how brave he'd been. 'The battery was dead on my phone, so I walked to that bus stop. There was an old lady waiting for the bus and she loaned me her phone so I could call you, Mum. Yours was the only number I could remember.'

Angie inwardly sighed. So much for needing a mother's comfort!

'And that's all I know.'

Henry looked exhausted and Angie suspected there was little more he could tell them about his ordeal. At least not straight away. After a meal and a good night's sleep, other stuff might come back to him.

'Take him back to yours, Angie,' Callie said. 'You'll be safe enough. Whoever took him obviously got what they wanted from Paul.'

'Your turn now, Mum.' Henry turned to look at her, granite forming the bedrock of his expression. The image of his father at that age. 'Where's Dad and what aren't you telling me?'

Angie hesitated, but only momentarily. 'Your dad hasn't been seen since you were taken,' she said, opting for the brutal truth. 'He's obviously gone off to do whatever those men wanted of him so that you'd be released.'

'Christ! I hope you didn't tell the police I was missing, in that case.'

Angie's heart went out to her son when his first thought

was for his father's safety. 'We didn't, love, but we've had people asking questions and shaking trees.'

'Sorry, Mum. It must have been horrible for you, not knowing where either of us were, or what to do about the situation.' Henry briefly hugged her. 'But you did the right thing, not involving the police.'

He sounded so mature that Angie wanted to weep.

'I brought you some of your things, Henry,' Tom said, indicating the bag of clothes on the floor at his feet.

Without another word about his father's disappearance, Henry pushed himself to his feet and left the room.

'Well then.' Darren broke the silence that reined once the door closed behind him. 'What do we make of that?'

'Absolutely no idea,' Angie replied. 'All I do know is that when I get my hands on Paul, he'll regret the day his mother gave birth to him.' She exhaled loudly. 'How could he be so irresponsible as to take our son to a contentious meeting in a brothel?'

'One thing we do know now, though,' Callie said, 'is that Melody was economical with the truth, to put it mildly.'

'She told me she'd never laid eyes on Henry,' Angie replied, nodding. 'But it seems they knew each other quite well.' She frowned. 'Why lie about something that could so easily catch her out?'

'Unless she knew Henry had been abducted and assumed he wouldn't live to tell the tale,' Tom said, squeezing Angie's shoulder as he put into words what they had all probably been thinking. 'So we have to assume that she's up to her neck in this business.'

'Why am I not surprised,' Angie replied, fuming still.

Henry returned, dressed in jeans and trainers and looking almost recovered.

'All set?' Angie asked, standing and summoning up a smile that probably didn't reach her eyes.

'I'll drive you,' Tom said, his tone brooking no argument. 'You can pick your car up from the showroom tomorrow.'

Angie nodded as she stood. Her concentration was shot, and she'd be a danger to herself and other road users if she got behind a wheel.

'Thanks for your help, Callie,' Henry said.

'Any time, although I hope it won't be under the same circumstances.'

'Oh, just one thing I've remembered,' Henry said, turning back from the open doorway. 'I don't know if it means anything, but I heard the man and woman mention Liverpool several times.'

Callie and Angie exchanged a look and simultaneously shook their heads. No one else seemed any the wiser either.

Only when Angie was home and Henry was upstairs, on the phone to his girlfriend, did Tom mention to her that they had a contract with a main dealership in Liverpool.

11

Left alone, Callie and Darren stared at one another for a protracted moment, attempting to get their heads round what they had just heard.

'What the hell!' Callie threw up her hands.

'I hope you don't expect an answer,' Darren replied. 'Whatever's going on, it beats the hell out of me. All we know for sure is that someone at Phoenix is up to their neck in it. If we hadn't thought so before Lucy was attacked, then we sure as hell know it now.'

'Someone thought she'd told tales out of school? Perhaps because we visited.'

'Precisely.'

'Paul was coerced into doing something he didn't want to in order to save Henry.' Callie said. 'At least we know why Henry was taken, if not by whom. So what's going on? And does it involve Gavin?'

'This all went down ten days ago, and Gavin's been in the wind for a lot longer than that.'

'True, but that doesn't mean he's not pulling strings from

wherever he is now.' Callie rested her elbow on her desk and her chin on her fisted hand. 'Poor Henry had been held for a week before Angie even realised that he was missing. From Angie's perspective, that's probably just as well. She'd have gone out of her mind with worry, and I would have felt compelled to put Fallow on the case. And if he'd gotten involved, that would have sealed Henry's fate.'

'Just having the police looking for him might have been enough to do that. Although, I don't think there was ever any intention of killing Henry.'

'What makes you think so?' Callie asked.

'Well, he wasn't physically harmed, he was fed, and they didn't let him see their faces. All the time Paul did as they wanted, Henry was in no real danger.'

'I see what you mean.' Callie leaned back in her chair, her mind alive with increasingly unrealistic scenarios.

'Two close friends and business partners are on the run at the same time but for different reasons,' Darren said dubiously. 'What are the chances? There has to be a connection.'

'Absolutely no idea, but if you're suggesting that Gavin had to coerce Paul by abducting his son then you've got it completely wrong. Gavin is many things, most of them unethical, but he wouldn't drag women or kids into his nefarious activities. Look at the way he's always kept me out of his business.'

'You haven't wanted to be involved. Henry, on the other hand, idolises his father and wants to emulate him.' Darren held up a hand to prevent Callie from protesting. 'He took him along to a brothel, for fuck's sake. How many fathers would do that?'

Callie had never really taken to Paul. He was given to bragging, to flashing the cash and putting himself about. Before

Angie had been forced to see him for what he was, she'd adored him. Callie's loyalty towards her friend was solid but she'd never have told Angie about Paul's extramarital activities. If Angie had wanted to think her marriage was made in heaven, Callie hadn't wanted to disabuse her, but now the blinkers had well and truly come off and Callie was glad, especially since she too was ready to jack her marriage in. She and Angie were no longer in the first flush of youth, but they weren't too old to have some long overdue fun.

'Anyway,' Callie said, sighing. 'I think our next task is to grill the lovely Melody. She's involved somehow; I'd bet my bank balance on it.'

'I agree, but she's probably too scared to talk. Still, it's worth a try. I suggest bringing her in here. She will be less confident away from familiar surroundings and perhaps scared enough, after what happened to Lucy, to drop a few clues.'

'Anything's possible.'

'I'll go and fetch her first thing in the morning,' Darren said. 'In the meantime, I'll have Pete make sure she doesn't leg it.'

'You can trust him?'

Darren waggled a hand from side to side. 'As much as it's possible to trust anyone in this game. Until we know what they've got going in that place, it's impossible to be absolutely sure. Pete and Gavin go way back, though. I think they grew up in the same part of town which, I guess, counts for brotherly bonding, or some such shit.'

Callie stretched her arms above her head and yawned, feeling weary and every second of her age. 'God, this business is getting to me. I'm exhausted!'

'Take yourself home and have some you time.' Darren chuckled. 'I'm sure the boss won't mind if you leave early.'

'Oh, I dunno about that. I hear she's a bit of a slave driver.'

Darren winked at her. 'I'll put in a word for you.' He picked up her jacket and held it out to her. 'Come on. Get out of here.'

'Yes, sir!'

Callie slipped her arms into the sleeves, picked up her phone and bag and fished out her car keys.

'I'll go to Phoenix first thing, drag Melody out of bed and have her here when you arrive.'

'Thanks, Darren. Have a good evening. I appreciate your help.'

'No worries.'

He smiled as he opened the door for her. Callie walked through it and let herself out the back way to avoid being detained by any of the regulars in the spa.

She drove home swiftly, trying not to overthink the situation with Paul and Henry. Sometimes, not thinking about something made obvious answers pop into her head but this time, it didn't work.

At home, she carefully double locked the front door behind her, put on lights everywhere and checked the app on her phone to ensure that the cameras outside were recording. She wouldn't admit it to anyone, but she was spooked.

'What did you get yourself into, Gavin, you twat?' she asked aloud, grateful for the sound of her own voice.

She put some music on, just to make the house feel a little less empty, and poured herself a glass of wine. She sipped at it as she kicked off her shoes and made her way upstairs. In her massive bedroom, she put her glass down on the side of the bath, turned the taps on, poured ruinously expensive bath oil into the tub and then lit the candles that surrounded it.

Having created a relaxing ambiance, Callie stripped off her

clothes in the bedroom and walked back into the bathroom, phone in one hand. She left it on the side and lowered herself into the fragrant waters, already feeling some of the tension draining out of her. She leaned back and closed her eyes, letting her thoughts run amok. Instead of focusing upon Henry and what they'd learned from his captivity, her mind seemed determined to focus on Darren and her heavy reliance upon him. It wasn't wise to put so much trust in anyone, she reminded herself, but so far, he'd given her no reason to doubt his integrity.

Besides, she was out of her depth with this business. Abductions, attacks on madams and sex workers with different agendas were all above her paygrade. It felt as though she was attempting to hold back the tide with a teaspoon and needed someone to have her back. Darren insisted that he was on the side of the angels, but he came from a tough criminal background, had contacts in surprising places and knew how to fight dirty.

She needed him.

Callie closed her eyes, allowing the soothing water to do its work. In danger of dropping off to sleep, her phone chirping into life on the edge of the bath brought her swiftly back to full consciousness.

'How is he?' she asked, seeing Angie's name flash up on the screen as she took the call.

'He's eating.' Callie could hear a combination of relief and amusement in Angie's tone. 'A lot.'

'Well, that's a good sign, isn't it?'

'Yeah, I guess. I have to say, he seems to be taking what happened to him in his stride. I've told him he can't talk about it to anyone, which I think he was gagging to do. You know, talking it up and everything. But when I said that Paul's safety depended on his discretion, that did the trick. He's really worried about his dad.'

'Well, he would be.'

'And seems to think that I don't give a shit.'

'In fairness, you've had a lot to take,' Callie reasoned.

'Yeah, but I don't want to make the kid take sides, so I've told him that Paul'll be fine. It's hard for me to be convincing though when I could cheerfully strangle the bastard for dragging Henry into his dodgy doings.' Callie could hear Angie's sigh echo across the connection. 'It was *the* one thing he promised me faithfully that he'd never do. A line he would never cross. He said he wanted a better start for our kids than he'd had, and I stupidly believed him. Well, not any more.'

'I don't know what to say. I can't even begin to imagine how anguished you must be.'

'Thanks. It's hard. I want to lock Henry in his room and never let him out of my sight again. But he's resilient and is already pushing me away. It's only a matter of time, I guess, before he probes me about his father and what I'm doing to find him. He'll blame me if he thinks I'm not looking hard enough. He's still very much a child in that respect.'

'Refer him to me if he gets antsy. Say Paul and Gavin are off together, or something. That will buy us some time.'

'Thanks. I hope in some respects that Henry's release means Paul's done whatever was asked of him and he'll walk through the door. That way, I won't have to hunt him down in order to throttle him.'

Callie laughed. 'That's the spirit!' She paused. 'Is Tom still there?'

'No, I sent him home. But he's why I'm calling you.'

'Really?' Callie chuckled. 'Something I should know about you two?'

'Absolutely not! Behave yourself.'

'Sorry. Okay, what about Tom?'

'Liverpool. He told me out of Henry's earshot that they have a regular run up to Liverpool from the showroom to a dealer there. Cars go back and forth between them all the time.'

'Do they indeed.' Callie let that sink in for a moment. 'So this *is* to do with the movement of cars.'

'Apparently so. Paul deals in new and nearly new cars, as you know. Demonstration models, short-term lease cars, stuff like that. And he has a regular supplier in Liverpool for the new ones. There's something not quite right about it, I've always thought. I mean, new cars have to be legit, don't they? It's not as if they can fall off the back of the lorry that's transporting them.'

'Something is being taken to or from Liverpool in cars that are being moved around, perhaps on trade plates,' Callie suggested.

'Drugs is the obvious assumption,' Angie said. 'Especially since we thought that might be what was going down at Phoenix; Paul had his meetings there and it's where Henry was taken from.'

'Paul got into something, then wanted out, but his paymasters were having none of it.'

'Whatever it is, he's been gone a hell of a long time. He probably doesn't even know that Henry's safe,' Angie pointed out.

'Perhaps he insisted upon him being released before completing whatever it is he's doing.' Callie paused. 'Has his passport gone?'

'He always carries it with him.'

'Yeah, Gavin does too. I guess they were both boy scouts.'

Angie laughed. 'Yeah, right!'

'Did you ask Tom for the name of the supplier in Liverpool?'

'No. Should I have?'

'I have absolutely no idea, babe, but we're a step closer to getting answers, that much I do know. Darren's bringing Melody here first thing tomorrow. Liverpool is something I can throw at her. See how she reacts.'

'I'll be there.'

'Not in the interview,' Callie said, her voice firm. 'You're emotionally involved and predisposed to dislike Melody. Leave it to Darren and me. I'm hoping that we can scare her enough, dangling what happened to Lucy and Henry in front of her, to make her tell us what she knows.'

'Ha! Good luck with that one. She's as tough as old boots beneath that lovely exterior.'

'Yeah, I know. I don't expect her to roll over, but she must be spooked by what's happened so hopefully, she'll let something slip.'

'Okay, I'll let you get on. I'll be in work tomorrow.'

'Don't worry if Henry needs you.'

'He doesn't.'

Callie could hear the sorrow in her friend's voice. 'Even so, be there for him. He's trying to be a man and pretend he doesn't need his mum but we both know differently.'

'See you in the morning.'

'Yeah, later. Love you.'

'You too.'

The water had turned tepid, so Callie climbed out of her bath, towelled herself dry and drank the last of her wine. Wrapped in a warm robe, she wandered downstairs and vaguely thought about eating something. Not having the energy to cook, she eventually rang for a home-delivery

Chinese, consumed less than half of it when it arrived, drank more wine and then locked up and went to bed early.

The wine worked its magic, and she slept soundly for eight hours solid.

Callie awoke refreshed and determined to get some answers. She dressed with care, aware that she would be confronting a probably disgruntled and antagonistic Melody. Callie needed to be at the top of her game and refused to entertain the possibility of being intimidated by anyone.

She arrived at her office at eight thirty, consulted with her duty manager to iron out any problems that had arisen overnight and placed a few business calls. By nine thirty, when there was no sign of Darren, she began to worry. On the point of calling him, she held off. Darren was more than capable of collecting Melody and if something had happened to prevent him from bringing her in, he would have let her know.

Angie put her head round Callie's door.

'Hi.' Callie got up to hug her. 'How's Henry? No nightmares, I hope.'

'Nope. Seemingly not. He got annoyed when I woke him up to ask if he was all right. Anyway, I left him sound asleep again.' Angie sat down, frowning. 'My only concern is that he might go to Phoenix to try and find out what happened to his dad.'

'Don't worry. Pete won't let him in. It's Friday today. Encourage him to see his girlfriend over the weekend and do normal stuff. Then on Monday, he could go back to working at the car lot. That way, Tom will be on hand to look out for him.'

'Yeah, that's a plan. I don't want to depend too much on Tom, though.'

'You don't think he's involved with Paul's dodgy dealings, do you?'

'I'd like to think not but...' Angie threw up her hands and

spread them wide. 'I appear to be a lousy judge of character when it comes to men.'

Callie chuckled. 'I feel the same way about Darren. He's almost too good to be true, but we both need someone to lean on, just a bit, and the way I see it, if they are working with our useless husbands then our being so proactive might actually bring them to their senses.'

'Because we might be putting ourselves in danger and they will be our Sir Galahad's riding to our rescue?' Angie gave a bitter little laugh. 'Anything's possible, I suppose.'

'My point is, we haven't found out anything that they don't already know, so they'll think we aren't doing any harm. If Darren or Tom try to steer us away from a particular course, *then* we'll know we're onto something.'

'I hear you!' Angie paused. 'Where's George Markham? Haven't heard anything about him for a while.'

'He has a building project going on in Kent and spends time there. All legit. I don't think he knows where Gavin is or why he's gone but I do think he relishes the opportunity to get on with his own stuff without Gavin pulling his strings.'

'Ah well, I guess that's what Paul's doing too but making a right old cock up of it.'

Darren put his head round the door at that point.

'Morning, ladies. She's here and not too happy about it. I had to literally drag her from her bed.'

'Give her some coffee and keep her waiting for ten minutes,' Callie replied. 'Then bring her in here and stay yourself.'

'Will do.' Darren disappeared again.

'Go and get some work done, Angie.' Callie stood again and gave her friend another hug. 'I'll buzz you as soon as I've spoken with her.'

'It's probably better if I don't see her again,' Angie conceded. 'You're right about that, even if your reasons don't match my own. I can't guarantee that I wouldn't do her serious bodily harm for messing with my husband *and* my son.'

Angie flashed a sympathetic smile. 'I hear you. Now scoot! Get out of here.'

Callie pulled up documents on her computer that she'd put off studying, aware that her concentration was shot, and she'd never make sense of hoops she had to jump through in order to turn the adjacent land which she'd just acquired into a golf course. It would be useful to be absorbed when Darren tapped at the door and ushered Melody through it, Callie knew, and so she deliberately didn't look up for several prolonged seconds, making the woman stand in front of her desk like a recalcitrant schoolgirl.

'Thank you for coming in,' Callie eventually said, glancing at the woman and finding it hard to disguise her reaction. Without make-up and dressed in jeans and a sweatshirt, Melody didn't look nearly so sophisticated. Her hair was a tangled mess, she had a spot on her chin and her expression was mutinous. 'Sit down.'

'I did not have a lot of choice about coming in. What's this all about and why do I need to be here?'

When Callie made no reply, Melody flounced in her chair like a stroppy teenager and crossed one denim-clad, impossibly long leg over its twin.

'Now then.' Callie removed her reading glasses and lent towards Melody. 'You would not be here now if you'd been truthful.'

'I do not lie!'

'Really!' Callie subjected the younger woman to a

prolonged look. 'Remind me again what you said to Angie about never having met her son?'

'What did you expect me to say to his mother?' Melody tossed her hair over one shoulder. 'I could tell she did not like me or approve of the way I make a living. Few women do. They like to feel superior, just as you are at this moment. Mrs Dalton was angry because Paul chose to fuck me and got obsessed.' She lifted one shoulder. 'It happens, but she wouldn't be pleased if she knew that her precious son enjoyed my company too.'

'And yet thanks to you, Henry has been abducted.'

She looked worried by the accusation. 'That had nothing to do with me!'

'My understanding is that Henry came to the brothel with his father in the hope of spending time with you. He was abducted from the brothel, so how can you not be to blame?'

'You are just like all the rest.' Melody leaned forward, her features rendered temporarily ugly by her spiteful expression. 'I am a prostitute, so it follows that I have no morals.'

'Do you?' Callie asked, unmoved by her clumsy attempt to play the martyr. 'Have a conscience, that is? I wonder, you see, because you have yet to ask me if there's any news of Henry. Do you even care?'

'What's the point of telling you that I do?' Melody actually pouted, and irritatingly, the gesture looked attractive on her. 'You will believe whatever you want to and anyway, you have already made up your mind about me.'

Darren, who had been leaning against the wall, stepped forward. 'Who were the two men that Paul argued with on the evening that Henry was taken?' he asked.

'I don't know. I didn't see them, or Henry that night. I was with a client.' A sly smile replaced the pout. 'Ask Superintendent Fallow if you doubt my word.'

'Fallow was there that night?' Callie shared a look with Darren. It was the first thing the girl had said that surprised her.

'He is there far too often and gets whatever he wants without paying.' Melody looked resigned. 'It is always that way for men of influence.'

'Right.' Callie took a moment to assess the implications of Fallow's presence at the club on that particular night. Could he have been one of the men who Paul argued with? 'Did he visit you on a regular basis? On the same nights?'

Melody shrugged. 'He comes to the club at least twice a week, but it is not always me that has to entertain him, thank goodness.' She paused. 'He also comes for the game, of course.'

'The game?' Callie and Darren asked together.

'There's a poker school every Wednesday night. Gavin started it. High stakes, of course, and Fallow is a regular.'

Callie nodded. She knew there was a poker school but hadn't been aware that it was run from Phoenix. She wondered if that was significant, especially since Henry had been taken and Paul had disappeared on a Wednesday.

'Very well, we'll leave that aside for a moment. Tell me instead who you think it was that attacked Lucy so viciously and why?'

'I have no idea.' But she looked away, avoiding eye contact.

Darren again stepped forward and this time thumped his clenched fist against the surface of Callie's desk. Hard. Melody flinched. 'Try again,' he said.

Callie almost flinched too. She had never seen Darren in such an uncompromising mood before and she was almost afraid of him, even though his ire wasn't directed at her.

'I really don't know and that's the God's honest truth. We are victims of our own success in some respects. We get the cream of the local custom. Lucky us.' Melody rolled her eyes. 'Other establishments are always sniffing around us girls, trying to lure us away with unrealistic promises. Lucy is our gatekeeper. Not that we're prisoners but it's in her own best interests to keep us happy and protected. That way, we all benefit.'

'Do you really expect us to believe that some rival madam or her associates beat Lucy to a pulp simply so that she could filch some of her girls?' Callie widened her eyes, making it obvious what she thought of that possibility.

'I'm not trying to make you believe anything.' Melody seemed more confident now and sent Callie a mocking smile. 'I am simply telling you the way that it is. Our business is extremely competitive. I hardly ever leave the club alone. I've been approached more times than I can recall with offers of alternative employment whenever I have done so, and that makes me uncomfortable. I am happy enough where I am. I can work as much or as little as I please. I make my own hours and have no interest in leaving. Not yet anyway.'

Callie glanced at Darren, who shook his head. Callie was convinced that Melody knew a great deal more about what went down at Phoenix that she was willing to share but it would be a waste of time pressing her. Beneath that pretty exterior, she was as hard as nails and wouldn't tell them anything unless she herself felt under threat.

'What do you know about Liverpool?' Callie asked, watching Melody closely as she posed the question.

'Only that it is a city in the north. I have never been there.' Her reaction appeared genuine and this time, she was able to hold Callie's gaze. 'Why do you ask?'

'Has Paul ever mentioned going there?'

Melody shrugged. 'Not as far as I can recall. But a lot of men say a lot of things to me. I hardly bother to listen. They are all so self-centred that it becomes boring.'

'Okay,' Callie said. 'That'll be all. I'm sure you're well able to take care of yourself but I would strongly suggest that you stay at Phoenix and continue your habit of not going out alone if you feel the need to go anywhere. Whoever attacked Lucy isn't done yet, I sense, and you could well be in that person's sights.'

'When can we reopen? Time is money.'

'If and when I say you can. And, although you haven't bothered to ask, I thought you might like to know that Henry has been found safe and well.'

Relief and a spontaneous smile spread across Melody's face as she muttered something beneath her breath in a language Callie didn't understand. 'Thank God for that!' she then said in English. 'Is he all right? Does he know who took him? What happened to him? Where is Paul?'

It was the most animated that Melody had been. Genuine relief that the kid was safe, or did she have an ulterior reason for her questions? It was difficult for Callie to decide.

'Thanks for your time,' she said. 'Darren will show you out.'

12

Angie burst into Callie's office a few minutes after Melody quit it. She was breathless and red in the face.

'What have you been doing?' Callie asked. 'You look as though you just ran a marathon.'

'Never mind all that. What did she have to say for herself?'

Before Callie could respond, Darren joined them. Unlike Angie, he looked suave and sophisticated, not a hair out of place.

'I put her in a cab,' he said. 'She is not a happy bunny.'

Callie indicated the comfortable chairs in front of the full-length windows, from where they could see the activity in the reception area below them, but no one could see them. There was a lot to be said for one-way glass. Coupled with cameras in almost every area of the spa, Callie sometimes felt as though Big Brother had taken over. But that was a small price to pay for having overall control. Not much went down in her empire without Callie being aware of it. Attention to detail, she often thought, was one of the reasons why she'd made such a success of the place.

Darren wordlessly went to the coffee machine, produced brews for them all and handed them round.

'What did you make of her performance, Darren?' Callie asked, once he'd taken the chair beside hers and briefly checked his phone.

'It *was* a performance,' Darren replied thoughtfully. 'I agree with you there. That one thinks on her feet and told us as little as possible. But she knows much more than she let on, that's for sure.'

'She didn't let on about anything,' Callie replied, venting her frustration with a wave of one arm.

'She's scared and trying hard not to show it. What's frightened her is another matter and not something she's likely to admit to. Her only genuine reaction was when we told her that Henry was safe and well. Interestingly though, she didn't press for details about his captivity.' Darren waved the hand not holding his coffee. 'She's a mass of contradictions and I'm not sure what to make of her.'

'Do you think she's involved in any way with whatever led to Henry's abduction?' Angie asked.

'I don't think we can ignore the possibility,' Callie replied. 'What she did tell us that I found interesting is that there's a weekly poker school at the club. I remember Gavin starting it years ago but didn't know it was still running. But apparently it is, and for high stakes. But get this: Fallow is not only a regular visitor to the brothel where he gets away with taking what he wants without paying, but he was also there for the poker game on the night that Henry was abducted.'

'He *has* to know what went down then!' Angie cried, bouncing on the edge of her seat. 'We need you to press him on that, Callie.'

'For what reason?' Callie asked gently. 'Henry's safe now. If we find out who took him, what will you do about it and what will that achieve? These are dangerous people. Look what happened to Lucy. And it's not as if you're desperate to find Paul.'

'I'm thinking of you, Cal. You've said yourself that you'll be under all sorts of pressure until Gavin resurfaces. And, I suppose, there is an outside possibility that both of our husbands are in above their heads.'

'Even if that's true,' Darren remarked, 'how do you suppose the two of you will be able to extract them?'

'Angie makes a good point,' Callie said, sighing. 'I need some answers if I'm ever to be free of the demands made by Gavin's associates. And since he's gone to ground for so long, I can no longer mark time, waiting for him to return and get them off my back. And until I have some idea what caused Gavin to run scared, I'm flying blind.'

'Whatever made Paul run, and we know his hand was forced by Henry's abduction, might be entirely separate from Gavin's dealings,' Darren said.

'Yeah, I know, but it's the only avenue we have so far. Anyway, I'm pretty sure Melody knows who Paul was arguing with that evening,' Callie said, 'but short of torturing her, she'll never say. Same goes for Fallow. He's always been out for number one and will lie and prevaricate unless there's something in it for him.'

Angie rubbed the back of her neck. 'Could one of the people Paul fell out with have been Fallow?' she asked.

'It wouldn't surprise me,' Darren said. 'But we don't actually know he was at the club at that precise time.'

'Melody implied that he was,' Callie replied. 'But we can't believe what either one of them says, so there's absolutely no point in asking Fallow if he strongarmed Paul into doing...

something. He'll only deny it and we'll have shown our hand for no reason.'

'Then we're no further forward in finding our husbands, Cal,' Angie said, pouting. 'I don't much care if I never set eyes on Paul again, but I know that having Gavin on the missing list leaves you treading water, so what now?'

'I think we need to pursue the Liverpool angle,' Darren remarked. 'Perhaps we should ask Tom more about that. Melody seemed genuinely ignorant about it but if Tom can tell us who Paul's dealer friend is in that part of the world, we could do some digging.'

'I'll call him in a minute and ask him,' Angie said.

'Go and see him in person, Ang. You need to keep showing your face at the dealership anyway. You'll get a better idea if he's telling the truth if you can see his reaction. As for us,' Callie added, glancing at Darren, 'I think another visit to the hospital would be in order.'

'We don't even know if they've brought Lucy out of her coma,' Darren pointed out. 'Shouldn't we ring and ask?'

'No. If she is conscious, I don't want her to know we're coming. That would give her the opportunity to say she doesn't want visitors, whereas if we just turn up with a bunch of grapes...'

'You want me to come with you?' Darren asked.

Callie grinned at Angie. 'Just in case the nurses get all protective and need to be persuaded.'

Darren winked at her. 'Charming nurses isn't in my job description, but for you, I'll see what I can do.'

'I'm going to pop home and check on Henry,' Angie said, picking up her bag. 'It's on my way to the showroom and... well, I just need to make sure that my first born isn't suffering from delayed shock, or anything. I tried to get him to see our GP, but he came over all macho and was having none of it.'

'Okay, babe.' Callie gave Angie a hug. 'Catch up with you later.'

A short time after that, Callie and Darren arrived at the hospital. As Callie had predicted, they were told that Lucy had been brought out of her coma. She was awake and lucid.

'She's very fragile and still in intensive care,' the nurse told them. 'But since you're her employer and she doesn't seem to have any family, seeing a friendly face will help her. I can let you have five minutes. No more than that and try not to say anything to get her agitated or it's my neck that will be on the line. She needs to remain calm. She's very ill.'

'Yeah, we know,' Darren said, flashing a smile that caused the pretty young nurse to blush. 'We just want to make sure she's as okay as it's possible for her to be under the circumstances.'

The nurse nodded. 'The police were here earlier. They asked to be told when she was conscious, but I don't think she could tell them anything about who attacked her.'

The nurse pressed a door code that let them into intensive care. Darren thanked her and headed for the cubicle that she indicated with Callie at his side.

'How do you do that?' she asked, grinning.

'It's what you asked me to do,' Darren replied, his expression so innocent that Callie burst out laughing. Her laughter seemed out of place in intensive care, though, and several castigating looks were sent her way by stressed visitors.

They found Lucy propped up with pillows. Her eyes were closed but Callie didn't think she was asleep. Her face was a puffy mass of cuts and bruises, and her breathing was shallow. One wrist was in a cast and the frame that elevated the bedcovers implied that there was damage to her legs. Someone had really given her a going over. Callie's blood ran cold. If they could do this to a person just for talking to her, what would they do to Callie if she stood in their way?

Gavin, what the fuck did you get yourself into?

'Hey,' Callie said softly, touching Lucy's good hand gently. 'How do you feel?'

Lucy's eyes flew open. 'Who let you in here?' she asked in a raspy voice.

'Who did this to you?' Callie asked, ignoring the venom behind Lucy's words.

'If I knew, do you think I'd tell you?'

'We thought you'd like to know that Henry Dalton has been found safe and unharmed,' Darren said, smiling at her.

To Callie's surprise, that knowledge seemed to cheer Lucy up. 'So, it's all over,' she muttered, closing her eyes again.

'What's over?' Callie asked. 'What do you know about this business? Where's Paul? You really need to tell us. We can't help you if you don't.'

'Your help I can do without. You need to go.' Lucy kept her eyes closed. 'Tired. Need to sleep. Just stay away from me.'

'I've closed the club until you're fit enough to return and take control,' Callie said. 'Did I do the right thing?'

'Why ask me?' Lucy's voice was so low, so raspy, it was hard to make out the words, but there was no mistaking the combination of fear and animosity that radiated from her. 'You'll do what you want anyway.'

'The girls are being paid by me to do nothing, so we don't think any of them will abandon ship,' Callie continued, undaunted.

'Well, aren't you just lady bountiful.' Lucy's voice had been reduced to a whisper. Callie could see that it was an effort for her to speak and that she really was exhausted. Besides, they'd not get anything out of her. It had been naïve of Callie to suppose otherwise, she realised.

'Get well soon.' Callie stood. 'Oh, and does Liverpool mean anything to you?'

Lucy's eyes flew open. She looked terrified. 'Nothing. Just go away.'

She closed her eyes again and Callie gave up.

'Liverpool's definitely the way to go,' she said to Darren as they left the hospital and climbed into Darren's car. 'Hopefully, Angie will get something from Tom to point us in the right direction.'

'Perhaps we should talk to Fallow after all before we do anything else. At the very least, we need to know why he didn't mention being at the club on the night Paul and Henry disappeared.'

'Like I said to Angie, he's unlikely to tell us the truth but it will be interesting to see his reaction, I suppose,' Callie agreed. 'I'll call him when we get back to the spa.'

But upon their return, all thoughts of Fallow were put on hold. Ryan O'Keefe, a tall, immaculately dressed older man with a mane of silver hair artfully swept back from a high forehead, awaited her. He'd leaned himself against the reception desk, avidly watching the activity as he peppered the receptionist with questions.

'Oh shit!' she muttered beneath her breath. 'That's all I need.'

O'Keefe turned as she approached, offering her a charming smile and his hand simultaneously. He repeated the gesture with Darren, addressing him by name. Callie wasn't aware that the two of them had ever met, causing her to doubt her own judgement about Darren's integrity. Then again, she reasoned, if O'Keefe was here to strongarm her then he would have made it his business to find out who she surrounded herself with. He would also be aware of Darren's father's situation and probably assumed that Darren would be open to bribery. Either that, or Gavin had taken Darren with him to a meeting with O'Keefe in the past. That seemed the most likely explanation.

'I apologise for calling without an appointment, Callie,' O'Keefe said, leaning in to kiss her on both cheeks. 'I know you are a busy woman, and I dare say that Gavin's disappearance has increased your burden.'

'Hello, Ryan. How are you?' Callie schooled her features into an impassive expression. He had her at a disadvantage as it was. The slightest sign of fear and he'd walk all over her. *Not happening!* 'How's the family?'

Callie had met Ryan O'Keefe on several occasions. Whenever Gavin was in the mood to impress by entertaining lavishly, O'Keefe's name was always on the guest list. As was Stafford's and a few other local unworthies.

'We're all good, thanks. It's been too long since we saw you.' *Not long enough!*

'What can I do for you, Ryan?' she asked briskly.

'Can we talk somewhere more private?' He glanced around the busy reception area, where a sea of robe-clad figures moved in gaggles as they made their way from one treatment area to another. 'Business is booming, I'm glad to see.'

Callie wanted to tell him that it was nothing to do with him, but that wasn't an option. She didn't have a death wish.

'Of course.'

Callie led the way up the sweeping staircase and entered her private domain. O'Keefe stood at the full-length windows, glanced down at the area they'd just left, then took in the bank of screens that covered most areas of the facility and nodded his approval.

'Classy,' he said.

Callie offered coffee which thankfully, O'Keefe declined.

'Just a word in private,' he said, sending Darren a significant look. Darren took the hint and left the office, closing the door quietly behind him.

'How can I help you?' Callie asked, taking the chair behind her desk and indicating the one in front of it to O'Keefe.

He sat down and fastidiously adjusted the crease in his trousers before returning his attention to her.

'Do you have any idea when Gavin will be returning?'

'You came here to ask me that in person?' Callie raised a brow, keeping her voice calm and conversational. 'A phone call would have been less trouble.'

'I also wanted to see how you're coping, obviously.' His smile showed early signs of strain. Stafford was a pussycat compared to O'Keefe, who was definitely not accustomed to anyone, especially a woman, questioning his conduct.

'I run this spa on my own. Gavin's little jaunt makes no difference to its popularity or profitability.'

O'Keefe flashed a reptilian smile and said nothing. Callie knew she was supposed to fill the ensuing silence with syco-phantic chat but was in no mood to play O'Keefe's games. In the end, it was O'Keefe who spoke again, and she felt as though she had achieved a small victory.

'You didn't tell me when you expect Gavin to come back?'

'Because I have absolutely no idea and frankly, I don't much care.'

He flexed a brow and probably didn't believe her. 'Well then, in his absence, I shall just have to transact my business with you.'

'In the market for a massage, are you, Ryan? I can arrange that. Ordinarily, there's a waiting list but for you...'

O'Keefe's expression darkened. 'Let's not play games, Callie. I have no beef with you, and I don't approve of Gavin legging it and leaving you to take the flack. Let's not make this any harder than it needs to be.'

'What flack?'

O'Keefe shook his head. 'You really don't know, do you?'

'Ryan, you've lost me. If you and Gavin had some business going, then you know very well that he won't have discussed it with me, so there's nothing I can do to help you.'

'He would have had to discuss the sale of this place. On paper, you're its owner.'

'What!' Callie half rose from her chair, shocked to the core. 'No, there must be a misunderstanding.' She slowly sank back down again. 'This is my business, registered in my name and Gavin has nothing to do with its running. If Gavin felt the need to sell then he would have to discuss the matter with me, which he did not.'

'You really are charmingly naïve, my dear.'

And you're fucking patronising!

'Call me what you like but I know my own business and it cannot be sold without my signature on the documents. End of.' She stood this time, trying not to let Ryan see that her legs, her entire body was shaking with a combination of fear and anger. Why the devil would Gavin agree to sell *her* business, a business that she loved and that she'd made a success of, without at least talking to her about it? 'I'm sorry that you've had a wasted journey, Ryan, but the spa is not for sale.'

'You're right insofar as you will need to sign the contract, but I have a written assurance from Gavin that you will do so. A price has been agreed. A very advantageous price from your perspective.' He threw a document onto her desk. In spite of herself, Callie picked it up and scanned its contents. It was a letter of intent, signed by Gavin. It wouldn't stand up in a court of law, and O'Keefe would be aware of that, but then he wasn't the type to trouble the legal system when it came to his business affairs. He preferred the more direct, hands-on approach when resolving disputes.

'I can see that this has come as a bolt out of the blue and I'm sorry.' O'Keefe lowered his voice to a seductive purr that made Callie's skin crawl. 'Even so, a promise is a promise, and I shall have to hold you to it.'

Callie knew there was no point in reminding the wretched man that she'd made no promises at all.

'Why do you want it? It's not in your line of business.'

'Why did Gavin offer it to me? I got the impression that he was short of cash and had people chasing him for it. Nasty people. He showed me your books and I have to say, I'm impressed. Even so, I thought I was doing him a favour. But now I've become accustomed to the thought of owning the place. I have plans for it and need to get the ownership transferred pronto.'

'He would have told me, talked to me about selling. He knows how much I've enjoyed building the business up.'

Callie spoke with more conviction than she actually felt. Could the debts that O'Keefe had referred to actually exist? The one thing that Callie had never had to worry about during the course of her marriage was money. There had always been an excess of it. Since making a success of the spa, she'd been financially independent and had never given Gavin's personal finances a passing thought. But Gavin had recently decided to go mostly legit. Had he sunk his capital into something that was too good to be true? Callie wished now that she'd paid more attention when he'd spoken of the opportunities available to a man of courage and vision.

'Gavin has got himself in a bit of a tight spot and taken the cowardly way out by doing a runner. But he can't hide forever and those who want an urgent word with him will find him eventually. And if they don't then they'll turn their attention to you.' O'Keefe fixed her with a hard look. 'If they haven't already.'

Callie thought of Stafford and swallowed. She didn't actually say anything but suspected that her expression did the talking for her.

'I thought as much.' O'Keefe nodded, his expression grim. 'Take a few days to think it over and I'll come back for your answer. If you get any hassle in the meantime, let me know. I'll have your back. You don't deserve any of this.' He leaned across the desk and kissed her cheek again. 'I'll be in touch.'

Callie, unable to say a word because she was too angry and too choked with emotion, watched the door close behind him. She then sank back into her chair and swore vociferously, feeling deflated and all out of options. This couldn't be happening! And yet it was, and she would have to find a way to deal with it. The spa was the one thing she had done completely on her own. It was never supposed to have been a success, she knew, but more a means to an end for Gavin's money laundering.

Callie was immensely proud of what she'd achieved. She hadn't known that she had so much natural business acumen. The Falls had been the making of her and had worked wonders for her ego. Now it was about to be snatched away from her by a vicious thug in a Saville Row suit who wanted to add it to his criminal empire and as things stood, she couldn't think of a single thing she could do to prevent him.

13

Angie drove home quickly, her progress aided by unusually light traffic. Henry was on the sofa, talking animatedly on his phone. He quickly cut the connection when Angie called out to him.

'You look a little brighter,' she said, sitting beside her son and ruffling his hair. 'Who were you talking to?'

'No one. What are you doing home? I don't need babysitting.'

'I know, but I'm a mother. It's part of the job description for me to worry when my son's abducted. Anything could have happened to you.'

'You didn't even know I'd been taken, Mum.'

'Not immediately, no,' she replied, hating to see the accusation in Henry's eyes. 'You live independently now, and I don't see or hear from you every day. And frankly, I'm glad I didn't know. I would have gone mental and could have inadvertently put you in more danger.'

Henry grunted. 'So, what are you doing to find Dad? Do you even care that he's missing?'

'Where would you suggest that I look, Henry?'

Another grunt. 'You could ask questions. I bet he's with Gavin Renfrew. Those two are joined at the fucking hip and Gavin's always getting Dad into dodgy stuff.'

She opened her mouth to chastise Henry for his language but closed it again without speaking. In the greater scheme of things, it didn't seem important.

'Callie's trying to find him. That's why any clues you can give us, any idea where to start looking, would be immensely helpful. Like you say, find Gavin and the chances are we'll find Paul too.'

Angie smiled at her son, but he wouldn't meet her gaze. He was angry and upset, as he had every right to be after what he'd been through, but his ordeal wasn't Angie's fault. Pointing out that it was his useless father who'd endangered him didn't seem worth the effort. Despite everything, Henry still appeared to worship the man. So too had Angie, for far too long, until her eyes had finally been opened.

'Has anything else occurred to you?' she asked, when Henry remained sullenly quiet. 'Anything about where you were held? That would be a good starting point.'

'The room I was in was modern.' Henry made the admission grudgingly.

Angie had imagined him being held in a grungy flat in an old tower block somewhere, with rodents having the run of the place.

'That's good. Anything else?'

'It was clean, and I could hear the sea. And boats too. Sometimes I think I heard fishermen going out early in the morning.'

'The marina?'

Henry shrugged. It seemed his willingness to cooperate had

run out of steam. Even so, he'd been more help than he probably realised. The fishing fleet was restricted to a particular part of the marina. It was surrounded by housing but not all of the flat had lifts, she knew, having visited several when Paul was going through a property-owning phase a few years previously.

She almost elevated from her chair when a thought occurred to her. As far as she was aware, Paul still owned a couple of flats in the marina. They were let out long term. Could Henry actually have been held in one of Paul's own properties? It seemed surreal and yet also made a bizarre kind of sense. Quite why the abductors would use Paul's property when needing a place to hold his captive son, she was unable to decide. Be that as it may, the possibility refused to let up and she sensed that the marina was somehow central to whatever Paul had gotten himself into.

'Are you hungry?' she asked Henry, careful not to let him see her animation. She most definitely didn't want her son to go charging off in a futile and misguided effort to find his father.

'I could eat something,' Henry replied grudgingly.

Angie quickly knocked up a plate of ham and chips and left Henry tucking into it. Barely able to contain her excitement, she headed for the showroom. Paul kept all his business records on his computer there. If she could crack his password and get into his files, she'd be able to find the addresses of the flats and the names of the tenants.

She called Tom from the car and warned him to expect her. Besides, she had to talk to him about Liverpool, which provided her with a legitimate excuse to see him.

'Hey,' he said, wandering outside and opening her car door when she pulled into Paul's regular spot. 'How's Henry?'

'Eating me out of house and home,' she replied, grinning.
'Excellent!'

She went inside with Tom. The place was quiet, no potential customers browsing, and no sign of any salespeople other than Tom. Angie nodded to Beccy as she entered Paul's office. The girl looked as though she'd been crying. Tom closed the door behind them and lowered the blind.

'What's wrong with Beccy?' she asked. 'She looks morose.'

'I probably shouldn't tell you that she's been that way for a while.'

Angie nodded. 'Since Paul did a runner? Yeah, I guessed as much.'

'Don't think Paul's encouraged her. The attachment is all on her side.'

'It really doesn't matter to me,' Angie said wearily, surprised to discover that she actually meant it. Thinking she was through with Paul was one thing. Coming close to admitting it to a man she didn't know very well was entirely another.

'Okay,' he said, 'I can see that you're bursting to tell me something, so out with it. How can I help?'

Angie reiterated what Callie had told her about Melody's enforced visit to the spa. 'She's running scared, Tom,' she finished by saying.

'Slow down.' Tom waved a placating hand. 'Does Callie think that Paul's involved Henry in whatever he's up to?'

'No, but Paul is fixated on Melody.' Angie growled. 'And Callie reckons she's scared of something or someone and probably knows more than she's letting on.'

'She'd see and hear a lot in her line of work and will know better than to speak out of turn.'

'She did mention that Fallow was at the brothel on the night Henry was taken.'

Tom shrugged. 'That doesn't surprise me.'

Angie let out a long breath. 'One of the reasons why I'm here is that Callie asked me to find out the name and contact details of your dealer in Liverpool. It's the only clear lead we have.' She wagged a hand from side to side. 'Well, almost.'

'Sure, I can do that but what do you intend to do with the information?'

'That's a very good question and not one that I can answer on my own. Callie is the one in charge so I think we should have another get-together tonight at the spa. You and me, Darren and Callie, to compare notes and think of a way forward. Are you good with that?'

'At your service, ma'am.'

Angie smiled, wondering once again why she felt such a pressing need for Tom's company. His protection. That wasn't like her, but then again, she'd never found herself in such dire circumstances before. Besides, Paul playing away had knocked her self-confidence and made her feel inadequate. Tom's open admiration was working wonders to repair the damage. Her instincts told her that he was one of the good guys but if they did run down the Liverpool angle and found that they were expected, then she would know who'd tipped the dealer the wink. Trusting Tom was, she decided, a test, of sorts.

'There's something else. I need to get into Paul's computer and check some stuff. Do you know his password?'

'I don't but Beccy probably does.'

Angie rolled her eyes. 'Yeah, I'm sure she does but I don't want to ask her.'

'Why not?'

Why not indeed? 'Because I think she might know where Paul is.' She threw back her head. 'Don't ask me why I think that way. It's just a gut feeling.'

'If that's true, wouldn't you want Paul to know that you're being proactive and delving into his affairs?'

'He will know that already because she will have told him I was here yesterday. And that you're helping me.'

'Well then, there can be no harm in asking her for his passwords. It might even bring him out of hiding.'

'True.' Angie paused. 'You haven't asked why I need to get into his records.'

'No.' Tom sent her a sexy smile. Angie was annoyed with herself for reacting to it. Now wasn't the time. Then she thought of Paul and Melody, and of Paul taking Henry to a brothel and her irritation evaporated. 'But you're going to tell me.'

Angie returned his smile as she explained Henry's recollections and the deductions she'd made.

'Does he still own flats in the marina?' she asked.

'No idea. He doesn't discuss his other business interests with me,' he said. 'But you're right. The answers will be in his online records, always assuming that the leases are legit. Just a mo.'

Tom disappeared for longer than Angie thought strictly necessary but eventually returned clutching a slip of paper.

Angie moved to Paul's desk and fired up his desktop.

'Here goes nothing,' she said, when the machine asked for a password. 'Melody69?' She wrinkled her nose. 'He really is into her, so to speak.'

'Sorry.'

'Don't be. I'm not.' Angie searched through her husband's files, looking for anything to do with his property acquisitions. 'The more I find out about his activities, the bigger fool I think myself for sticking by him all this time.' She paused her search and fixed Tom with a reflective look. 'I've never had much time for women who claim they weren't aware that their husbands were being unfaithful. Surely, they must have known, I've always thought. There must have been tell-tale signs they chose to ignore. But now I know that's not necessarily the case. I hate thinking of myself as one of those pathetic creatures who sticks by her man come what may. I'm worth more than that.'

'That you are, darling. That you are.'

'Anyway, here we are.'

Tom leaned over her shoulder as she found details of two property purchases in Brighton marina.

'It doesn't look as though he's sold them on,' Angie said, tapping a pencil against her teeth.

'Easy way to find out.'

Tom jotted down the addresses and then did an online search of the property register on his phone. 'They're owned by Dalton Associates still,' he said after a short pause. 'One ground floor and one penthouse.'

'Presumably, there's a lift in the penthouse block so if I'm on the right track then that's where Henry was held.' Angie frowned. 'What the hell does it mean, though? Surely Paul didn't have him abducted. Why would he? Who's the tenant?'

'There must be a tenancy agreement on Paul's computer somewhere.'

Angie did another search of his files and eventually found what she was looking for. 'It was let to April Morton six months ago on a year's tenancy.' She looked up at Tom. 'Who's April Morton?'

'Absolutely no idea. I've never heard the name.'

'Henry said he heard a woman's voice, so could it have been her?'

Tom shrugged. 'She was the one who insisted that Henry be moved out of the apartment, so it's reasonable to assume she called the shots. Either that or someone connected to her insisted upon keeping him there.'

'So, what do we do about it?'

'That's not for me to say. Best talk it over with Callie later.'

Angie nodded, printed out the details of the tenancy and made a note of the flat's address.

'Well, I guess that's it for now. Shall we meet at the spa at five?'

Tom smiled. 'Works for me,' he said.

* * *

Callie pulled herself together again seconds before Darren rejoined her.

'You look upset.' He scowled, his concern for her wellbeing etched into his expression. 'What did O'Keefe want?'

Callie moved to the comfortable seats. Darren followed her there and sat beside her.

'What he wants is for me to honour Gavin's commitment to sell the spa to him.'

'What!'

Callie sighed. 'My reaction precisely.'

'He's trying it on.'

'I think not. There's a letter on my desk,' she said.

Darren got up and read it. 'This is a photocopy,' he said, scowling.

'Well, he'd hardly leave the original in my safekeeping, would he now? What counts is that Gavin signed it – no question of that.'

'He can't agree to sell something that isn't his.'

'Ha! I don't think Ryan O'Keefe is too worried about the legalities. Bottom line, he expects me to honour Gavin's offer.'

'I can understand why you're so bent out of shape, Callie,' Darren said in a reflective tone. 'But would it be such a bad thing? I know you don't like O'Keefe, but you could sell to him, walk away and have nothing more to do with him. The price is generous. Very generous. You want to sell up and get away from Gavin's crowd, so it seems like a good opportunity.'

'Perhaps, but I don't like being coerced. I've worked hard to establish the spa, but I very much doubt whether O'Keefe will keep it running as a going concern. He wants it for another reason.'

'Yeah, good point.'

'Besides, Stafford won't take it lying down and will probably come after me anyway. Him and God alone knows who else. O'Keefe will keep them at bay until he gets what he wants, then it'll be open season on me. I'll never be safe.'

Callie felt the beginnings of a stress headache thumping at her temple and closed her eyes in a futile attempt to make the pain dissipate. Wordlessly, Darren got up, poured her a glass of water from the carafe on the side and produced a couple of paracetamol.

'Here,' he said, handing her both the glass and the pills. 'This should help.'

'Thanks.' She swallowed the pills, touched by Darren's empathy. She couldn't recall a single time during her long marriage when Gavin had noticed any discomfort she felt or became proactive in his desire to relieve her symptoms.

'You realise, of course, that O'Keefe will be difficult to get rid of.'

'Yeah, so we'll just have to outsmart him.' Callie leaned forward, her depression slowly giving way to a burning desire to stand her ground. 'We need to find out why he's so keen to get his hands on the spa. If we know that then we might be able to think of a way out.'

'The land you have earmarked for the golf course?'

'It's not suitable for building, if that's what you're thinking.'

'Well then, we need to find out who O'Keefe hangs out with. My understanding is that he buddies up with a few members of the local council.'

Callie glanced up at him. 'Even if that's the case, they can't grant planning permission on unstable land. There would have to be the usual soil tests, and the planning committee would then know about the silt.'

'Reports can be faked, especially by men with O'Keefe's contacts. Committees can be blackmailed or bribed. It doesn't have to be a unanimous decision to grant planning permission, remember.'

'Okay, I'll leave you to make checks on O'Keefe, Darren. I don't want to know who you use or how you do it but for God's sake, be careful!'

Darren flashed a compelling smile. 'Glad to know you care.'

Callie chuckled. 'Good PAs are hard to find.'

Just then, her phone chirped into life.

'It's Angie,' she said, taking the call. 'Hi, Ang, what's going on?'

'I have a lead,' Angie said excitedly. 'Can Tom and I come over and talk it through with you at about five? Darren needs to be there.'

'Sure. Give me a clue.'

'Best to talk in person. See you in a bit.'

'Well,' Darren said, when Callie related Angie's news. 'Might be best to see what Angie has before we go after O'Keefe.'

14

Callie tried to concentrate on her regular work and put all thoughts of O'Keefe's demands from her mind. It was near impossible, of course, and in the end, she gave up and took herself off for a massage. There had to be some advantages to being the boss insofar as she could jump the queue. There always was a queue, but any reminders of her success failed on this occasion to cheer her up. She had one of the beauticians sort her hair out and apply her make-up. Feeling more relaxed and looking good helped to restore her waning self-confidence.

She returned to her office just as Angie and Tom arrived.

'Hi, guys,' she said. 'Come on in.'

Seated in their usual spot in front of the long windows, Callie got straight down to business.

'Come on, Angie,' she said, smiling at her friend's animated expression. 'I can see you're bursting to share. What have you found out?'

'Henry remembered a few things about where he was held. Nothing specific but enough for me to have a good idea where it might have been.'

Callie grinned when Angie and Tom went on to explain the snooping they'd carried out and the conclusions they'd reached.

'What the hell!' Darren said, when she ran out of words.

'My thoughts exactly.' Callie shook her head. 'Henry was held captive in one of Paul's flats. It hardly seems credible.'

'I don't think much of Paul right now,' Angie said, 'but even I can't believe he knew where our son was taken. I would like to think that if he'd even suspected then he would have got him out somehow, but right now, I'm not so sure what to think.'

'We need to find out more about the tenant, April Morton,' Callie said, reaching for her phone and googling the name. She was met with a dozen different choices and at a glance, none of them appeared to have any connections to Brighton.

'I can get someone onto digging,' Darren said, making a note, 'and watching that flat, if you think it necessary.' He glanced at Callie and Angie as he spoke and they both nodded.

'Do you suppose that Paul gave April the tenancy *because* she was involved in his business, whatever it is?' Callie asked.

'Either that or he's screwing her,' Angie replied, a bitter edge to her voice. 'Can't afford to ignore either possibility.'

'Does Paul have much to do with O'Keefe?' Callie addressed the question to Tom, thinking he would know more about his business associates than Angie.

'He's been to the showroom a few times and closeted himself away with Paul. I have no idea what they talked about, but I remember one recent discussion got heated. I could hear raised voices even though the door was shut, but they'd closed the blind so I couldn't see who was doing the shouting. O'Keefe wasn't there to purchase a car, that much I do know.'

Angie frowned. 'Why are you so interested in O'Keefe, Cal? What's he got to do with this mess?'

'I didn't think he had anything to do with it,' Callie replied. 'But after what Tom just told us, I'm not so sure.' She sighed. 'The long and the short of it is that he's trying to buy me out of the spa.'

'What! He can't do that.'

'Yeah, my sentiments entirely. He says Gavin signed a letter of intent, which he did. I've seen it.'

'What on earth does he want with this place?' Angie looked as mystified as Callie felt. 'Anyway, you own it so he can hardly force your hand.'

Tom and Darren shared a look, both very aware that he could and very likely would.

'We think he wants to develop it in some way. Either that or he wants to have a direct market for his dirty money without involving Gavin. Darren's on the case.'

'We're thinking he might have plans to develop the golf course land, which isn't suitable for building, but that won't stop O'Keefe. The only access to it is through the spa's grounds, obviously.'

'Even he has to abide by the planning laws.' Angie's jaw dropped. 'You're thinking he's bribing someone on the planning committee?'

'The thought crossed our minds,' Darren replied. 'I'm having O'Keefe watched to see who he associates with.'

'Tread carefully,' Tom warned. 'O'Keefe won't take kindly to being spied on.'

'Yeah, I hear you.'

'So, what now?' Angie asked, sighing heavily. 'I don't give a rat's ass about Paul, but if you think we need to find him in order to get to the bottom of things then I'll bet you that his PA, the lovely Beccy, will be able to point you in the right direction. She can barely hide her hostility in her dealings with me. I'm just too stupid to have seen what's been going on beneath my nose before now because I trusted the bastard.'

Callie reached across to squeeze Angie's hand.

'I think we need to put a little pressure on Fallow,' Callie said musingly. 'I reckon he knows a hell of a lot more about what's going on then he'll ever let on. He was at Phoenix when Henry was taken so must have seen or heard something.'

'Or been one of the men arguing with Paul,' Tom added.

'That possibility had occurred to us.' Callie threw her arms above her head and stretched. 'Tell us more about your Liverpool dealer, Tom.'

'Not much to tell. Paul's been doing business with him for years. He imports a lot of high-end cars from abroad. They come into Liverpool docks, and we send a driver to collect any that we're likely to sell. Works in reverse too. If we take a decent car in part exchange and Bernie Bracewell has a buyer...'

'Would you buy a car from Bernie Bracewell?' Darren asked, making everyone laugh.

'Seriously though,' Tom said. 'Paul's had the car business for ten years and Bernie's been one of his main suppliers all that time. There's no car that he can't source. The man's a legend in the business.'

Callie took a moment to think that over. 'If we're right about the drugs angle being operated from Phoenix,' she said, 'could they be transported from Liverpool in the cars that go up and down between dealerships?'

'It's possible, I suppose,' Tom said, 'but I've worked at the lot for years and not even heard a whisper.'

'The drivers wouldn't need to know if the panels were packed with cocaine, or whatever,' Darren said. 'And anyway, the chances of them being stopped are minimal. It's my understanding that delivery drivers have commercial insurance arranged through Paul.'

Tom nodded when Darren glanced at him. 'That's right, and if they get clocked for speeding then their renewal rates go through the roof, meaning it would no longer be cost effective for Paul to employ the offender.'

'So, they abide by the rules of the road and make themselves virtually invisible,' Darren concluded.

'Who books the transfers or deliveries?' Callie asked. 'I assume not Paul because he's not always there and doesn't get involved with the day-to-day stuff.'

'Not me,' Tom replied. 'It would be Beccy.'

'Of course it would!' Angie rolled her eyes.

'I'll do a bit of delving into Bernie Bracewell's background. That *has* to be his real name,' Darren said, making a note of it. 'No one would choose to lumber themselves with such a moniker.'

Darren's phone rang. He checked the screen, excused himself and stood up to take the call. No one spoke as they listened to his end of the conversation.

'Hold on, I'll ask. It's Pete at Phoenix,' he said. 'He caught Melody trying to slip out unseen. There's a pedestrian gate at the back but Pete locked it. She was trying to climb over and it's six feet tall with barbed wire at the top.'

'Blimey, she *did* want to get out, didn't she?' Angie muttered.

'What do you want to do about her?' Darren asked. 'Pete's holding her, and I can hear her language from here.' He chuckled. 'Good job I don't speak Croat.'

'Have Pete get one of his men to bring her here,' Callie said.

Darren gave those instructions and cut the connection.

'The girls aren't prisoners,' Angie said. 'If they want to go out, or leave permanently, they can do so through the front gate. So, it follows that wherever Melody was going, she didn't want anyone to know.'

'Perhaps she was linking up with Paul. Sorry, babe,' Callie said, when Angie winced. For all her insistence that she was over Paul, word of his infidelity still clearly rankled.

'Hasn't she heard of phones?' Tom asked.

'It won't take them long to get here. Make yourself scarce please, boys.' Callie nodded at Darren and Tom. 'We don't need to confront her mobhanded. Angie and I will see her alone.'

'We'll be outside,' Darren said as he and Tom stood. 'Yell if you need us.'

'Oh, Darren?'

'Yes?' Darren turned as he approached the office door.

'Call Fallow. Tell him I need to see him immediately,' Callie said. 'Don't take no for an answer. Make sure he's in plain view in your office and that Melody sees him when she arrives. Watch their interaction and let me know what passes between them.'

'Will do.'

'We're getting somewhere,' Callie said, when the door closed behind Darren. 'I can feel it.'

'We're getting closer to finding Paul perhaps, but we're not making much ground when it comes to finding Gavin. And you now have to find him, you realise that?'

'Yeah, I know.' Callie sighed. 'It will be the easiest way to get O'Keefe off my back. Gavin's dug a hole for himself and made all sorts of wild promises, by the looks of things, to get himself out of it again. Except if he doesn't want to be found then he won't be. I have a feeling I'm not the only person looking for him. In fact, I know I'm not. But still, if we find Paul, I'll bet he'll be able to shed some light.'

'And I can beat him to a pulp, so it's win-win.'

Callie smiled. 'Yeah, that too.' She paused. 'You sure you're good with seeing Melody?'

'Oh yes! She and I have unfinished business.' Angie rubbed her hands together. 'She lied about knowing my son and I want her to explain why she felt that was necessary. I don't buy the feeble explanation that she gave you.'

'Fair enough. I'm going to put some pressure on her so go along with whatever I say.'

Angie grinned. 'When do I not?'

A short time later, the ladies heard a loud, bombastic voice echoing from Darren's office.

'Fallow!' they said together.

'He's not accustomed to being kept waiting, or to being so arbitrarily summoned, methinks,' Angie said, chuckling.

'But he came, and even quicker than I expected him to, which speaks of a guilty conscience.'

'Always assuming he *has* a conscience.'

'Well, there is that. I'm guessing he wants to know what we know. He will be aware that we've found Henry. I wonder what else he knows and is about to tell us. And who he reports to for that matter.'

'He's a worried man,' Angie agreed. 'But he's not stupid and will be looking out for his own hide.'

The door opened and Darren ushered Melody through it. She looked mutinous. And beautiful. Dressed to the nines in what could only be described as work clothes, Callie wondered how she'd hoped to scale a six-foot gate in a skirt that barely covered her buttocks.

'Planning on doing a little work off the books?' Callie asked, eyeing the girl with open amusement.

'Where I was going is none of your business,' she replied,

attempting for an aloof expression that failed to hide her anger and apprehension.

'Out to seduce vulnerable young men, I have no doubt,' Angie said, fixing Melody with a disdainful look.

'I am glad your son is safe,' she replied.

'The son you have never met and never spoken to.' Angie shook her head. 'How can you live with yourself?'

'Asks a woman who was born in a safe country and has never been coerced into doing anything she would prefer not to just to stay alive.' Melody tossed her head. 'You can judge me all you like, but you don't know me. You don't know what I've had to overcome in order to feel *safe* doing what I do now. We are not all the same. It's worth remembering that.'

'Thank you for the lecture.' Callie's tone of voice immediately silenced Melody. 'Sit down.'

She did so, crossing her legs and still looking mutinous.

'Why did you feel the need to climb a fence to get out of the club? You are well aware that you can come and go through the front pedestrian gate.'

'I do not have to tell you anything.'

'True,' Callie agreed. 'But then again, all the time you're working at Phoenix, you *are* answerable to me. In my husband's absence, I am responsible for hiring and firing. I assume you do wish to continue working at the place...'

'I had private business to attend to that I didn't want anyone else to know about.' She again tossed her hair, a gesture that presumably entranced her clients but cut no ice with Callie. 'I do have a life outside of my work.'

'You went out in your work clothes for a non-work meeting?' Angie sent the woman who had her husband wrapped round her little finger a sneering look. 'I would suggest it's more likely you were doing a little moonlighting.'

'Moonlighting?' Melody frowned. 'What does that mean?'

'My friend means that you were carrying on, business as usual. Except your customers cannot come to you and so you were going to them and pocketing the full fee.'

'Setting up on her own,' Angie suggested, 'or she would be but for the fact that business with nothing to do with sex keeps her bound to Phoenix.'

'I... I have no idea what you mean.'

But Callie could see that she was physically shaken by the suggestion. She knew what was going on at the brothel, was involved with it and probably knew the identity of Lucy's attacker too. Getting her to talk though would be an uphill struggle.

'When did you last speak with my husband?' Callie asked.

'What?'

'It's a simple enough question.' Callie tapped her fingers on the surface of her desk.

'I can't remember. When he was last at the club, I suppose.'

This time, Callie slapped the palm of her hand down hard enough to make Melody flinch. 'I don't believe you!'

Angie leaned towards her, looking lethally dangerous. 'It's in your best interests to tell us what you know.' She spoke softly, persuasively, but her features remained etched in concrete. 'We can protect you, but only if we know what we're fighting against.'

'No one can protect me. In my line of work, you learn early on to put yourself first. I do not want to end up the same way as Lucy.' She shuddered. 'Or worse.'

'And yet you seem to think that you will be safer at Phoenix than cut loose,' Callie said reflectively. 'And I will throw you out if you don't level with us.' She fixed the girl with a merciless look. 'Never doubt it. Is it drugs? Or something worse?'

'I don't know!' Melody leaned forward. 'I can't tell you what I don't know. It is better to see and hear nothing and to mind my own business. I want to stay at Phoenix, not because I am involved with whatever's frightened Gavin and Paul but because it's just about the safest environment for me. Trust me, I know other girls who work in the area, and they are all envious of my situation. Short of going to London, which I don't want to do for reasons of my own, Phoenix is as good as it gets.'

'Then tell us where you were going that's so secretive.'

Callie held up a hand to prevent Angie from speaking too. It was make or break time. Melody could either level with them or she really would be out of work.

The ensuring silence felt heavy, oppressive, as they left Melody to mull over her options.

'Very well,' she eventually said. 'I was going to visit my daughter.'

'Your daughter!' Callie and Angie spoke simultaneously.

'It is her birthday today.' A spontaneous smile graced Melody's lips. 'She's a year old. I had to see her. I promised.'

Callie shook her head. 'Then why not simply leave through the front gate?'

'Because she didn't want to risk being followed,' Angie said slowly. 'She cannot live with the child, or its father, because she's being made to work at Phoenix against her will.' She looked directly at Melody, her gaze unflinching. 'Have I got it right?'

Angie felt a chill trickle down her spine. She knew now with absolute certainty who the child's father must be.

'Paul,' she said slowly. 'Paul is your daughter's father.'

Melody lowered her head. 'Yes.'

She breathed the word so quietly that Angie barely caught it.

'How can you be so sure?' Callie asked briskly. 'In your trade, there must have been dozens of men.'

'I do not have unprotected sex with anyone,' she replied aloofly. 'Paul did not pay me for my services. We are in love. He was planning to tell you,' Melody said, speaking directly to Angie.

'So much in love that he let you carry on working,' Angie responded, a vicious edge to her voice.

'I had no choice. You are right, I was compelled to remain at Phoenix. I had debts that I had to repay, not in monetary terms. But Paul was... is, sorting things so that I will be free to leave. That is what he was attempting to do when...'

Her voice trailed off and Angie knew she had only just

stopped herself from speaking out of turn. She also knew that she wouldn't make another slip of that nature. She was terrified of whoever had brought her to England and forced her into prostitution. At least that person couldn't possibly be Paul. So, who? Someone local to the area with connections to Phoenix. She glanced at Callie and could see that her mind was similarly occupied.

'Sorting them by having our son abducted!' Angie cried, angry tears blurring her vision.

'He could not have anticipated that!'

'Then perhaps he shouldn't have taken our son to a brothel.'

Melody looked momentarily less sure of herself but quickly rallied. 'He wanted us to get along, to know one another before Paul moved on.'

Melody's words sounded weak. Unconvincing.

'Did Henry know that you planned to break up our marriage?' Angie asked.

'No, of course not. Paul told me the marriage was over. That you have drifted apart. The children were grown with their own lives and there was no reason for him to stay. I'm sorry,' she added, clearly realising how callous she sounded, 'but that is what he told me. I have seen it more times than I can recall.'

'In your line of work, that doesn't surprise me. Happily married men do not use the services of prostitutes,' Callie said, glowering at the woman. 'Was Paul arguing with the people or person who forced you into your trade? Did they take Henry to force Paul's hand when he refused to play ball?'

'I don't know who Paul was arguing with but I can say with certainty it was not that person.'

'Does the person have a name?' Angie asked, more in hope than expectation.

Melody simply shook her head. She was too afraid to say a word.

'Let's be clear on one thing.' Angie hardened her tone. 'You are more than welcome to Paul. I never want to set eyes on the cheating bastard ever again. But I do want to know where he is and why it was necessary for Henry to be abducted and since you can't or won't enlighten me, then I need to hear it from him.'

'I do not...' Melody's words stuttered to a halt.

'You know.' Callie dealt the woman a venomous look. 'You were going to meet him and celebrate your daughter's birthday. That is why you were so desperate to escape unseen, and why you dressed the way you did. You didn't want to be seen by whoever it is that frightens you rigid. You didn't know the gate would be locked and didn't expect to have to climb the fence, but you did so because if you were caught then the assumption would be that you were about to ply your trade elsewhere.'

'Paul is paranoid about me getting hurt.'

'Didn't seem to bother him when Henry was in the firing line, or that I'd be out of my mind with worry.' Angie shook her head. 'I can't get past the fact that Paul didn't even have the decency to call me.'

'Paul doesn't want anyone to know of our connection. It would not be safe for me and anyway, the people who brought me to England would not like it. We are not supposed to get emotionally involved with our clients.'

Angie blew air through her lips but refrained from comment.

'As soon as Paul knew that Henry was safe, he refused to do anything else to help the people who took him. He's laying low until they have no further use of his services.'

'Whatever they are doing is time sensitive?' Callie asked.

Melody shrugged. 'Perhaps.'

'And you really have no idea what it's all about?' Angie drilled the woman with a scathing look. 'Why do I not believe you?'

'I will not put Paul in further danger by telling you what I think and there is nothing you can do to make me.' Melody folded her arms. 'Be aware that if you try to evict me from Phoenix, you are the one who will be in danger, Mrs Renfrew. Anyway, what can two deserted wives do against such a ruthless operation? They wouldn't think twice of harming a woman if she got in their way. Look what happened to Lucy if you doubt me. Believe me, I am protecting you.'

Angie sensed Melody's intransigence. She was terrified of these people. What the hell had Paul got himself involved with?

'Paul's in hiding and anyone following you would be led straight to him,' Callie said. 'But Henry isn't in hiding, nor is Angie, and either one of those could be taken to force Paul's hand, so I really don't buy your story.'

'I cannot help what you believe. I have told you the truth, at least insofar as my situation is concerned. I am not prepared to say anything about other matters.'

Angie shook her head. 'I don't believe what I'm hearing,' she said. 'Where is Paul now?'

'With our daughter who is being looked after by people he trusts and no, I am not going to tell you who they are.' Melody sat a little straighter. 'Just be aware that if you make me leave Phoenix, the people who are using me will know it was not my fault, but that will not save me from a beating, or worse. And then they will come after you.'

'Why do they need you to stay?' Callie asked.

Melody sighed. 'I am not telling you anything else. I have

already said too much.' She paused. 'What do you intend to do about me?'

Callie glanced at Angie, who shrugged.

'Tell my miserable, cowardly excuse for a husband to at least call me,' she said. 'I will pack his things but need to know where to send them.'

'Go back to Phoenix,' Callie said, clearly struggling to conceal her frustration. 'Darren will arrange a cab for you. You know where to find me if and when you decide you need my help.'

Callie dismissed the woman with a wave of her hand. Melody got up and left without a backward glance.

'I feel as though we're taking one step forward and two back,' Callie said. 'But never mind all that. You've not only had it confirmed that your husband's a serial cheat but also that he's fathered another child.' Callie rounded her desk and hugged Angie. 'Are you okay? Stupid question, of course you're not.'

'Actually,' Angie replied, dashing at tears that she refused to let fall, 'in a way, what Melody told me was a relief. If Paul had convinced me that he'd made a mistake, that his dalliance with her was a one off, then I might have relented, put it down to a mid-life crisis, and taken him back. If for no other reason than Henry adores his father and appears to hold me responsible for the breakdown of a relationship that I had no idea was fractured. So perhaps I am partly to blame. I should have noticed the signs.'

'Don't you dare blame yourself! He's the one who's strayed and started another family without bothering to let you know.'

'Yes, perhaps you're right.' Angie grunted. 'Anyway, what now?'

'Now we have Fallow in here.' Callie pressed the intercom and asked Darren to step in.

'Fallow's about to burst a blood vessel because he's been kept waiting for so long,' he said, grinning. 'Oh, Angie, Tom had to run but he said he'd call you in a bit.'

'Oh, okay.' Angie didn't like the fact that Tom's rushing off disappointed her quite so badly. She absolutely could not afford to lean on him, or anyone else other than Callie.

'How did Fallow react to the sight of Melody?' Callie asked.

'He paled and then sent her what I'd term a warning look, but she didn't even glance at him. Blanked him like he wasn't there.'

'Okay, wheel him in and stay yourself.'

'What the hell's going on?' Fallow burst through the door, bellowing like a bull. 'I am not accustomed to being kept waiting.'

'Then perhaps you should have levelled with me when we spoke before,' Callie replied, the epitome of calm. Her manner appeared to knock the wind out of Fallow's sails. It was hard, Angie knew, to rant and rave at a person who remained implacably cool. 'You are on my husband's payroll and in his absence, I expect you to keep me in the loop.'

'What loop?' Fallow huffed. 'You don't have any idea what you're talking about.'

'You'd be surprised what I've found out over the past few days.' Callie leaned back in her chair, her gaze not once moving from Fallow's blotched face. 'Tell me, are you a shareholder in Porchester Investments?'

'What!' Fallow's face turned crimson. 'Why do you ask?'

'I'm growing weary of you answering my questions with questions. It's worth bearing in mind that I possess the ability to ruin you, so it's time to cooperate.'

'You wouldn't dare!'

'Really?' Callie fixed the superintendent with a hard look that made him squirm. 'You know what they say about the female of the species. Both of our husbands are on the missing list, we're being pressurised by certain unscrupulous people who are making outrageous demands and Angie's son was abducted. Do we look like the type who will sit back and do as we're told? Our backs are against the wall, and so we fully intend to fight against the people attempting to manipulate us. And you, Superintendent Fallow, are going to share what you know with us.'

'Now just a minute!'

'You are really not in any position to negotiate,' Angie added, when Fallow tried to protest. 'Whatever scam you're running resulted in my son being abducted and believe me, Callie's anger at being left to deflect the flack is nothing compared to the way that a mother feels when her child is drawn into her husband's dodgy dealings.'

'How many more times?' Fallow raked a hand through his sparse hair. 'I have no idea why Henry was taken or who Paul was arguing with that night. I'm Gavin's pawn, in too deep to get out from under, much as I'd like to, but Paul had something going on that didn't involve Gavin and he sure as hell didn't ask me to smooth his path. Paul has something to prove to himself and others, if you ask me.'

'Then work with us,' Callie said, leaning towards him and doubtless sensing an opportunity. Fallow had his sticky fingers in no end of questionable pies and his loyalty was far from certain. The only person he cared about was himself. Turning him would be a high-risk strategy, if that was what Callie had in mind, but Angie could see that it was their only course of action.

'What do you propose?' he asked cautiously.

'What is going on at Phoenix, other than the obvious?' Callie's gaze remained focused on Fallow's face. 'Let's start with Melody. She's working off a debt to the people who brought her to the UK, or so she would have us believe. Who are they? Did they beat Lucy for talking to us?'

'I honestly don't know.' Fallow spread his hands. 'I wish I did. Some foot soldiers, for want of a better description, have been picked up and deported without spilling the beans, so no one knows who's at the top of the pile. Whoever it is will be surrounded by others taking all the risks. That's the way these things work, but I can tell you that they're vicious thugs, and clever too. They bring in class girls who know what they will be expected to do when they get here, lured by the huge amounts they can earn in a short space of time.' Fallow grunted. 'They just don't realise how long they will have to work before they're debt free. It's not as though they have written contracts and can resign.'

'How is Gavin involved?' Callie asked. 'I had no idea he had illegals working at Phoenix, but it seems there's a lot I don't know about his various operations.'

Fallow sent her a look that implied she was being naïve. 'It's not an industry with a complaints procedure,' he pointed out.

'Okay.' Angie could see the strain etched around Callie's eyes as she spoke. 'Leaving aside Gavin's machinations for a moment, let's concentrate on Paul. You are aware of his attachment to Melody?'

Fallow glanced at Angie and just for a moment, his expression softened, making him appear almost human. 'Yeah, I know,' he said, 'the stupid bastard!'

'Don't waste your sympathy on me,' Angie said briskly. 'I just need to find him and assure myself that my family will be safe from these horrible people in future. Then he can ride off into the sunset and play happy families.'

'I don't know where he is and that's the God's honest truth.'

Angie didn't like Fallow but got the impression that he was being honest, partly because Paul had taken so much trouble to hide himself away.

'Does the name April Morton mean anything to you?' Callie asked.

Fallow blinked at her. 'Can't say that it does. Should it?'

'We're not sure,' Angie said, 'but we think she might have held Henry at a property of Paul's in the marina.'

'Of Paul's?' Fallow looked astounded.

'Yeah. Nothing like keeping it in the family,' Angie said bitterly.

'I'll run a check and get back to you.'

'Right.' Callie's tone remained brisk, businesslike. 'You have yet to tell me what Porchester Holdings means to you.'

Fallow hesitated.

'Now isn't the time to turn coy,' Callie said. 'You want out from under Gavin's thumb, and I can make that happen, but my co-operation comes at a price. I need you to work for me now. I'm being pressured by O'Keefe.'

'Christ!'

'He wants to buy the spa. Any idea why?'

'Nope. He's one vicious thug. I steer well clear of him.'

And also turned a blind eye to his activities, Angie didn't doubt.

'I did hear some talk, can't remember where, about using the land you want to turn into a golf course for a private clinic.'

Angie and Callie exchanged a glance.

'Doesn't sound like something O'Keefe would want to involve himself with,' Callie said.

'Well, it would never have got permission anyway, so that can't be it.'

'See what you can find out for me,' Callie said.

Angie imagined that Fallow would turn bombastic again but to her surprise, he gave a meek nod.

'Anyway, about Porchester Holdings: Gavin paid me in shares from time to time. Said they'd be a good investment, and they have been. I couldn't keep having cash going into my account.' He rubbed the side of his nose. 'A few people have been making comments about my association with Gavin: people who are anxious to see me booted off the force. If professional standards got involved, I couldn't have unaccounted-for deposits going into my account and the cash under the mattress was getting a bit bulky.'

His feeble attempt at humour fell flat.

'The trials and tribulations of bent coppers,' Angie remarked scathingly.

'Who are Porchester Holdings?' Callie asked. 'There is suspiciously little about them online. They appear to be a finance company, but we have no idea what they finance and who the directors are.'

Fallow shrugged. 'They rescue failing companies, strip them of their assets and turn them round, is my understanding. It doesn't pay to ask too many questions.'

'They launder a lot of their dosh through this place, we've discovered,' Callie said, 'so they are not exactly white knights.'

'I'd steer well clear,' Fallow advised.

'We'll ask Paul when we find him,' Angie said, grinding her teeth.

'I doubt whether he'll know. Porchester is Gavin's baby and I'm pretty sure that Paul has no connection.' He paused. 'You're aware that Gavin and Paul's friendship, business association, call it what you will, has cooled over the past year.'

Both ladies shook their heads.

'We have socialised less as couples, I suppose,' Angie remarked pensively. 'I hadn't really thought about it, but now I know Paul was playing away, I guess that entertaining his wife came low on his list of priorities.'

'It's down to Gavin overreaching himself and getting on the wrong side of some seriously heavy guys. And to Paul's jealousy of Gavin's success. Friendly rivalry turned into a competition from Paul's perceptive, I think. He got tired of being number two. Then he got involved with Melody and I know he and Gavin fell out big time over that one. Gavin looked upon her as his personal property, you see, but Melody made her preference for Paul clear.'

'How touching,' Angie said scathingly.

'Well, anyway, Paul started his own moneymaking scheme, wanting to get one over on Gavin. And no,' he added, holding up a hand, 'I have no idea what it involved, but I do know that he overreached himself, got too ambitious, got in over his head and wanted out. Which is why Henry was taken, I'm guessing. Paul's hand has been forced. Anyway, if you want to find Paul, Melody will lead you to him eventually.'

'Gavin taking off has got nothing to do with Paul scarpering?' Angie asked.

'Nope. Not as far as I'm aware.'

'Do you know who Gavin crossed badly enough to make him run?' Callie asked.

'No, and I haven't tried to find out.'

'You don't seem to know very much,' Angie said.

'Because I don't want to. I supply information when needed, or let Gavin know if my colleagues are intent upon collaring him. I don't know, and don't need to know what he gets up to, or with who. I'm just glad that he's off the grid and I don't have to dance to his tune for the time being.' Fallow scowled at nothing in particular. 'I'm thinking of putting my papers in and taking early retirement. I've had enough of this. It's wearing on my nerves.'

'Are we supposed to feel sorry for you?' Callie asked. 'You're the one who swore an oath to uphold law and order and then reneged on it.'

'Is it drugs being run through Phoenix?' Angie asked.

'I don't think so. I'd have heard a whisper. They have a strict no-drugs policy there and the girls are regularly tested to make sure they're not using.'

'Okay.' Callie raised her arms above her head and stifled a yawn. 'See what you can find out about April Morton and anything else about Paul's location. We need to find him as a priority.'

'I'll make sure Melody's actions are carefully monitored,' Darren said, speaking for the first time. Up until then, he had remained at the back of the room, quiet and watchful, missing nothing.

'Right, thanks. Keep in touch,' she said to Fallow as he headed for the door.

Fallow stood and turned to face Callie. 'I'll stick my neck out and do all I can to help you,' he said. 'But in return, I need your assurance that Gavin will back off if... when he returns. I mean it, Mrs Renfrew, I've had enough. I know where a lot of the bodies are buried, and I can and will take Gavin down with me if the shit hits the fan and I'm implicated in any way.'

Callie nodded. 'I hear you. We both want the same thing.'

'Right. Just so long as we're clear.'

'I'll let you out the back way,' Darren said, opening the door for Fallow.

'Phew!' Callie got up, went to her bar and opened a bottle of Chablis. She poured two glasses and handed one to Angie. 'After all that, I think we've earned this.'

'Do we believe a word that Fallow said?' Angie asked, raising her glass in a salute and then taking a healthy swig.

'Actually, I think for the most part that I do. He's running scared. His colleagues are suspicious of his association with Gavin, and he must be aware it's only a matter of time before he's investigated. But with Gavin on the run, he sees an opportunity to retire, and no doubt take himself off to sunnier climes in order to enjoy his questionable gains. But he also knows we can turn the screw if he doesn't help us, so...'

'We're looking at two different reasons for our husbands having taken off then.'

'Seems that way. I didn't realise they'd fallen out. Did you?'

Angie shook her head. 'But like I said, I didn't even realise that Paul and I were socialising less. Familiarity and all that.'

'Well anyway, finding Paul and figuring out how to stop the people who are after him is our first priority.'

'We could ask George,' Angie said, referring to the third business partner.

'He won't know,' Callie replied. 'But yeah, I'll have a word when I next hear from him.'

16

Callie glanced at Darren when he returned to the room.

'Did you know that Gavin and Paul had fallen out, Darren?' she asked.

'Nope. My main focus has been on this place for ages now. Gavin only calls on me when he needs an errand boy. Mind you, Fallow's right about one thing: their businesses are largely separate. Paul has always been second best, in Gavin's eyes and, I suspect, in his own. Gavin leads and Paul follows.'

Angie nodded. 'Yeah. Thinking about it, he's whinged a bit about Gavin thinking he's top dog recently, but I never thought much about it.'

'They've had a few barnies over recent months,' Darren said. 'Differences of opinion about the direction of their joint ventures. In Gavin's eyes, Paul was being overambitious and in too much of a hurry.'

'Perhaps because he wanted to prove he has what it takes,' Callie remarked.

Darren shrugged. 'Possibly, and if Paul has tried to go solo and prove something to himself and others then it wouldn't surprise me.'

'The idiot!' Angie let out a frustrated breath. 'The sensitivity of the male ego never ceases to amaze me. Gavin has the pizzaz to be an instinctive leader, even I can see that. You either have it or you haven't. It's not something that comes with training.'

'So, what now?' Darren looked at Callie as he posed the question.

'Well, keeping Melody under surveillance is our first priority. She will lead us to Paul eventually.' Callie turned to Angie. 'Any idea who Paul might have asked to care for their child? Sorry,' she added, when Angie winced.

'Don't be,' Angie replied. 'I'm done with the dirty nappies, disturbed nights and perpetual worry. Not that Paul will do any of that stuff. Well, he didn't first time around, but still...'

'I'm assuming that Melody doesn't know anyone around these parts well enough to trust them with her child,' Callie said, 'so Paul must have made the arrangement.'

'I can't think of anyone off the top of my head. I'll ask Tom when he calls later.'

Callie grinned. 'You be sure and do that,' she said.

Angie sent her a *what-the-hell* look but failed to suppress a responding grin.

'I've got people watching that apartment in the marina. They'll take pictures of people coming and going and I have someone who can run a facial-recognition thingy,' Darren said. 'So, if Fallow can't find out who April Morton is, we might have more luck.'

'You're full of surprises,' Angie said. 'I think we'll keep you around for a while.' She picked up her bag and grabbed her jacket. 'Anyway, I'm off to check on Henry. Again. Not that he'll appreciate my fussing, but I'm his mum so he'll just have to put up with it.'

'Catch you later,' Callie replied, standing to give her friend a hug.

Left to themselves, Callie smiled her thanks when Darren topped up her glass.

'You okay?' he asked, concern etched into his features.

'Things are getting better by the minute.' She sighed. 'Have one yourself.' She indicated the bar with a jerk of her thumb. 'I think we've both earned it.'

'Thanks, I will.'

Darren opened a beer and then sat opposite Callie, legs splayed, the bottle dangling from his fingers.

'Any further suggestions would be gratefully received,' Callie said, watching him. 'I'm up against it here. O'Keefe will be back, and soon, and this time, he won't be asking quite so nicely. Nor, for that matter, will Stafford.'

Darren leaned across the space that separated them and gently touched her hand. Callie was unsure how she felt about his spontaneous gesture. Grateful for the attention at a time when she felt as though she was at sea in a sinking dinghy, she reminded herself that she had to remain focused without leaning too heavily on him. On a personal level, he was far younger than her and anyway, she absolutely wasn't in the market for a relationship. She removed her hand from his reach and used it to pick up her glass.

'O'Keefe is very much a family man, did you know that?' Darren asked.

'Can't say that I did. He trotted his wife out on social occasions back in the day, when Gavin was still attempting to mix it with the high-flying criminal fraternity, but then so did everyone else. Can't say I even recall what Mrs O'Keefe looks like so she can't have made much of an impression on me. Most of us wives tended to gravitate together, as usually happens at any social gathering, but I can't recall Mrs O'Keefe joining in our general whinging about the men. I can't even recall her Christian name, come to that.'

'They're childhood sweethearts, apparently. They have half a dozen grown kids. Four boys who work for their dad and two girls married to associates of his who are busy giving him a plethora of grandkids.'

'Blimey, talk about keeping it in the family!'

'Yeah, his clan are everything to him, which is why he would never go to Phoenix for anything other than a business meeting. He's famous for not putting it about, but do you know who rules the roost?' Darren smiled. 'I'll give you a clue and it ain't O'Keefe.'

Callie widened her eyes. 'His dowdy missus?'

'Got it in one. Word is she's the only person O'Keefe's afraid of. Not that anyone would dare to pull O'Keefe's leg about it. I've heard it said that he talks to her about his business problems and she's often the one to come up with fresh ideas. She's hard as nails and ruthless with it.'

'A woman with a brain.' Callie tutted and shook her head. 'What is the world coming to?'

Darren laughed. 'We're doomed.'

'All well and good.' Callie's expression sobered. 'But how does that help us?'

'I have absolutely no idea, but I do have a few useful connections who keep their ears to the ground.' He paused to take another swig of his beer. Callie watched with teenage-like fascination as he swallowed and then forced herself to look away again. *Stay professional!* 'We really need to find out, and find out fast, why O'Keefe wants this place so badly.'

'I agree, but even if we manage to, I'm not sure what we can do about it.'

Darren winked at her. 'Knowledge is power.' Darren put his empty bottle aside and shifted his weight into a more comfortable position. 'If he does want to develop the golf course land for some reason and aims to bend members of the planning committee to his will, and if we know in advance then we can...'

'Can what?' Callie threw up her hands. 'It's hopeless. He won't be strong-arming any officials until he owns the land in question.'

'Yeah, point taken.' Darren fell momentarily silent as he thoughtfully rubbed his chin. 'A clinic. Fallow mentioned a clinic. What the hell does O'Keefe need a clinic for?'

'Perhaps a member of his precious family is seriously ill.'

'Now that,' Darren said, leaning towards her, 'is a very real possibility. I have heard that his younger daughter, who's his favourite, hasn't been seen for a while.'

Callie frowned and tilted her head, openly curious. 'Where do you hear these things?'

Darren waggled a hand from side to side. 'Here and there. I might not be a criminal myself, but I can't change my background and can't avoid mingling with my family's connections on occasions. Besides, no offence intended, but I do work for a gangster and the fact that I know my way around some of the shadier characters in town is probably one of the reasons why I was hired.'

'As long as you don't mean me then no offence is taken.' Callie smiled, enjoying Darren's teasingly enticing smile a little too much. *Down, girl!* 'Anyway, even if your theory about a sick relation is true, O'Keefe can afford to fly that person to the best medical facility in the world. Building a clinic to treat her seems far-fetched to say the least. Anyway, by the time the place was up and running, if she's that ill then it would be too late.'

'Yep, but even so...'

'I still think the business at Phoenix is drug-related,' Callie said, articulating her thoughts as her mind jumped from one situation to another.

'The business with O'Keefe won't be,' Darren replied with authority. 'Like I already said, he hates the sex trade and more to the point, so does—'

'Mrs O'Keefe,' Callie finished for him. 'God, there's so much we don't know. I wish I'd taken more notice of Gavin's wheeling and dealing but I made a point of not being involved. Better that way, or so I thought.' She sighed. 'Anyway, I guess we have to concentrate on the area that we know most about whilst your people do their digging. In other words, we need to find Paul and to do that, we need to find his daughter. We can't wait days or weeks. We have to shake the tree somehow and find her now. Today. Tomorrow at the latest.'

'The alternative is to agree to sell to O'Keefe.' Darren held up a hand to stop Callie from protesting. 'It's not a deal until the legal bods have done their bit, which we can delay and that will buy you some time. And he'll keep Stafford off your back.'

'I had thought of that, but I can't agree to the sale and then renege. My life expectancy wouldn't be worth diddly squat.'

'Swallow your pride if necessary and walk away with the money. Start a new life free from all these scumbags.' Darren looked almost vicious in his determination. His reaction, she assumed, was an indication of the resentment he felt towards his criminal father and the difficult choices he'd been obliged to make when he didn't go into the family profession. 'I know that's not what you want but at least it will leave us with the opportunity to find out what O'Keefe wants the place for and to stop him if possible. If we can take away the need then he'll probably lose interest in purchasing.'

'I can't fault your logic, but that doesn't mean I have to like it.' She sighed. 'So, we concentrate upon running Paul to ground then. He and Gavin might have had a falling out but I'm betting that Paul will still have heard something about O'Keefe's reasons for wanting this place.'

'I can't think of any other way,' Darren said, regret in his tone.

'Well, we've said all we need to. It's now a waiting game. Patience isn't one of my strong points and I won't be able to concentrate on anything else, so I'm going to take myself off home.'

'What would you say to a night on the town? A few drinks and a nice meal somewhere. It would do you good to take your mind off things.'

Callie hesitated. She was tempted, very tempted, but would it be wise? They would be seen by someone but... so what? Gavin was the only person who'd give a shit, but he wasn't fond enough of her to break cover just because she was out on the town.

Was he?

'You're on,' she said, thinking of all the evenings when she'd sat at home alone whilst Gavin had entertained his floozies. 'Pick me up at seven.'

Callie reached for her phone, but it chirped into life before she could return it to her bag.

'Fallow,' she said, checking the caller ID and hitting the green button. 'You have something for me?' she asked, putting the call on speaker.

'April Morton, maiden name Nilssen, is a Swedish pharmacist,' he said without preamble.

'Pharmacist?' Darren mouthed, looking as perplexed as Callie felt.

'She worked for a big pharmaceutical company in Stockholm but came to England a year ago and married Graham Morton.'

'Is she still employed by the pharmaceutical company?' Callie asked.

'Nope. She held a senior position but resigned. That's all I know.'

'Why come here?' Callie asked, her mind going into overdrive. 'What do we know about Graham Morton?'

'He's known to us professionally. Did a five stretch for narcotic violation. He's on parole and gave his address as that flat in the marina, which is how we found April.'

'He's a drug dealer?'

'Yeah, but not the sort of drugs you're thinking about.'

'Then what?' Callie sent a helpless look Darren's way.

'We're talking prescription drugs at knock-off prices.'

'Thank you, Superintendent,' Callie said. 'You've just made my day.'

'Happy to oblige,' he said, cutting the connection.

* * *

Tom rang Angie whilst she was still driving home.

'Sorry to run out on you,' he said. 'Something came up at the showroom and I was needed to prevent a big deal going west.'

'No worries.'

'What happened? No, don't tell me now. I'm on my way over.'

'But Henry—'

'Henry's a big boy and I have a legitimate reason for wanting to see him. He is supposed to work at the showroom, and I am technically his boss.' She could hear the smile in his voice. 'Stop worrying and trust me, I'm a car salesman.'

'I can't argue with that.' She laughed, something she found herself doing all too readily when in conversation with the enigmatic Tom. She had clearly misjudged him before now. He had hidden depths and wasn't the wide boy that she'd had him pegged as being. More to the point, he appeared to be on her side, but appearances could be deceptive, she reminded herself. It would be better not to let him get too close, but she so needed some company right now and would put herself first for a change. 'Okay, come over as soon as you like. Perhaps you'll be able to get more than monosyllables out of my son. Anything's possible.'

Angie arrived home to find Henry in the same place she'd left him: on the sofa, surrounded by empty junk food packets, TV blaring and his phone in his hand. The room stank of cigarette smoke. He had his headphones on and didn't at first realise she was there. Angie watched him for a moment, thanking every deity she could think of for his safe return, at the same time vowing to disembowel her husband for putting him at risk when he finally broke cover.

'Hey,' she said, tousling his hair. 'Into healthy eating, I see.'

Henry barely looked up and didn't acknowledge her presence, which caused something to snap inside of her.

'I know you've been through a lot,' she said, snatching the headphones off his ears and throwing them down, 'and I'm trying to make allowances, but ignoring me is insulting.

Smoking in my lounge is a no-no, as you are well aware. Even your father wouldn't do that, and God alone knows, there's little else he wouldn't do.'

'Well, you would say that.' He turned to look at her, his expression full of raw pain. 'It's true what they say about a woman scorned, obviously.'

'Do you really want to have this conversation now?' Anger and disillusionment caused Angie to blurt out the question more acerbically than had been her intention. Henry sent her a caustic look, perhaps because she'd almost never lost her temper with him before now, even when he was going through the stroppy teenager with a grudge against the world phase. Perhaps that was her problem, she reasoned. She tended to make excuses for her nearest and dearest and tolerate their moods, which explained why she was taken so much for granted.

She was a doormat.

Correction, she had been. But the worm had finally turned.

'There's nothing to talk about,' he said sullenly. 'You've driven Dad away with your nagging. End of.'

'Oh, grow up, Henry! Not that it's any of your business, but I loved your dad. Past tense.' Angie was in full stride now and stood over her son, fisted hands planted on her hips. 'I thought the feeling was reciprocated. Ha!' She shook her head. 'Talk about naïve.'

Something in her attitude clearly struck a chord with Henry and he looked at her now with stupefaction rather than resentment. 'Dad will be back,' he said.

'No, he won't because I won't have him.'

'Don't be daft. This is just a blip.'

'You were abducted because he's got himself in above his head in some dodgy deal. You could have been badly hurt, even killed, and yet you're still making excuses for him?' Angie let out a frustrated breath. 'It's time to face reality. Your father is in love with a sex worker and she's welcome to him.'

Henry looked relieved. 'He's not in love, Mum. It don't mean nothing.'

'Really?' Heavy sarcasm underlined the one word.

'He's just finding an escape. You let yourself go, took him for granted, and so he looked elsewhere.'

Angie sighed, not bothering to take him to task for the letting-herself-go dig. 'So where is he now?' she asked instead.

Henry stared at his hands and had nothing to say.

She focused her gaze unflinchingly on her son as she awaited his response. 'Has he been in touch?'

Henry shook his head with obvious reluctance. 'His competitors used me to force his hand,' he said weakly.

'Well, if your father didn't take you to brothels when he knew these guys were after him, then they couldn't have used you, could they?' Angie chose to ignore the fact that Henry, or any of her other children, could have been snatched from the street at any time. Her blood still ran cold at the thought but now wasn't the time to fall apart.

'I like going there. Talking to Melody—'

'Who wanted to get to know you, but not for the reasons you hoped. She's your father's mistress, Henry, and for all we know was responsible for your abduction.'

'Don't be daft!'

'Daft, am I? Who encouraged you to chat with Melody? Time to take your dad off that pedestal you've put him on and see him for what he is. It's taken me long enough but now that I've opened my eyes, I don't much like the view and won't be taken for a fool any more.'

'You're not being fair to him, Mum. All couples have rocky

patches, but you'll get past this. He needs your support, not your censure.'

'Even if I wanted to, I'm not sure I could ignore your half-sister,' Angie replied, losing all patience with Henry's unrealistic view.

'Half-sister?' His mouth fell open. 'What are you on about?'

'Ask your friend Melody if you want to know because I don't suppose you'll believe me. You'll put it down to the menopausal ravings of a deranged woman, but Melody just told Callie and me that Paul fathered her daughter. Yeah, it took me by surprise too,' she said, taking in Henry's slack-jawed expression, 'given that the child is a year old, and I didn't have a clue that he was dissatisfied with life at home, but there you go.'

'Oh God, Mum!'

There were tears in Henry's eyes and she spontaneously opened her arms to him, all anger forgotten. He was her little boy again who needed his mum. She hugged him close and let him sob on her shoulder. To the best of her knowledge, he hadn't shed a tear since being released from captivity and so part of this was delayed reaction, she knew, but she didn't care. All she knew was that she and Henry were friends again and right now, that was all that mattered.

Perhaps she should have treated her son as an adult before now and shared some of her concerns with him. But it hadn't seemed fair to burden a child with adult worries. Besides, he would have taken his father's side if she uttered one word of censure about the wretched man.

'It's okay,' she said gently, soothing him with sweeps of one hand down his back. He was so tall now, well over six foot, but would always be her baby. 'No matter what happens, Paul will always be your dad.' That was a ridiculous remark, she realised, as soon as the words left her lips. She'd just pointed out that he hadn't even checked in on Henry and when that fact registered with her child, perhaps the blinkers would finally come off. 'It's a difficult time but we'll get through it.'

Henry pulled out of her arms, looking embarrassed by his meltdown. 'I didn't mean the things I said about you,' he told her, unable to meet her eye.

'I know.' She tugged at his hair which was, as always, too long.

'Who's that?' He walked to the window, and she saw his face fall when he realised it was Tom who'd pulled onto their drive. A part of her boy was still hungry for his dad's return, she realised with a sinking heart.

'It's Tom,' Angie said, stating the obvious. 'He said he'd be over. He wants to talk to you and he's also trying to help me find your dad.'

'Whatever.'

The sullen young man was back with a vengeance. Perhaps he didn't like Angie associating with Tom, but she was damned if she'd let her son's views influence her choice of friends. Even the knowledge that Henry had a half-sibling didn't appear to have destroyed his faith in his father and he was doubtless already making up excuses for Paul in the back of his mind.

Angie opened the front door before Tom could knock.

'Hey,' he said, strolling into the lounge and shaking Henry's hand, the swagger in his step that Angie disliked so much back in place now that they had company. It was almost as though he was playing a part, she thought, hoping that she'd seen the real Tom on the recent occasions when they'd been alone. The Tom that she'd found herself getting to like. 'You okay, mate? You had us all worried there for a while.'

'Yeah, I'm good.' Henry's attitude was brash yet subdued.

'We're ready for you to come back to the showroom when you are.'

'I'll be there tomorrow. It will be good to do normal stuff again.'

'Are you sure?' Angie asked.

'I'm off home now, Mum,' Henry said. 'Helen's coming round.'

'Okay, darling, but ring me later or I'll worry.'

'Yeah, yeah.'

Henry shared a *what-can-you-do* look with Tom, picked up his jacket and left.

'That went well,' Tom said, smiling. 'Has he upset you?'

'We had a heart-to-heart. It took him a while to accept that he has a half-sibling but now that he has, my boy will have some thinking to do.' She chuckled. 'He harbours romantic notions over Melody, so knowing his dad is already in there might make him reassess his father's character.'

'Half-sibling?' Tom blinked at her.

'Sorry, you don't know, do you. Sit down. Would you like a beer? I'm going to have a wine. After that showdown with Henry, I need it.'

'A beer would be great, thanks.'

Angie arranged the drinks, cleared the remnants of Henry's junk food from the couch and sat beside Tom. She then told him everything they'd learned from Melody.

'Bloody hell! The idiot!' Tom shook his head. 'What the hell was he thinking?'

'If he was thinking at all, it sure as hell wasn't with his brain,' Angie said bitterly. 'The thing is, Melody was sneaking out to attend their daughter's first birthday party and we literally spoiled the reunion. We assume she was going to meet Paul there but didn't make it.'

'They must have a means of communication.'

'I'm perfectly sure that they do but even if we search every inch of Phoenix, if she has a burner phone hidden, we're never likely to find it. Besides, what good will it do? Paul will know what's going on from her.'

'He'll also know that you've gone on the offensive. That will surprise him.'

'Why?' Angie shot him an affronted look. 'Because the meek little woman indoors, who's so trusting that she never asks questions, has grown a pair, figuratively speaking?'

'Yeah, something of that nature and good for you.'

Angie smiled, her annoyance dissipating. 'You're right though, but when he involved Henry, he crossed a line. Any mother worthy of the name would have reacted in the same way.'

'So, what now?'

'Now we try to find Paul. I won't feel safe for myself or my kids until I know what he's got himself into. And to find him, we need to find his child. I get the impression that's where he and Melody meet at present, but we have absolutely no idea who's looking after the child and Melody is refusing to say.' Angie turned sideways on the cushions and looked Tom directly in the eye. 'I thought you might be able to shed some light. You've seen more of him than me for a long time now.' She paused. 'Why had that not occurred to me before now? Perhaps because I didn't mind his absences,' she added, answering her own question. 'I got caught up with my work at the spa. Having a career again, one that I'm good at, gave me a purpose and I was no longer dependent upon Paul.' She smiled. 'I rather like the new version of me.'

'So do I,' Tom said softly.

'So, do you?'

'Do I what?'

'Have any idea where the child might be? Does anyone connected to the showroom have kids, or know anyone that looks after them?'

'Not offhand.' Tom slowly shook his head. 'Sorry, Angie, but nothing springs... holy shit!'

'What?' Angie half rose from her seat. 'What is it?'

'Beccy.'

'Paul's assistant. What about her? She doesn't have children, does she?'

'No, but her sister does, and she dotes on her nephew and niece. She has their picture on her desk, and she talks about them all the time.'

'She dotes on Paul, too,' Angie said. 'It makes sense.' She reached for her phone.

'What are you doing?'

'Calling Callie. She needs to know about this.'

17

Callie dressed for her evening out with more care than usual. It had been a *long* time since she'd dated, if that was what this was. Her preparations had nothing to do with impressing Darren who, she reminded herself, was much younger than her, not interested in her romantically and anyway, she still wasn't entirely sure that she trusted him.

'Keep the faith,' she muttered as she examined her reflection and felt satisfied with the image that stared back at her. In a pale-blue jersey dress that fell to mid-calf and clung to all her curves along the way, she felt that she still had what it took to make a statement. She donned four-inch heels which pushed her height to a confidence-giving five-ten. She would still be at least three inches shorter than Darren but her height and the air of self-confidence she had perfected over the years to hide her insecurity would, she hoped, make her seem like a woman not to be messed with.

The chances of encountering some of Gavin's old sparring partners was highly probable – there were limited watering holes in their village – and she didn't want any of them to get the impression that she was all at sea without Gavin to hold her hand. It would be interesting to learn what they made of Darren stepping into his shoes, which is the conclusion wagging tongues would likely reach. Perhaps word would reach Gavin too, wherever he was. That possibility caused Callie to smile.

See how you like it.

She had just put the final touches to her make-up when her phone rang.

'Hey, Angie,' she said, taking the call.

'Can Tom and I come over?' she asked, excitement in her voice. 'I think we might know where Paul's baby is being kept.'

'Sure. Darren's due at any moment so you can tell us both.'

'Is he now.' Angie's chuckle sounded over the airwaves. 'Is there something you need to tell us?'

'Don't go there! I'll see you in a bit.'

The doorbell sounded ten minutes later. When Callie opened it, Darren swept the entire length of her body with an unmistakably approving look.

'Wow!' he said.

'I need to let the local worthies know that I'm not down and out without Gavin around,' she said, wondering why she felt the need to explain herself to a man who was effectively the hired help.

'No one would ever think that of you,' he replied, with an easy smile. He strolled into the house with one hand casually thrust into his trouser pocket. 'Are you ready?'

'Actually, Angie and Tom are on their way over. They think they know where to find Paul's child.'

'Do they indeed.' Darren flexed a brow. 'This calls for a drink. Shall I do the honours?'

Without waiting for a response, he went to her drinks cabinet, extracted a bottle of Krug from the fridge and expertly popped the cork. He poured the frothing liquid into two flutes without spilling a drop and handed one to her.

'What are we celebrating?' she asked.

'A breakthrough? Any excuse will do.'

She smiled, clinked her glass against his and took a sip before leading the way into the conservatory, where comfortable chairs surrounded their indoor pool.

'Do you use it?' he asked, nodding towards the turquoise water.

'Hardly ever. Nor does Gavin since he can't actually swim. He insisted on having it installed though, just to impress people.'

'It's a far cry from the social housing where I grew up,' Darren remarked. 'The only swimming any of us ever got to do was in the local pool, and then only when we could afford to get in.' He chortled. 'Or if we could duck past the barrier when no one was looking.'

'I didn't grow up in luxury either,' Callie felt the need to point out. 'And all of this has come at a heavy cost. You can never entirely relax, always expecting that knock at the door late at night. The spa was supposed to be my release but instead, I found myself worrying about the increasing amounts of dodgy money that Gavin put through it. I own the place so the buck stops with me, but of course he was having none of that and simply told me that I worry too much.' Callie snorted. 'Easy for him to say. Even with the likes of Fallow on his side, there's only so much protection he can depend upon from that quarter. I mean, we're seeing it now. Fallow is running scared and thinking about saving his own hide. He'll drop Gavin in it if he has to. And me as well.'

'Well, if you take O'Keefe's—'

The doorbell sounded, cutting off whatever Darren had been about to say. Callie suspected that he would have used the opportunity to again point out the benefits of selling up, putting the past behind her and creating a new life for herself. His urging her to bail made her wonder if he was thinking about her best interests or working at someone else's behest. Could he be working with O'Keefe? She chased the thought away, telling herself she was becoming paranoid. So far, Darren hadn't given her any reason to doubt him.

Hold that thought!

'Hey!' she said, opening the door to Angie and Tom.

'Wow,' Angie said as she walked in, dressed in the same clothes as earlier. 'Are we keeping you from something?'

'Nothing that can't wait. Hey, Tom.'

'Callie.'

'We're in the conservatory, drinking champagne for no particular reason.'

'I'll pour two more glasses,' Darren said, joining them and doing precisely that.

'Okay,' Callie said, when they were all settled with their drinks. 'Give. Where do you think Paul's child is being cared for?'

Tom told them his theory.

'It would explain why Beccy's attitude was borderline hostile when I showed my face at the car lot,' Angie added.

Tom nodded. 'Beccy thinks Paul walks on water. She'd do anything for him.'

'Even arrange for her sister to care for his love child?' Darren asked, his expression sceptical.

'He won't have told her he's the father but will have spun

some line about Melody being unable to care for the child currently.'

'Hang on, though,' Callie said. 'If Paul and Melody go to see the child at the same time, then her sister is bound to catch on. Beccy might be fixated on Paul but I'm guessing that even she has her limits, especially if she's seen Melody, who is absolutely, lethally gorgeous. Mere mortals can't compete.'

'I hear what you're saying,' Angie replied. 'The same thought had occurred to me, but it's also the only lead we have so we need to follow it up.'

'Do we even know where the sister lives?' Darren asked.

'Palitine Way. I know because Beccy mentioned the house is directly across from the local school in a good catchment area, which is important, apparently,' Tom said.

'Okay.' Darren stood up and pulled his phone from his pocket. 'I'll arrange for the place to be watched for signs of Paul.'

'Is he likely to...' Callie stopped talking, wondering what point she was trying to make.

'Melody loves that kid,' Darren said. 'You said the only genuine reaction she showed was when talking about her. She missed her birthday so will try again, likely later tonight or tomorrow. Paul, if he's as involved with her as we think, will be there for this momentous occasion. Apart from anything else, he will want to know why we pulled Melody in and how much we know about whatever he's involved with.'

Callie and Angie both nodded their agreement.

Conversation stalled whilst Darren made his call.

'Okay, all set up,' he said, rejoining them.

'Ask your mate at Phoenix to turn a blind eye if Melody tries to sneak out again and then tell us,' Callie said.

'Good thinking.'

Darren made another call. 'Done,' he said, pocketing his phone.

'You told me Fallow had news about April Morton,' Angie said.

Callie told her and Tom what they now knew.

'So,' Tom said when she ran out of words. 'We're talking about prescription drugs. I never thought that Gavin or Paul would involve themselves in the recreational drug trade. Quite apart from anything else, Stafford has the market cornered and wouldn't take kindly to the competition.'

'The bastard launders his money through my spa,' Callie said, an edge to her voice.

'I've heard there's a thriving market for medical drugs,' Darren said.

'Why?' Angie asked. 'If someone's ill and needs medication, they can go to their GP and get it prescribed.'

'If they're here legally,' Tom said.

Darren nodded. 'Everything we know or suspect seems to centre on drugs. And don't forget, people with untreatable conditions who have a few bob will pay almost anything for drugs that are still not on the market.'

'Ah, I see what you mean.' Callie put her empty glass aside. 'You hear about trials of new drugs that show promising results in the experimental stage for just about every life-threatening condition, but they still have to jump through dozens of hoops before they're approved for the market and that can take years. So how would they be available for sale on the black market?'

'Think April Morton,' Darren replied. 'She was a high-flying pharmacist who's finished up in this country married to a guy with form. She will have contacts. She was probably caught either stealing drugs or making them herself but that would never have come out in the open for fear of adverse publicity, to say nothing of the company's share price.'

Darren's phone rang and he checked the display.

'Excuse me,' he said standing. 'I need to take this.'

Callie and Angie both watched him walk away. Whoever had called him, Darren didn't want them to hear his side of the conversation. Either that or he was simply being polite. Callie chose to believe the latter.

'How's Henry holding up?' Callie asked.

'He's being stoic,' Angie replied. 'I don't think the reaction has really set in yet. But anyway, he reckons he's going back to work tomorrow, which is probably a good thing. Take his mind off it.'

Darren returned, pocketing his phone.

'I asked one of my dad's friends to get back to me, and that was him. He knows the O'Keefe's. Used to do some work for them back in the day. Low-grade stuff, but he went legit years ago and doesn't have anything to do with them now. Even so, he knows the family and what makes them tick.'

'You can trust him?' Callie asked, wondering if it was wise to involve so many outsiders in their quest. But then again, she reasoned, what would it matter if word of their activities reached the wrong ears? They were only asking questions, and perhaps it would spook someone into making a false move.

'I think so, yes. I promised him a few quid for his information, for which he was grateful. He's getting on a bit and could use the readies. Anyway, he confirmed what I told you earlier about O'Keefe being an out-and-out family man. Nothing is more important to him and as far as anyone is aware, he's never broken his marriage vows.'

'Wow!' Tom's shell-shocked look made everyone smile.

'What he also just told me is that O'Keefe's youngest, his daughter Chloe, had leukaemia a few years back. He took her to America to be treated in a specialist unit and she recovered. But here's the thing: her little girl now has it. One or two other members of his extended family on the male side have recovered. He doesn't know if the child's prognosis is terminal, but it isn't looking good. Word is, she's too sick to travel to America.'

'So O'Keefe is arranging for the drugs to come to her,' Callie suggested.

'Wouldn't you, in his situation?' Angie asked, looking sympathetic.

'More than likely. I never thought I'd feel sorry for O'Keefe. But anyway, it seems likely that we're right. O'Keefe wants to set up his own private clinic, probably because his wife insists. They want to make sure that help is immediately at hand for their own family, given its history, and charge anyone who can afford it a fortune to be treated when all else has failed and they're desperate.'

'Very possibly,' Darren replied, 'but that doesn't get us past the fact that the golf course land is not suitable for building, and it would take years to build and equip the place even if it was.'

'Not if they have a container building,' Tom said. 'You must have seen them popping up as temporary structures,' he added when met with a sea of blank faces. 'They don't need deep foundations, can be erected in weeks and can probably circumvent the planning rules if they're intended as a temporary structure.'

'It all fits,' Angie said, tapping her fingers. 'Right down to Paul having April Morton waiting in the wings.' She frowned.

'But what does it have to do with my husband? This is O'Keefe's baby.'

'I'm thinking we were right and that the drugs are coming in through Liverpool but brought down to this part of the country in Paul's cars,' Callie said. 'Presumably, there's some sort of underground clinic in operation where they're already being dished out to the privileged few.'

'And Beccy schedules the drivers for those trips,' Angie said, scowling. 'Perhaps she isn't just fixated on Paul. Perhaps she's also up to her neck in this business.'

'Paul decided enough was enough,' Callie added, 'and wanted out, but O'Keefe wasn't about to let him go and forced his hand by abducting Henry. If O'Keefe is a family man fixated on his kids, it would explain why Henry wasn't harmed. He wouldn't raise a hand against an innocent youngster.'

'I'm sure it's a very lucrative business,' Darren mused, 'so why would Paul want to give it up now? He was trying to get one over on Gavin, and it's a bit late for him to develop a conscience, isn't it? Besides, it's not as though they're recreational drugs that can ruin lives. These are drugs that are supposed to help sick people who have got nothing to lose by trying them.'

'Perhaps something went wrong?' Tom suggested. 'There have been deaths...'

'How would Paul know that?' Angie asked.

'A better question to ask,' Darren said, 'is why Paul hasn't resurfaced. We're assuming he did what O'Keefe wanted, which is why Henry was released, so why continue to keep his head down?'

'Perhaps O'Keefe knows he'll toe the line now but isn't finished with him,' Angie mused.

'He didn't need to hide away before, and we assume he was

working for him then,' Tom pointed out. 'What can have changed?'

No one seemed to have a clue, and the conservatory fell silent.

'We're clutching at straws,' Callie eventually said. 'I don't think there's much more we can achieve until Paul surfaces, and we can ask him those questions for ourselves.'

'Before or after I throttle him?' Angie asked with a growl.

'Well then,' Tom said, glancing at his watch, 'there's somewhere I need to be, so I'll drop you home, Angie, if you're ready to go. Let me know if you need me to do anything, Mrs R.'

'It's Callie.' She smiled at the ambitious younger man, as sure as she could be that he wasn't caught up in Paul's shenanigans. 'Just keep things ticking over at the showroom and an eye on Beccy. Don't spook her if you can help it. Hopefully, Melody will make a fresh break for freedom soon and then we can take a step forward.'

'Well,' Darren said once the others had left, 'we're making progress, of sorts. Are you still up for that drink?'

'Absolutely! I'd like to go out for a while, do something normal to take my mind off my problems.'

'That can be arranged.'

Darren drove them to an out-of-town restaurant that had recently opened, and Callie had been meaning to try. But she hadn't been out much since Gavin's disappearance. She wondered why. She was used to Gavin going off-piste and his absences didn't ordinarily mess with her social life. She had a wide circle of friends and was never short of invitations but this time, for some reason, she'd been keeping a low profile. It was almost as though she had something to hide, she realised, always supposing that her absence from the local social scene had been noticed.

'This is more than a drink,' she said, stating the obvious, when a waitress led them to a table for two and handed them menus.

Darren smiled at her across the table. 'I figured you could use the distraction.'

'That's thoughtful but this place is expensive,' she said, glancing at the prices on the menu and trying not to wince. 'You must either let me pay or ask for a pay rise.'

'I wouldn't have brought you here if I couldn't afford it.'

'Sorry, I didn't mean to offend you.'

Darren waved her concerns aside and ordered an expensive bottle of wine. He tasted it, declared it to be fine and the waitress poured for them both.

'Cheers,' he said, raising his glass and clicking it against hers.

He was easy company in a social situation, Callie found. He was far better educated than she'd realised, as became evident when he spoke intelligently on a number of subjects. Darren intuitively didn't mention her problems and she felt herself relaxing.

'We're being watched,' he told her.

'I know. The Griffiths at the table in the corner. I'm pretending that I haven't seen them.'

'Consider them unseen.' Darren picked up his glass. 'He does legitimate business with Gavin; that's how I know him.'

'They've been to one of Gavin's gatherings at the house. They're a nice couple but they're clearly wondering what I'm doing here alone with you.'

'Let them wonder.'

'Why *are* you here with me and not wining and dining some young woman?' she asked, pushing her empty main course plate aside with a wistful sigh. 'I'm sure you have them queueing up.'

Darren laughed. 'Not exactly. I'm no monk but I'm not in the market for settling down either. I've seen too many of my mates do that and live to regret it. I suppose, if I meet the right woman, I'll know it, but it hasn't happened yet. Besides, who'd want to marry into my dissolute family?'

'I'm sure they're not that bad. Besides, they should judge you, not your relations.'

'In an ideal world, perhaps.' He metaphorically appeared to dust his hands together, as though not wanting to pursue that line of conversation. 'Now,' he said, 'can I tempt you to dessert?'

'Not a chance. I've already eaten too much.' She smiled at him. 'Thank you. It was lovely. I had no idea I needed a night out quite so badly. I will definitely talk to the boss about that pay rise.'

He winked at her. 'Ah, so my ploy worked then.'

She laughed, watching him as he tapped his card against the machine and made the young waitress blush when he smiled at her.

'All set?'

'Yep. And ready for my bed.' She covered her mouth with her hand. 'Sorry, that came out wrong.'

Darren said nothing. Instead, he unlocked his car and opened the passenger door for her. He drove the short distance to her home with swift economy, saying nothing, as though realising that she needed a little quiet. He had the radio tuned to an oldies station, the volume turned down low.

'Thank you,' she said, when he pulled into her driveway. 'I enjoyed that more than I expected to. No, don't get out. It's late and I need my beauty sleep.'

'Okay.' He leaned across and pecked her on the cheek. 'Sleep well.'

'See you tomorrow,' she said, climbing from his car and waving.

But sleep, she knew, would be a long time coming. She had forgotten her tribulations for a couple of hours but alone in her massive bed, she knew that all her demons, her insecurities, would come out to haunt her and she would pay a heavy price for her brief respite.

18

Callie's disturbed and unsavoury dreams were interrupted by her phone ringing at six in the morning. Groggy and disorientated, she reached for her mobile that she'd left charging on her bedside table.

'Yes,' she said, not bothering to check the display to see who was calling. 'What is it?' Whatever it was, she knew that people didn't make social calls at such an ungodly hour and so it had to be important.

'Hey.' Darren's gravelly voice echoed down the line. 'Sorry to wake you, but I thought you'd like to know that Melody just left Phoenix.'

Callie was instantly awake. 'Is someone following her?' She sat up and pushed the hair from her eyes.

'Of course. I'll pick you up in half an hour if you want to be in on this.'

'You bet your sweet life I do! I imagine that Angie will too. I'll ring her now and we can pick her up on the way.'

'Okay. See you in a bit.'

Callie took a ninety-second, lukewarm shower, sufficient to

wake her up, and threw on the first clothes that came to hand: her favourite jeans and a sweatshirt. She thrust her feet into flats, brushed her hair and didn't bother with make-up. She made a quick call to Angie and was at the door when Darren's car drew up outside.

'Hi,' she said, climbing into the passenger seat.

'Hi yourself,' he replied, pulling out onto a deserted street. It was still dark and there were no other vehicles on the move in the sleepy hamlet of Frenchurch. 'She's heading for where we think her daughter is being looked after.'

'But surely the child will be sound asleep at this hour, as will the people caring for her. What can she be thinking?'

Darren shrugged. 'Melody probably figured that the early hours would be the safest time to get out of Phoenix unseen. She may not actually go to the house until later. Or then again, she might have arranged to meet Paul somewhere else entirely.'

Callie nodded. 'True.'

Angie was waiting for them when they reached her house. She jumped into the back seat, looking fraught. Not surprising, Callie thought, given that she was very likely about to be reunited with Paul. Callie had never seen her friend half so fired up before and almost felt sorry for Paul.

Almost!

'You ready for whatever we find?' Callie asked.

'Oh yes! I want this to be over with, but most of all, I want answers.'

'I understand.' Callie reached between the gap in the seats and touched Angie's knee.

By the time they reached Palitine Way, it was gone seven and completely light. Callie could see activity in a number of the houses. Breakfasts being prepared, nothing out of the ordinary.

'Number seven. Here we go.' Darren pulled up a little past the house in question and pointed to it.

'Someone's up,' Callie said. 'I can see activity in the kitchen.'

'They would be if they have one or more children in there,' Angie replied. 'Take it from one who knows. Lie-ins are not an option until they hit their teens, then you can't get them out of bed.'

'So, what now?' Callie asked.

'Now we wait. Melody doesn't have a car and so unless Paul picked her up somewhere, she's going to have to make her way here by public transport or in a taxi.'

'How do we know she isn't already in there?' Angie asked, her knees jiggling with obvious frustration.

'We don't,' Darren said. 'The guy following her lost her when she got on a bus. He sounded frustrated. But there's only one way in and out for her. There's no back entrance with direct street access. I know because I had someone check the place out when it was first mentioned.'

Callie nodded her approval. She should have thought to suggest it, but it seemed there had been no need. Darren was one step ahead of her.

Angie nodded. 'So, they will have to arrive or leave by the front door.'

'They're here!' Callie cried.

Angie leaned forward to check the wing mirror and saw a cab pull up outside number seven. She gasped when Paul climbed from the back and held out a hand to assist Melody from it. She muttered something incomprehensible beneath her breath when he took Melody in his arms and kissed her long and deep.

Before Darren or Callie could prevent her, she opened her

door and ran towards her husband. He was so engrossed in the kiss that he obviously didn't hear Angie, or Callie and Darren, who'd followed close on her heels, approaching.

'How touching,' Angie said, resting her fisted hands on her hips, presumably to prevent herself from planting one of them in the centre of Paul's face.

'Angie!' Paul looked at her, his jaw slack with shock. 'What the hell are you doing here?'

'Get in!' Darren indicated his car with a jerk of his thumb.

Paul walked up to Darren and thrust out his chest. 'Who the hell do you think you are to give me orders?'

'It's this or having it out in front of your daughter,' Callie said sweetly, her tone silk on steel. 'Your choice.'

Paul glanced at Melody.

'I told you they would work it out,' she said, her tone bereft.

'It's all right, darling.' His entire focus was on Melody's face, his voice a tender caress which doubtless further infuriated Angie. How could he be so insensitive! Callie wanted to throttle him and save Angie the trouble. 'We'll sort this out. You don't need to be involved.'

'Oh yes she does!' Callie and Angie said together.

Paul glanced around like a rabbit caught in headlights, as though it had only just occurred to him just how much trouble he was in. His first thought seemed to be to bolt but to do that, he'd need to get past Darren, who had a good three inches on him. He went to the gym regularly. His muscles were toned and there wasn't an inch of fat on him. Paul was also twenty years older and wisely decided against taking Darren on.

'Be a man for once and face up to your actions instead of running away, like you always do when the going gets awkward, leaving your kids to take the flack,' Angie growled, when Paul still hesitated.

Without another word, Paul sighed, took Melody's hand and led her to Darren's BMW. They slid into the back seat. Callie pushed Angie towards the passenger seat and herself occupied the remaining space at the back, next to Melody, who was wedged in the middle with nowhere to put her long legs, looking uncomfortable in every sense of the word.

'Where are we going?' Paul asked, when Darren started the engine and did a one-eighty.

No one answered him and the journey back to the spa was made in uneasy silence.

They made their way directly to Callie's office. Darren closed the door and wedged his shoulder against it, just in case Paul decided to make a run for it. Callie wouldn't put it past the snivelling coward. Melody and Paul stood together, attempting to look as though they were in control, but Angie was having none of it. Pushed beyond her limits by the damage Paul had done. No one spoke as Angie walked up to him and slapped his face as hard as she could. Her hand making contact with his skin sounded like a gun shot in the otherwise quiet room.

'That was for endangering Henry and introducing him to a prostitute,' Angie said. 'And this is for being a cheating scumbag.'

She lifted her knee and placed it with considerable force in the centre of his scrotum. Paul screamed and doubled over, clutching his crown jewels as he howled with pain.

Callie wanted to applaud. Damn, that must have felt good! Images of doing something similar to Gavin flooded her mind. She shared a high five with Angie as they sat together, united on one sofa. Paul and Melody occupied single chairs across from them. Paul had managed to sit upright but still let out the occasional groan. Angie's knee must have done considerable damage, but he appeared determined to front it out whilst he searched for his lost dignity.

Melody seemed indifferent to proceedings, as though she had retreated to a place in her mind where nothing could reach her, in much the same way that presumably she got through her day job. Paul's face, where Angie had struck it with such force, looked angry and red. But not as angry as Angie who, seated beside Callie, was as wired as a tightly coiled spring. Clearly, her friend still had a lot of pent-up emotion to release.

'Okay, Angie,' Callie said. 'This is your show. Ask your questions.'

'I have just one. Leaving aside the fact that you're a pathetic excuse for a man, Paul, explain to me how you could possibly have drawn our son into your criminal activities? It was the one thing we agreed we would never expose them to. And yet he was abducted for fuck's sake, and you didn't even let me know.'

'I couldn't.' Paul ran a hand through his hair. 'It wasn't supposed to get that far and when it did, I knew you'd go dashing in, all guns blazing, if you knew he'd been taken. I'm sorry, Angie, truly I am. But I did what they wanted and knew Henry wouldn't be hurt so he was never in any real danger.'

'Only traumatised,' Angie hissed.

'Start at the beginning,' Callie said. 'Tell us what you got involved with and how it got so out of hand.'

Paul folded his arms and shook his head. 'Not happening,' he said decisively. 'It's safer if you don't know.'

Angie half rose from her chair and Callie could sense just how badly she wanted to beat the man senseless. She placed a restraining hand on her friend's arm.

'Not yet,' she said. 'Give him one more chance before you pummel him.'

'Spoil sport!' Angie muttered, sending death looks Paul's way.

'I knew you would be like this,' Paul said in a patronising tone. 'But our marriage has been dead in the water for a long time. You're the only one who didn't realise it. Life's too short to try and fix the unfixable. I've moved on and you should too.'

'Do you really think I'd take you back after this?' she asked, her eyes agog. 'Is that what you think this is all about? You have a very inflated opinion of your own self-worth, is all I can say. You're history, Paul. I'll pack your things for you, and you can let me know where to send them. The brothel, perhaps?'

Paul scowled at her. 'This doesn't have to be uncivilized,' he said, reaching for Melody's hand and lacing his fingers with hers. 'We're adults after all.'

Callie and Angie exchanged an incredulous look, for once both lost for words.

'Why don't we tell you what we've found out about your activities,' Darren said, stepping forward and filling the awkward silence. 'Gavin had been holding you back for too long, not giving you enough responsibility or trusting your judgement. You grew tired of being his bag carrier, so you set out to prove to the world in general and Gavin in particular that you're the big man.' He waved Paul back to his seat when he half-stood. 'So you started bringing illegal prescriptions drugs into the Brighton area for O'Keefe.'

'What the fuck!' Paul dropped Melody's hand and scratched his head, looking totally bewildered. 'How the hell did you find that out?'

Callie and Angie exchanged a satisfied nod.

'We didn't know, not for sure,' Angie said, 'but you've just confirmed our theory.' She clearly enjoyed his discomfort.

'Never play poker, Paul. No wonder Gavin didn't let you take more responsibility.'

'Tell us what went wrong,' Callie said. 'You obviously refused to do something for O'Keefe, but he forced your hand by abducting Henry.'

'That should not have happened.'

'Damned right it shouldn't have!' Angie said, seething.

'O'Keefe wants to build a clinic on the land I've purchased to make a golf course.' Callie spoke as if she knew it was the truth, unsurprised when Paul gave a reluctant nod.

'He wants to help his own family but also sees an opportunity to make money from those in need of urgent medical help not available in this country or on the NHS.'

'You were helping him, so what changed?' Darren asked.

Paul allowed a long pause. No one attempted to break the silence, but Callie and Angie kept their gazes firmly focused on him.

'He's gone too far,' Paul eventually said. 'He's moved into organ transplants.'

'Fuck!' Darren muttered.

Callie felt shell-shocked. 'I assume the donors are not necessarily willing,' she said.

'Some are. There's a market amongst desperate illegals who'll donate a kidney, but when I was asked to bring a heart in, I drew the line.'

Angie inhaled sharply but remained silent.

'Who harvests the organs?' Darren asked.

Paul shook his head. 'I have no idea. O'Keefe has an outbuilding at his home where he conducts a private clinic, if you like.'

'You brought that heart in because Henry was held,' Angie said, grinding her teeth.

'What else could I do? The heart was in Birmingham.' He held up his hands. 'Don't ask me about that because I have no idea what set-up O'Keefe has in that city, and I have no desire to know.'

'April Morton is involved?' Darren asked.

Paul nodded. 'Yes,' he said. 'She runs the clinics but who performs the transplants, I have no idea. Nor do I want to know.'

'Is O'Keefe running the business from Phoenix?' Callie asked. 'We know he goes there, but not for the same reason as most men. And more to the point, is Gavin involved?'

'Gavin knows nothing about it.' Paul looked agitated. 'I don't know where he is and why he's been gone for so long. A lot of people are looking for him. All I do know is that he was completely ignorant about the drugs. He would have vetoed the business if he'd known, even though they weren't recreational drugs, and we were providing a service for desperate people. You know how much Gavin hates anything to do with drugs,' he added, making it sound like an accusation.

'You probably regret not telling him now,' Angie said, sending her husband a scathing look loaded with disdain. 'Then he could have reined you in and you wouldn't be in O'Keefe's pocket. No wonder Gavin didn't trust you with anything important. You're barely capable of tying your own shoelaces.'

'Phoenix is only used for meetings,' Paul said.

'Then why was Lucy beaten up for talking to us?' Callie asked.

'People are nervous. It's a highly lucrative business designed to help the terminally ill. These drugs save lives, they don't destroy them, but still, it's illegal.'

'So is harvesting organs from unwilling donors,' Callie

pointed out. 'I keep thinking about that heart and guessing that the donor didn't die of natural causes.'

Paul lowered his head. 'I knew better than to ask, but yeah, you're probably right, which is why I decided things had gone too far. Lucy knows what goes on, she doesn't miss a trick, and probably gets paid by O'Keefe to facilitate meetings and keep her mouth shut.'

'What about you, Melody?' Darren asked. 'What binds you to Phoenix?'

Melody, who hadn't spoken a word up until that point, glanced at Paul, as though seeking permission to open her mouth, which surprised Callie. She had been sassy and upfront in all their previous meetings and Callie hadn't expected her to kowtow to any man.

'O'Keefe hasn't finished with you, has he?' Callie said slowly, as the truth dawned. 'He knows of your attachment to Melody, probably knows about the baby too, and all the time she's working at Phoenix, he's assured of your co-operation.'

Paul gave a grim nod. 'O'Keefe only agreed to release Henry if Melody stayed in place,' Paul said. 'She knew the score and agreed, even though we'd decided to cut and run.'

When Paul glared at Angie as though he expected her to be grateful, Callie could see that her friend was on the verge of losing it. Once again, she restrained her with a gentle hand on her shoulder. Now was not the time.

'What more does O'Keefe want from you?' Darren asked.

Paul spread his hands. 'No idea, but something big is on the agenda, that much I do know. His wife is the driving force behind this business. A lot of her relatives and direct family have hereditary illnesses and she is determined to save them all, no matter what it takes.'

Melody nudged him when Paul paused. 'Tell them,' she urged.

'Okay, why not? If they have a death wish then that's on their heads.' Paul cleared his throat. 'O'Keefe's younger daughter has a little girl of three. There's something seriously wrong with her. She needs a transplant but no suitable donor is available. They're running out of time.'

'Christ!' Callie tugged at her hair. 'I'd feel sorry for them but for the fact that...'

'That they're probably looking for a suitable match so they can kill that child off and harvest its organs,' Darren finished for her.

'What I don't understand... one of the many things I don't understand, Paul, is why you're needed as a courier,' Angie said. 'Surely anyone could drive the organ to its destination.'

'Because he wanted out, is my guess,' Darren said, answering before Paul could. 'Now that he's driven illegally harvested organs around the country, he's up to his neck in the business, and if he's developed a conscience then he can't be trusted to keep his mouth shut. He's O'Keefe's puppet to do with as he wishes. Hope you're enjoying being the big man, Dalton.'

'How's your old man?' Paul asked in a sarcastic tone. 'Still doing time, is he?'

'Stop it!' Angie cried. 'You're in no position to adopt the moral high ground, Paul, so just shut up and tell us what we want to know.'

'It's because of me,' Melody said. 'O'Keefe got me into the country. I am not here legally. He can drop me in it to the authorities any time he likes.'

'Fallow must know that,' Callie said.

Melody snorted. 'Why do you think he can take what he likes from me whenever he wants to without paying?'

'So, I'm assuming your last job is to collect the organ for O'Keefe's granddaughter and take it to his place,' Callie said.

'Yep.'

'You really think he will let you go after that?' Angie shook her head. 'You're even dafter than I thought.'

'Why have you laid low since Henry was released?' Callie asked.

'To avoid this conversation, I expect,' Angie replied for him. 'He doesn't even have the bottle to tell me to my face that he's leaving.'

'You've been doing this for a while, haven't you?' Callie frowned at Paul, who couldn't meet her hostile gaze and looked away. 'Porchester Investments is your baby, and you've had the nerve to launder the funds through the spa.'

'Gavin said it would be okay,' he said, sounding as feeble as he looked.

'You needed to ask him, just so he'd see how well you're doing and have him think he'd misjudged you.' Angie sent him a scathing look. 'How pathetic can you get?'

'When are you due to bring in the organ?' Darren asked.

'Tomorrow night, then we'll both be free and clear. I know what you're thinking, but O'Keefe is a man of his word.'

'He's a villain. A people trafficker who condemns lone illegals to death if their organs happen to be a match for one of his customers,' Angie said. 'But that's okay because he's a man of his word.'

'If O'Keefe has such a good thing going, a clinic that flies beneath the radar, why does he want to expand and put one on my land?' Callie asked. 'It will draw attention to his activities, surely.'

'I don't know,' Paul said sullenly. 'But he's an ambitious man and sees an opportunity. Organs can be purchased legally from abroad. Perhaps he wants to go legit.'

Melody slowly shook her head. 'It's time to tell the truth,' she said. 'I am tired of all the lies and prevarication.'

'Go on.' Callie leaned towards the younger woman, sensing her need to unload.

'There was a fatality,' she said. 'A child did not survive the operation.'

'That's awful,' Angie said, clutching her cheeks.

'How do you know?' Callie asked.

'I told you when you first came to see me that my work is like being a priest. Men don't only want sex; they want to talk their problems through.'

'The child's father was a customer?'

She nodded. 'His daughter had been on the NHS waiting list but no suitable organ had been found. He tried to buy from abroad without success. Going out of his mind, prepared to do anything, he heard about O'Keefe's experimental drugs. He heard because I told him. I thought it would earn me some kudos with O'Keefe, not seal his child's death warrant.'

A tear trickled down her cheek and Callie realised then just how much she loved children. All children, not just her own and Paul's. She had wondered why she'd not terminated her pregnancy. It would be an impediment in her line of work. She knew now that she had the baby because she desperately wanted to.

Callie wondered if she had been selfish, bringing a child into such an environment but then again, the maternal instinct overrode all other considerations in some women, or so she'd been told. Personally, she would have no idea. She'd been vaguely disappointed when she never fell pregnant, but not once did it cross her mind to try IVF. Or to adopt. She'd simply got on with her life, accepting that she wasn't supposed to be a mother. Given Gavin's unethical means of making a living, that hadn't seemed like such a bad thing.

'Do you know the man's name?' Darren asked.

'Yes, George. Gerry Fanshaw.' Melody absently threw her hair back over her shoulder. 'O'Keefe charged him double what it would have cost to get an organ elsewhere.'

'He traded on the man's desperation,' Angie muttered, disgusted.

'Yes. George had to use up all his savings and remortgage his house. He lost everything. After the death of their child, his wife left him and... well, I haven't seen him since. He came to me one last time and told me everything. I was the only person he could talk to about it who would understand, which he said helped. And yet I feel so guilty for putting him in touch with O'Keefe that I decided, I wanted out.'

'I'm sure you did,' Callie said with a shudder.

'The tragedy with the child is why Mrs O'Keefe is insisting upon a proper clinic with more state-of-the-art equipment,' Melody said. 'She seems to think it can be registered legally, and that the illegal stuff can go on beneath the radar.' She threw up her hands. 'I do not know about that.'

Everyone was momentarily quiet.

'Okay, Paul,' Callie eventually said, sitting forward. 'This is what you're going to do.'

'Hang on a minute!'

'Shut up and listen.' Callie's commanding tone had the desired effect. Paul immediately closed his mouth and sat staring sullenly at his hands, a beaten man. A follower, never a leader. Gavin had got that part right. 'You are going to give us your contact number and keep in touch with us every step of the way.'

'Why? There's nothing you can do to stop O'Keefe, and I would strongly advise you not to take him on. He'll crush you like an irritating fly if he catches on to what you're doing, and believe me, not much gets past him.'

'Perhaps because you think like a man and brute force and intimidation are your only solutions. There are more ways to get the upper hand.'

'What ways?' Paul frowned. 'You're delusional if you think you can get one over on O'Keefe, or his missus. Quite frankly, she terrifies me more than he does, what with her quiet voice, dead eyes and steely determination. She won't let anyone or anything come between her and the well-being of her family. Take my word for it.'

Callie ignored Paul. 'In case you're thinking of running to him and telling tales,' she said, 'this entire discussion has been recorded.' She held up her phone to emphasise her point.

'Great minds!' Darren smiled at her and held his up too.

'If O'Keefe comes after me then this recording will be released to a copper who can't be bought. Surprising as it might seem to you, they do exist. And Fallow will change sides quicker than you can change your shirt. He's a survivor that one and is already thinking twice about crossing me. Mrs O'Keefe is not the only deadly female in this fiasco.'

'What are you going to do?' Paul asked.

'Better you don't know. Just keep me in the loop and O'Keefe will never know where I got my information until it's too late for him to do anything about it.'

'Okay, I guess.'

'No guessing necessary, which ought to be a relief for your lonely braincell,' Angie told him. 'Just do as you're told, then you and Melody can ride off into the sunset and live happily ever after.'

'Now then,' Callie said, leaning forward. 'One more thing. Where is Gavin and why did he leg it?'

Paul spread his hands, looking relieved by the change of subject. 'I have absolutely no idea, but you know Gavin, he's always got a finger or two in one dodgy pie or another, despite going increasingly legit. People are coming to me, asking where he is all the time, but I honestly don't know. Nor do I know what spooked him.'

Callie studied him for a long time but on this occasion, he looked right back at her without flinching. It was the first time since he'd walked into her office that he'd told the complete truth, she sensed.

'Okay, give Darren your number and then get out of here.'

'How are we going to get O'Keefe?' Angie asked, the moment the door closed behind Paul.

Callie looked straight back at her and sighed. 'I don't have a goddamned clue,' she replied. 'But I know someone who will have,' she added, reaching for her phone.

19

Angie struggled to overcome a whole raft of conflicting emotions, her oscillating feelings in danger of overwhelming her. Her marriage *was* dead in the water, no question of that. She'd accepted the fact before today's confrontation but seeing Paul so totally wrapped up in Melody had briefly reminded her of the way they'd been in the early days, before a succession of children took priority in their lives and they slowly drifted apart. She allowed the silence in Callie's office to seep into her bones, grateful to her intuitive friend for giving her space.

'I never saw any of that coming,' she said on a heavy sigh. 'The connection to a thug like O'Keefe. Only Paul could get himself involved in something so unethical.'

'If it helps, he obviously didn't think it through.'

Angie harrumphed. 'Thinking isn't one of Paul's strong points.'

'It's got completely out of hand, and he obviously drew a line when he realised that human organs were involved.'

'Is that supposed to make me feel better?'

'Nope. Just saying it the way I see it.'

'Paul is right in some respects though, much as I hate to admit it.' Angie sent Callie a supplicating look. 'How can we possibly bring O'Keefe down? He's untouchable.'

'No one is untouchable, Angie. There will be a chink, a weak link somewhere, and I think I know how to find it.'

'Care to share.'

'In a mo.' Callie smiled at her friend. 'How are you bearing up?'

Angie shook her head. 'I have absolutely no idea. I don't think the extent of my husband's stupidity and selfishness has properly sunk in yet.'

'I know this isn't what you want to hear, Ang, but in some respects, I admire Melody. If she hadn't told us about that fatality, Paul sure as hell wouldn't have.'

'She obviously likes kids,' Angie conceded, a grudging edge to her voice.

'And probably hopes we can do for O'Keefe, then she'll be free to have her child with her *and* give up her occupation.'

'Yeah, I guess she's a victim too in some respects.' Angie let out a long sigh as she made the concession. 'Anyway, who did you just call?'

Darren walked into the room before Callie could respond.

'Phew!' he said, heading for the coffee machine. 'I never expected any of that.'

'Well, we absolutely can't confront O'Keefe, Angie, you're right about that.' Callie nodded her thanks when Darren placed a flat white in front of her. 'But there are more subtle ways to bring a man to his knees that don't have to involve brute force.' She took a sip of her coffee and smiled at them both over the rim of her cup. 'Speaking of which, Dawn's on her way.'

'That's genius!' Angie's radiant smile quickly faded. 'I think.'

'She likes nothing better than delving into local stories, especially if there's any chance of the nationals picking them up. And this has all the right ingredients, if she goes about it the right way.'

It was true, Angie conceded. Dawn worked for a local cable news network and contributed to online news networks too. But she was still looking for her break into the big time.

'Except she can't print and expect to continue breathing,' Darren pointed out.

Callie flashed a mischievous grin. 'Who said anything about printing?' she asked.

Darren responded with a slow smile of his own. 'Have her start a campaign about illegal transplants.'

'How will—'

Dawn burst into the room. 'Hey, everyone. Where's the fire? Your call made you sound desperate, Cal.'

Vibrant and oh so sophisticated, Dawn hugged Angie and Callie and blew Darren a kiss. He responded by grinning and making her a coffee.

'You're an angel,' she said. 'I'm gasping for a brew. Been listening to my editor banging on for over an hour about a lack of human-interest pieces. I mean, that presupposes that humans are actually interesting and that everything under the sun hasn't already been done to death. I blame blogs, vlogs, webinars, and all the other amateur stuff online. Honestly, the world and his wife seem to think they're in line for the next Pulitzer... What?' She looked up, clearly just noticing that their collective attention focused upon her with varying degrees of amusement and impatience. 'What did I just say? Why are the three of you looking at me like I'm the answer to your prayers? I probably am, of course, but even so...'

'Stop talking a mile a minute and we'll tell you,' Callie said, laughing and flapping a hand.

'I'm all ears,' Dawn replied, making a zipping motion across her lips.

It took Callie, assisted by Angie and Darren, a good ten minutes to tell the complete story. Dawn, now in professional mode, nodded and asked the occasional pertinent question.

'Wow!' she said, when Callie came to an end. 'You have been busy.' She turned to Angie. 'I'm so sorry that Paul turned out to be such a spineless rat, but that's men for you. No offence intended,' she added, grinning at Darren.

'None taken,' he assured her.

'Don't feel bad for my sake,' Angie said. 'I'm glad he's shown his true colours. I can now make a life for myself on my own terms before senility hits.'

'Is Henry okay?' Dawn asked.

Angie waggled a hand from side to side. 'It's hard to be sure. He's certainly putting a brave face on things. I reckon the reaction will kick in some time soon but he's going back to work, and Tom will keep an eye on him. And at least he no longer thinks his dad walks on water, which is a result of sorts.'

'So, what are we going to do to stop this O'Keefe fellow?' Dawn asked casually, as though it would be the easiest task in the world.

'The problem we have is that it's time sensitive. He could be back here as early as tomorrow demanding that I sell the spa to him,' Callie said, looking furious, as well she might. Having dealt with Paul, Angie was on a roll and would happily pulverise Gavin on her friend's behalf for getting her into this quagmire, should he have the nerve to show his face again. 'That means you can't do your usual diligent research resulting in an in-depth expose. Well, you couldn't anyway and name names. We would none of us be safe if you did that.'

'What Callie means, I think, is that something online sent from an untraceable email address, highlighting the flood of unauthorized medical drugs in the area would be a good place to start,' Darren said, tapping his index finger against his teeth as he articulated his thoughts. 'Canvas people's opinions, get them talking about it on all social-media platforms, keep stoking the fires and hope that it goes viral. "Would you do this as a last resort if your loved one was at death's door," and so on.'

Dawn nodded. 'Yeah, I was thinking along the same lines.'

'I'll tell O'Keefe that I'm willing to sell, to buy us some time,' Callie said. 'That way, he'll keep Stafford off our backs too.'

'Will enough people see your posts, though?' Angie asked, frowning. 'Dawn can't do this through the paper's official website because she needs to remain anonymous.'

'Oh, I have my ways of covering my gorgeous backside,' Dawn replied, patting the backside in question and making them all smile. 'I'll post online under a false name.'

'I can set that up for you,' Darren said.

Dawn blew him another kiss. 'I will need to interview Gerry Fanshaw and put his side of things in a follow-up piece, explaining how desperate he felt, what lengths he was prepared to go to in order to save his child. Without actually naming him, obviously.'

'But O'Keefe will know who he is,' Angie said.

'Indeed, and I'll explain the risks to the poor man,' Dawn replied. 'But if, as you suggest, he lost everything in his quest to save his kid's life, then I'm betting he'll jump at the opportunity to speak about the decisions he took and explain why he took them.'

'But if he knew his daughter's new liver was harvested illegally, he committed a crime,' Callie said.

'I very much doubt if he did know for sure,' Dawn replied. 'He probably made a point of not asking. Suspecting is another matter, but there's no law against not acting on one's suspicions. Well, not yet anyway, anything is possible in the future.' Dawn paused and Callie knew her journalistic brain would be ticking over with possibilities. 'I would imagine Gerry was conflicted though and that's what I'd like to get across. There will be sympathy, I suspect, for the illegal medicines but outright hostility on the organ-donning front. Saving one child's life whilst sacrificing another...' Dawn shook a finger. 'Uh-huh.'

'Are you absolutely sure you want to get involved?' Angie asked. 'It could be dangerous.'

'Are you kidding me?' Dawn rubbed her hands together, eyes gleaming. 'Try stopping me. This could become big. Nationwide even. I'm sure it doesn't only go on in this quiet backwater and I could blow it all wide open. It has everything. Prostitutes, illegal drugs, murder, criminal kingpins, greed.' She counted the points off on her fingers. 'The list is endless. Most journalists would cut off your hand to have a pop at it and you ask me if I'm sure.'

Angie chuckled. 'Just checking.'

'I'll set you up that email address now if you're ready,' Darren said. One of his many skills included fluent cyber-speak. Angie knew he'd created whatever identities Dawn needed and that no one would track them back to her. 'It will be impossible to trace, trust me on this.'

'On I do trust you, honey bunch.' Dawn gathered up her

things, motivated because she sensed the scoop of the century. Angie really hoped that ambition didn't make her incautious. 'But now, I'm out of here. I have work to do. Criminals to expose. A scumbag of an editor to impress.' She blew them all a kiss. 'Laters!'

She fluttered her fingers and left the office at Darren's side, chattering to him ten to the dozen, as was her style.

'Phew!' Angie fanned her face with the side of her hand. 'Dawn's energy wears me out.'

Callie chuckled. 'I know.'

'Well done for thinking of her. At least one of us had her brain in gear.'

'You were a little preoccupied with pummelling your ex-nearest-and-dearest.'

'Shit, that felt good! Kneeing him in the goolies, I mean.'

Callie chuckled. 'I know what you meant.'

'God, but he's a wimp. Why hadn't I realised that about him before now?'

'Because you loved him. Because he's the father of your brood. Because you thought you'd be spending the rest of your lives together. Besides, I can hardly talk. I've always known about Gavin's womanising but still stuck with him.'

'I know,' Angie said softly. 'But Gavin is the type of man you simply don't walk out on. He has something special, some sort of charm or charisma... hell if I know what it is, but I have always understood why you stuck by him.'

'We tend to overlook our husbands' shortcomings, I guess. Familiarity and all that. Take it from one who knows. It's always been easier to keep the peace by not criticising or questioning and instead getting on with my own life. I can see now that's what I've been doing all these years, so in a way, Paul's done us a favour by forcing our hands.'

'You really intend to give Gavin the boot when he comes back this time?'

'You bet your life I do! He's finally gone too far, leaving me with all this crap *and* simply assuming that I'd sell the spa because he wants me to.'

Darren rejoined them.

'I've set up the email for Dawn and she's toddled off to make a start. I'll create a couple of online accounts on the major social platforms in a mo and she can start posting as soon as she's ready. She says she'll be in touch as soon as she issues something, which will be later today.'

Darren left them, presumably to set up the accounts in question. How he would make them appear vintage rather than brand spanking new, Angie didn't bother to ask. She probably wouldn't understand the technicalities even if Darren explained them to her in words of one syllable.

'So, what now?' Angie asked.

'Now we wait, which is often the hardest part.'

'In that case, I might drop by the showroom, just to check on Henry.'

'Henry?' Callie waggled her brows.

'Well, all right, and to talk to Tom as well. He's been a big help and deserves to know. I underestimated him before. The face he shows to the world, all swagger and self-assurance, is very different to the sensitive man lurking beneath.'

'Make sure Henry doesn't get wind. If he knows his father has resurfaced, after a fashion, he will want to have things out with him and now isn't the time.'

'Yeah, I know.'

Callie and Angie embraced.

'Let me know as soon as you hear anything,' Angie said as she left the room.

* * *

Left alone, Callie closed her eyes, weary after too little sleep. She mulled over what they had learned and the actions they had put in place. She wondered if it could be that easy. If O'Keefe would buckle beneath the weight of public disapproval. Almost certainly not, she knew, but it was a start. If Dawn's campaign did gain momentum, then the police would have to investigate. O'Keefe couldn't buy the entire constabulary.

Could he?

He didn't need them all, of course. Just men like Fallow in senior positions who could close down investigations if they got too close for O'Keefe's comfort. The alternative was to do nothing at all and let O'Keefe win. At a push, she could be coerced into selling the spa to him and ridding herself of the pond life who were determined to manipulate her at every turn. She had been seriously considering doing so, but now that she knew *why* he wanted the spa, it was simply no longer an option.

She worried that Dawn would get overenthusiastic and take unnecessary risks in her quest to make the journalistic big time and get one over on her boss, with whom she was constantly at odds. Dawn was a Rottweiler at the best of times when she got her teeth into a story. Admitting defeat wasn't built into her DNA. She had never had such a potentially explosive break before, and God alone knew what lengths she'd go to in order to exploit the situation. Part of Callie wanted to call her, to tell her it was a mistake and to back off, but she knew that she'd be wasting her breath.

Dawn was focused and wouldn't even hear her.

There must be another way to get O'Keefe to back off from

her *and* to stop him from trading in human organs, Callie decided. Some way that didn't mean one of her closest friends took all the risks whilst Callie sat back twiddling her thumbs. She racked her brains and came up short. O'Keefe was the local criminal kingpin and even the likes of Stafford were only able to operate on his patch because he allowed them to. A hard man who ruled the roost through a regime of violence and intimidation.

He was untouchable.

However... Callie drummed her fingers on the surface of her desk. Stafford was no slouch in the criminal world either. The two had different operations but for the loan sharking and existed in hostile harmony, one never encroaching on the other's territory. Stafford had a pressing need to launder his funds through the spa, but if Callie were to tell him that O'Keefe wouldn't permit it, would that be enough to start a turf war between the two men?

It was risky but better than doing nothing at all, she decided. O'Keefe had made his disapproval of the drug trade apparent to everyone who knew him, but was also aware that the demand would never go away. And all the time there were customers, someone would supply their needs. Better the devil you knew and could control from O'Keefe's perspective, she assumed. If he put a stop to the money laundering, then either a turf war would ensue, or Stafford would take his business elsewhere. Either way, the disruption would distract both men and give Dawn's campaign a chance to gain momentum.

Did Callie really have the courage and the will to start a fight that had nothing to do with her and that would drop her right in the middle of full-scale criminal warfare?

The possibility had only just taken hold when Darren

buzzed to say that Stafford had arrived, asking to see her. It seemed like an omen and made Callie's mind up for her.

'Send him in,' she said, sitting a little straighter as determination spiralled through her bloodstream. She could do this. She absolutely could!

'Any news of your husband?' Stafford asked, striding into her office as though he owned the place.

'Good morning,' Callie said, politely. 'What can I do for you?'

'Don't play games, Mrs R. I ain't got all day. Have you considered my proposition?'

'I haven't been propositioned since I was in my twenties.'

Stafford looked edgy today, twitchy, as though he was overdue for a fix of his own product. He declined the offer of a chair and pranced around Callie's office like a caged tiger. 'Save the sassy mouth,' he growled. 'I need to get some funds moving and I need it doing quick.'

'Then look elsewhere. The spa is under offer.'

'You what!' He spun on his heel and glared at her. 'Nah! You're having me on.' He shook his head, as though trying to convince himself. 'You can't sell as a going concern. The books would never stand the scrutiny. I know how much of my dosh has passed through them.'

'I'm not going to discuss my business affairs with you,' Callie said, managing to look down her nose at the drug dealer, even though she was seated, and he loomed over, red in the face. Perspiring. 'But what I will do is inform my prospective purchaser of your requirements. I dare say he'll let you know if he's happy to accommodate you.'

'Who is it?' Stafford slammed the flat of his hand against the surface of Callie's desk. 'Who have you got into bed with?'

Callie flinched but otherwise didn't move. She knew it

would be a grave error to show any signs of weakness in front of a bully, a man who was clearly on edge.

'You just told me that it wouldn't be possible to sell,' she said, her calm tone at direct variance to her racing heart. 'Which is it?'

Stafford glowered at her, clenching and unclenching his fists, his expression thunderous. He was unpredictable and, Callie reminded herself, wouldn't hesitate to actually use those fists on her. She lost all thoughts of playing it cool at that point. Instead, she pressed the button beneath her desk that would sound in the outer office. Mere seconds later, the door flew open, and Darren's reassuring musculature filled the aperture.

'Mr Stafford is leaving, Darren,' she said with a negligent flap of her wrist. 'Please escort him from the premises and tell security that he is not to be allowed admittance again.'

Callie hadn't thought it possible for his expression to turn more menacing but clearly, she had underestimated the man. He was unaccustomed to being challenged by anyone, especially a woman.

'You'll regret this,' he growled, shaking off Darren's hand when he placed it firmly on Stafford's shoulder. 'Get your hands off me, you snivelling excuse for a man, and remember who you're dealing with. Taking orders from a woman.' He sent Darren a scathing look. 'What's in it for you? Hoping to take her old man's place, are you?' He sniffed, searching for his misplaced dignity as he turned to leave Callie's office, Darren dogging his footsteps. 'You ain't heard the last of this.'

Callie let out a sigh of relief when Darren turned to wink at her and then closed the door behind him. She unlaced her fingers, which were still shaking, wondering how things would have transpired if Darren hadn't been there to bail her out of trouble. Then again, she probably wouldn't have confronted Stafford if she'd been alone.

One thing she did know with absolute certainty: it had felt good to have told him no. But he would be back, she knew, demanding to know who the new owner would be. She couldn't afford to relax and must depend upon Dawn's campaign after all because something had stopped her from naming O'Keefe. Then again, she hadn't needed to. The moment she instructed her solicitors, word would get out and then the cat would be very much amongst the proverbial.

It was the best she could do.

'He's gone, turning the air blue with threats.' Darren returned to Callie's office and sat opposite her. 'You okay?'

'Kinda.' She smiled at the man who was starting to seem like her rock: solid and dependable. 'You heard it all, I take it.'

'Every word.'

'I know it wasn't wise to bait him, but it felt so damned good to stand up to him.'

'He won't take it lying down and will try to force your hand. He doesn't actually believe that the spa is being sold and thinks you fobbed him off, so you'd be best advised to call O'Keefe and tell him his offer has been accepted.'

'I know.' Callie fidgeted in her chair. 'But it feels wrong.'

'You don't have a lot of choice, Callie. Dawn is going out on a limb for you.'

Sighing, Callie dialled his number. He answered on the second ring.

'Mrs Renfrew,' he said, his suave voice echoing across the airwaves, making her feel nauseous. He thought he had won and was turning on the charm. 'What can I do for you?'

'I will honour my husband's offer,' she said bluntly.

'I am glad you have seen reason.' She could hear the satisfaction in his tone. 'You will do very well out of it and so we all win.'

'Let me know the name of your solicitors and I will start the ball rolling.'

'Very well.'

'Just one thing. Stafford was here this morning, attempting to strong-arm me.'

'Ah, I see.' O'Keefe paused. 'Don't worry. He will not trouble you again.'

'Right.'

Callie hung up, feeling as though she had been defeated, despite the fact that the pressure she'd been living with had also been relieved.

Darren smiled at her. 'You've done the right thing,' he assured her.

She leaned her elbow on her desk and her chin on her fisted hand. 'Then why does it feel so wrong?' she asked glumly.

20

Callie got through the rest of the day by applying herself to the work that had piled up whilst her concentration had been elsewhere. Angie popped back just as Callie was about to leave for the day, wondering how to occupy the time. She had resisted the urge to call Dawn. When she had news for her, she'd be in touch.

'Have you seen this, ladies?' Darren asked, entering Callie's office with his phone in his hand.

They both looked at the survey that had been started up online about experimental medical drugs. Callie hadn't really believed that it would get much notice, but it appeared that the world and his wife had lost no time in weighing into the debate.

'I can't believe so many people have seen this so quickly!' Callie said, her mouth hanging open when she saw the number of votes that had been cast, the overwhelming majority in favour.

'It's on Facebook, TikTok, Instagram and X,' Darren told them. 'It's being shared all the time. What with the health system being in the state it's in, it's clearly a subject that's struck a chord with a lot of people.'

'So many supportive comments, too,' Angie added, reading through them. 'People think the pharmaceutical industry is overregulated and overpriced. No one is actually admitting to having purchased unregulated drugs though, even though it's not a crime. Well, I don't think it is.'

'It's against the law for the companies to release them, but the chances are that they didn't,' Darren said. 'That's where people with the know-how, like April Morton, come in.'

Callie's phone rang.

'It's Dawn,' she said, checking the caller ID. 'Hey, girlfriend. I have to hand it to you, you don't hang about.'

'You've seen it then?' Dawn's voice, on speaker, echoed round the room. 'I can't quite believe it myself.'

'We have seen it,' Angie said. 'So has half the world, judging by the reaction. Good work!'

'It's just the start. O'Keefe, if he sees or hears about it, will look upon it as validation.' Dawn's throaty chuckle resonated. 'But tomorrow, I'm going to ask who would accept an organ as a last resort without knowing where it had come from. Whether the donor had been willing or duped, that sort of thing. It should create quite a stir.'

'Be careful!' Callie chided. 'Don't get carried away. I know what you're like when you get your teeth into a story. Just bear in mind who we're up against.'

'I've already fixed up an interview with Gerry Fanshaw,' Dawn replied, blithely ignoring Callie's warning. 'He's actually keen to talk about his daughter's illness, it seems. I'll let you know how it goes.'

They all said goodbye and Callie cut the connection.

'Come on!' Angie grabbed her bag and beckoned to Callie. 'You and I are having a long overdue night on the town.'

'In Frenchurch?' Callie smiled. 'There's one pub and a Chinese.'

'Don't be so negative. We're going into Brighton and we're gonna paint the town red. We both need it.'

'Then how can I refuse?' Callie replied, thinking it was indeed just what she did need to take her mind off things. Besides, it would be futile to argue with Angie when she was in such an intransigent mood.

'Well, you can't, obviously.'

Darren smiled. 'Have a good evening, ladies.'

'Oh, we intend to,' Angie assured him. 'I am newly single. Well, as good as, and my friend here will be in the same situation once she finds her louse of a husband and has the satisfaction of dumping him.'

'I think I'd better tell Gavin before you tell the world,' Callie chided.

'Whatever.' Angie waved a hand, in manic mode – a combination of relief and delayed reaction, Callie supposed. Whatever the cause of her elation, Callie was willing to go along with it. 'Darren's trustworthy.' She emulated Dawn and blew him a kiss.

'Right.' Callie laughed. 'See you tomorrow, Darren.'

'I'll have my famous hangover cure on hand,' he assured them.

'Where are we going?' Callie asked, as they piled into a cab. 'Don't we need to change?'

'Nope. We're perfect as we are.'

'Well, there is that.'

Angie gave the cabbie the address of a newly opened bistro

pub in the centre of Brighton. A trendy place that Callie had never tried.

They arrived, took seats at the flashy bar and ordered cocktails that didn't touch the sides. Only when they were on their third did they decide it would be as well to eat something.

'I feel like I'm a teenager again,' Angie said, once they were seated at a table for two, next to the window. She nodded towards two guys at the bar who had them in their sights. 'Seems we still have what it takes, girl!'

'I for one never doubted it.' Callie smiled. 'Even so, I'm not sure I'm on the market for another man right now. Still have to get rid of the one I already have.'

'You know what they say about getting straight back on the horse.' Angie grinned, but Callie got the impression that her heart wasn't really in it. She was simply trying to prove something to herself. She would probably have felt better if she'd gone out alone with Tom. 'When did I last let my hair down this way? It's like a ton of weight I didn't know I'd been carrying around for months has suddenly been lifted from my shoulders.'

'No regrets then? I mean, you and Paul were together for a long time.'

'Together but apart.' Angie sighed. 'I can quite see that now. I think I knew on some level that I'd lost him but I either didn't want to face the reality or I simply didn't care.'

Callie nodded. 'Whereas I always knew that Gavin liked to put it about a bit, but it didn't bother me. But enough is enough.' She clicked glasses with Angie. 'Here's to a new start.'

It was midnight by the time Callie fell out of a cab and into her house. Her head felt fuzzy, and she wasn't too steady on her feet.

'Whoops!'

She giggled as she tottered on her heels, heading for the kitchen and a pint glass of water. She kicked off her shoes, aware that she'd pay the price for overindulging the following day. But hell, it had been worth it! They'd drawn the attention and admiring glances of other diners which did a great deal for Callie's self-esteem, and Angie's too. Just what they'd needed, the consequences be damned.

Callie tumbled into bed a short time later and for the first time in weeks, she slept solidly, with no alarming scenarios invading her subconscious.

She woke to the sound of her mobile ringing. With aching head and heavy limbs, she sat up and groggily took the call, without first bothering to check who wanted her at such an ungodly hour.

'You okay?' Darren's voice was loaded with concern.

'You woke me up to ask me that?'

'It *is* half nine.'

'Shit! I'll be in soon.'

'No rush. I was worried because you're never late, that's all.' He chuckled. 'I take it the night out went well.'

'No idea. Don't remember a thing.' Callie threw the duvet aside. 'See you in a bit.'

'You might want to check your social media first. Dawn's survey has really taken off.'

'Okay.'

Callie cut the connection. First things first. She stood up experimentally and discovered that, all things considered, she didn't feel too bad. Only a mild headache and dry mouth to show for her night of overdoing it. She'd had worse hangovers.

She downed a glass of water, headed for the shower and

slowly came alive. In need of caffeine before she did anything else, Callie's next port of call was her kitchen. Only when she had a steaming brew in front of her did she log onto her Facebook account. And gasp.

'Bloody hell!' Over a hundred thousand people had now responded to Dawn's survey, the vast majority voting in favour of unregulated drugs being used for the treatment of the terminally ill, if all else had failed. 'How the hell did she garner so much coverage so soon?'

She wanted to call Dawn, wondering why her friend hadn't been in touch with her. This was monumental news, but they needed to discuss the next step and tread carefully. Dawn would be worried about other journalists picking up the baton and beating her to the spoils. That might cause her to act recklessly and forget what was at stake. O'Keefe would know about the survey, and despite supporting the use of the drugs, it still might make him edgy. It would probably make the mainstream news and create debates all over the place, possibly even in Parliament. Didn't the government have to debate petitions that received over a certain number of signatures? She couldn't remember what the threshold was but was pretty sure that one hundred thousand cleared the bar.

All thoughts of her hangover forgotten, Callie dressed quickly and drove to the spa.

'This is incredible!' she said by way of greeting to Darren, waving her phone at him.

He smiled at her. 'You have to hand it to Dawn, she gets the job done.'

'Has there been any reaction from anyone we know?'

Darren shook his head. 'Not as far as I'm aware.'

'I need to call Dawn and discuss where we go next.' Callie

felt concerned about the speed of events. She no longer felt as though she was in control. 'I wasn't prepared for such strong feelings.'

'I hear you.'

Callie made her way into her office and flipped through the messages that had been left for her in a neat pile by Darren. Nothing that couldn't wait. She picked up her mobile and called Dawn, who answered on the first ring.

'Who's a clever girl then?' she asked.

'I'm grateful but don't get carried away with journalistic fervour.'

'O'Keefe will be delighted with the good publicity, if he even knows about it.'

'Dawn, I've just logged onto a local news site and it's headlining.'

'I know.' Dawn's voice was filled with pride.

'Oh God!'

'Don't worry. I know what I'm doing. I'm going to follow up with a piece about organs. I'll send you my draft copy now. God!' she added, and Callie could imagine her friend jumping from foot to foot in her excitement. 'Jarred's going bananas, wanting to know who got the ball rolling, and I *so* want to tell him.'

'You'll be able to, darling,' Callie replied soothingly, aware that Dawn was referring to her editor, with whom she enjoyed a love/hate relationship. 'Just not yet.'

'And perhaps only after I've sold my exclusive to the nationals,' she replied smugly.

'That's the spirit!'

'Sending it now. Must fly. Scumbags to bring down. You know how it is.'

The line went dead but shortly thereafter, an email came

through from Dawn with an attachment. Callie called Darren into her office, and they read it together.

'Wow!' Callie sat back and absently ran a hand through the ends of her hair. 'She really doesn't pull any punches, does she?'

'This could get messy.' Darren's expression turned unnaturally serious. 'O'Keefe won't appreciate the publicity, even though it's favourable so far.'

'If it makes him think twice about continuing with the organs then the end justifies the mean.' Callie tapped her fingers. 'I keep thinking about those poor, witless victims.'

'I hear you.'

'It will unnerve O'Keefe, but just so long as he doesn't find out that Dawn's behind it all, then it might just work.' Callie wanted to believe that was the case but the uneasy feeling she couldn't shake concerned her. 'You sure he won't be able to trace her IP address?'

Darren looked offended by the question. 'Not a hope in hell.'

'Just checking.' Callie took a deep breath. 'Let's get on with our day and wait to see how things pan out. There's nothing more we can do about this for now.'

'Right. You have a working lunch with the managers at noon.'

'Yeah, I hadn't forgotten.'

'And a Zoom conference with the gym suppliers. They have some new instruments of torture they want to interest you in.'

'Okay, I've got it.'

In work mode again, Callie tried to put her concerns to the back of her mind and concentrate on her day. At the end of it, with Angie and Darren in her office, they checked social media.

'Fucking hell!' Darren breathed. 'This is a monster!'

A whole torrent of disapproval was the response to the question about organ donors. There were the usual trolls who seemed to think that gulling illegals was no big deal, but the majority of responders were adamantly against the idea.

'It will be picked up by mainstream media in a big way now,' Angie said, looking awestruck.

'Perhaps we've overreached ourselves.' Callie shuddered. 'I can't say why but it just doesn't feel right.'

'Too late to stop the juggernaut now.' Dawn breezed through the door, looking thoroughly pleased with herself.

'Well done!' Callie got up and hugged her friend. Even if they'd stirred up a hornet's nest that they could no longer control, Dawn had done a bang-up job and was justifiably pleased with herself.

'I have what it takes, even though I do say so myself!'

'Modest as ever,' Angie said, taking her turn to hug Dawn.

'So, what happens now?' Dawn asked. 'I did my interview with Gerry Fanshaw earlier today.'

'No!' Callie went cold all over. 'I told you not to. Not yet. He knows who you are and if O'Keefe asks him.'

'Calm down. I haven't published and won't until you give me the all-clear. I just wanted to have it ready. Anyway, there's no reason why O'Keefe will suspect Fanshaw.'

Callie thought there was every reason. She shared a glance with Darren and could see that he understood the ramifications too.

'It's dynamite, what he had to say to me.' Dawn bounced on the edge of her seat, high on adrenaline. 'If anyone can read it without shedding a tear then they don't have a soul. That little girl was his only child. He and his wife had had three rounds of IVF, all of which failed. They'd given up all hope, and then she fell pregnant naturally. The child was their world.'

'Was he aware that the organ she received was illegally harvested?' Callie asked.

'He says he didn't ask. He believed the people he dealt with, who told him that the donor had been in an accident in Europe somewhere. But yeah, he's not stupid. He was just a desperate father who bankrupted himself trying to save his only child and didn't want to face up to the consequences of the risks he took. Risks that, by the way, he assured me he would take again in a heartbeat.'

There was momentary silence in the room.

'O'Keefe will have the debate brought to his attention, if he hasn't already seen it,' Darren said. 'You mention the south coast several times, Dawn, so he's going to suspect that someone's on to him, which means he'll do one or two things. He'll either give up his dream, or should I say his wife's dream of saving the world, or he'll try and find out where all this has come from.'

'And you showed your face to Fanshaw,' Callie said, sighing.

'But he won't be aware that I've spoken to him. I offered him money for an exclusive, but he has to keep schtum until I'm ready to publish or risk losing his payday. He needs the dosh, Callie, and signed an agreement. He's living in a caravan, for God's sake!'

If O'Keefe knew of his reduced circumstances, he would be a prime suspect, Callie knew, but there seemed little point in reiterating the possible consequences of Dawn's over-enthusiasm.

'Okay,' Callie said, stretching her arms above her head and feeling the belated consequences of her late night. 'Let's call it a day. I'm bushed. Dawn, for goodness' sake, take care and keep a low profile. Don't go anywhere alone, especially after dark.'

'Stop fussing.'

'I'm serious. O'Keefe is dangerous at the best of times. If he thinks a couple of women have tried to get the better of him, God alone knows what form his retribution will take. So, I need you to promise me.'

'Okay, I promise.' She crossed her heart and grinned at Callie, irrepressible. 'Satisfied?'

'Same goes for you, Angie.'

'Yeah, I hear you.' Angie waved Callie's concerns aside with an airy flap of her wrist.

'I don't think Dawn realises what she'd gotten herself into,' Callie told Darren after she'd seen her friends off. Dawn was on another story. Angie had an appointment – she refused to call it a date! – with Tom. 'I'll never forgive myself if anything happens to her because of something I asked her to do, and all so I could keep the spa.'

'She'll be okay,' Darren assured her.

'Just so long as O'Keefe doesn't interrogate Fanshaw.'

'Don't invite trouble. Get yourself off home and stay there. Double lock the doors and call me at any time if you're worried.'

'Thanks.' Callie touched Darren's hand. 'You're a good man to have on side.'

Darren chuckled. 'If you say so, boss.'

Callie drove home, still deeply concerned about what they'd – what she'd – set in motion. She knew that what was started couldn't be stopped and that worrying wouldn't resolve anything, but she couldn't seem to stop her mind conjuring up ever more terrifying scenarios.

She pulled onto her driveway, the house in complete darkness. It was too early for the internal lights to have come on and so she felt comforted when the external security lights were triggered by her arrival.

She put her key in the front door and knew immediately that something was wrong. A feeling, a sense of foreboding, gripped her, and indecision temporarily rooted her to the spot. She tried to convince herself that she'd let her fanciful imagination spook her. The house was deadly quiet, just as it should be. She flipped on the hall light and immediately felt better. Everything looked just the way she'd left it, and she told herself that she was letting her fear get the better of her.

She walked into the kitchen, in urgent need of a chilled glass of wine. But she hadn't crossed the floor before a strong arm grabbed her from behind. She tried to scream, for all the good it would do her, but the arm had cut off her windpipe and she struggled to get air into her lungs.

'Evening, Mrs R.'

O'Keefe's voice echoed in her ears as he slowly released the pressure and she was able to breathe again.

'What the hell!' She spun on her heel and glowered at him, terrified out of her wits but damned if she'd give him the satisfaction of knowing it. 'What do you think you're playing at? You nearly gave me a heart attack.'

'I came to discuss our business agreement. It wasn't my intention to frighten you.'

His tone was suave, conversational, but his expression was set in stone. He was not a happy man, and Callie knew what had upset him so badly. The fact that he was here could only mean one thing.

He suspected Callie's involvement in the online campaign.

'What's to discuss? And anyway, how did you get in here?' *Stupid question, Callie.*

He leaned his backside against a work surface and watched her with unnerving stillness. Callie's wits were slowly returning to her. She hadn't seen any sign of his car outside, so he must have parked a bit further away. And he was alone, apparently convinced that he could handle her without help. It would be bad for his street cred, she supposed, if he required help to subdue a mere female.

Hold that thought!

'I smelt a rat when you gave in to my demands so readily. You don't strike me as the type of woman who likes to be told what to do, especially when her husband has made promises on her behalf without bothering to run them past her first.'

'You're right. I don't like it one little bit, but I'm not stupid and don't have a death wish. Anyway, I've had enough of dancing to Gavin's tune. He's gone too far this time, so I shall take the money and be off somewhere sunnier.'

Callie knew she'd over-explained and abruptly shut her mouth.

'I knew you were dead set against selling, so why change your mind so quickly?'

'I just told you...' Her words trailed off when O'Keefe glowered at her.

'Then that fucking online campaign sprung up out of nowhere.'

'Sorry, what?' Callie shook her head. 'You've lost me.' But she could see that he wasn't fooled by her protest, perhaps because her voice had developed an annoying quiver. Her phone was in her bag, on the hall table where she'd left it, but even if she could reach it, O'Keefe wouldn't permit her to call for reinforcements. Annoyingly, she'd left her coat, with Mace in the pocket, in the hall too.

Stupid, Callie. Stupid!

'I know you've been asking questions, poking your nose into my business.' He advanced towards her, and she instinctively took a step backwards. 'I'm guessing you got your little journalist friend involved. I'll deal with her later but first...'

He reached for her, grabbed her hair and pulled her head backwards painfully. She screamed but there was no one to hear her and anyway, her fear appeared to please O'Keefe. She bit her tongue, quite literally, and didn't make another sound, but her brain had gone into survival mode as she searched for a way to get out of this situation.

'Come on,' he said, dragging her towards the door, 'we're going for a little ride.'

Callie knew that if she left the house with him, it would be the last thing she ever did. He had a reputation for a reason, as attested by the stony determination reflected in his expression. Ordinarily, women and kids were off limits, but Callie had crossed a line and would now be fair game in his eyes.

'Stop fighting me, sweetheart,' he said, breathing heavily. 'You brought this on yourself and have no one else to blame.'

He fumbled for the kitchen door handle, still keeping a tight hold on her, but he momentarily allowed his grip to loosen as he fumbled with the unfamiliar lock. She knew that this was her one chance. Reaching abruptly towards the wall behind her, her fingers touched her magnetic knife holder. She snatched the closest one to hand, didn't allow herself to think about what she intended to do in the split second available to her before she thrust it with all her force into O'Keefe's gut.

He looked at her, eyes wide with dawning astonishment.

'You fucking bitch!'

Blood spilled from his lips as he tried to speak. A gurgling sound emerged as he slithered slowly to the floor, blood gushing from his belly. His eyes glazed over, and the gurgling stopped.

Callie watched him die, feeling absolutely nothing. No

remorse. No shock. Nothing. All she cared about was the blood fountaining onto her newly tiled kitchen floor. *Damn*, she thought. The blood would stain the grouting.

She walked into the hall on surprisingly steady legs given that she had just killed a man, reached into her bag for her phone and called Darren.

21

A month after O'Keefe's disappearance, Callie, Angie and Dawn sat on the wraparound terrace at the marina penthouse where Henry had been held, enjoying watching the boating activity. It had been totally redecorated and furnished with exquisite taste.

'I thought you'd lost your mind when you gave Paul the house and took this apartment instead,' Callie said. 'But now that I've seen it for myself, I can understand why.'

'The house was too big for me and held too many reminders of family life,' Angie replied, pouring champagne for them all. 'I wanted a fresh start. Paul has given me a very large sum of money as well as this apartment and I got the better end of the deal.'

'Too right!' Dawn lifted her glass high in a toast. 'To strong women.'

They clinked glasses.

'How are the kids dealing with their dad?' Dawn asked.

'Henry isn't talking to him. I think he's secretly distraught because his father's taken the woman he was fixated on. As for the others, they're keeping him at arm's length. The horrible part is that I don't think Paul cares. He's so fixated on Melody and their child that nothing else matters to him. Anyway, I can do no wrong in the kids' eyes at present so I'm making the most of it while it lasts.'

'Melody's still working at Phoenix, is she?' Dawn asked.

'Yes.' Callie answered her. 'She doesn't dare to leave, it seems, until O'Keefe either resurfaces or a body is found.'

Only Darren knew that he was dead, and that Callie had killed him. She had decided against telling her friends. Not because she didn't trust them but because she didn't want to put them in a position of having to lie if hard men came asking questions.

Darren had rushed to her aid like a guardian angel the moment she'd called him and took control. He found O'Keefe's car parked up the road and took his body away in it. That was all she knew. He said it was safer that way.

'He has to be dead,' Angie said for the hundredth time. 'I mean, he hasn't even instructed his solicitors about the purchase of the spa.' She shook her head. 'And apparently, no one knows anything about his abrupt disappearance.'

'The men in our lives are good at going AWOL,' Callie remarked.

'What about Stafford?' Angie asked. 'Won't he come crawling back, expecting you to dance to his tune, Cal?'

Callie chuckled. 'He's welcome to try but I very much doubt whether he will. The whole criminal world is discussing O'Keefe. His wife has offered a hefty reward for information, which implies that she thinks he's dead.'

'Word is that they almost never spent a night apart and that she always knew when not to expect him, so Tom tells me,'

Angie said, 'so yeah, I guess she thinks the worst. Couldn't happen to a nicer woman.'

'Unless or until he's proven to be dead, no one will dare to encroach upon his territory,' Callie said, 'so Stafford won't come sniffing round. I'm free to run the spa the way I see fit.'

'And Gavin?' Dawn asked. 'Any news?'

'Nope.' She smiled at her friends. 'And you know what, I really don't care any more.'

'Are you really in demand with national TV, Dawn?' Angie asked.

'You bet your life I am.' Dawn grinned. 'My interview with Fanshaw airs tonight. Opinion about what he did and why is already causing endless debate.'

Callie for once felt totally relaxed and allowed the conversation to flow around her. At least O'Keefe wouldn't be able to offer his questionable services to any other desperate person, she thought with considerable satisfaction, and so she had done the world a favour. Mrs O'Keefe was a tough nut, but Callie was counting on the adverse publicity making her think twice about pushing for the clinic.

She felt safe. At least for the time being.

* * *

Darren lurked in Callie's office, checking the bugs he'd planted months previously and which Callie knew nothing about. It meant that he could listen to all her conversations if he felt the need and report back on her activities.

A phone that only one person had the number to, rang, distracting Darren. He had been expecting the call and answered straight away.

'How's it going?' a voice asked.

'All quiet.'

'How is she?'

'Stoic.'

A chuckle echoed down the line. 'Yeah, she would be.'

'When are you coming back, Gavin?'

'Soon, I hope. Just keep an eye on things for me and make sure she stays out of trouble.'

'Christ, you don't want much!'

'Just remember how much I pay you to look after what's mine.'

The threat was obvious. As the line went dead, Darren wondered if Gavin knew how much his wife's attitude had changed during the course of his latest disappearance. Very probably not since Darren hadn't bothered to enlighten him. Arrogant men of Gavin's ilk thought they ruled the world, and he probably assumed that he'd be able to bend Callie to his will the moment he breezed back into her life.

Unfortunately, Gavin currently ruled Darren's personal world and he was obliged to dance to his tune. Nothing lasted forever, though, Darren reminded himself, and his time would come, hopefully before Callie discovered that he was playing both sides against the middle. She would not, he knew, ever forgive him, even if he was able to make her understand that he had no choice in the matter.

* * *

MORE FROM EVIE HUNTER

Another book from Evie Hunter, *The Takedown*, is available to order now here:

www.mybook.to/TakedownBackAD

ACKNOWLEDGEMENTS

My thanks as always to the wonderful Boldwood team and in particular to my eagle-eyed editor, Emily Ruston.

ABOUT THE AUTHOR

Evie Hunter is a British author, who's spent the last twenty years roaming the world and finding inspiration from the places she's visited. She has written a great many successful regency romances as Wendy Soliman but has since redirected her talents to produce dark gritty thrillers.

Sign up to Evie Hunter's mailing list here for news, competitions and updates on future books.

Follow Evie Hunter on social media:

X x.com/wendyswriter
f facebook.com/wendy.soliman.author
BB bookbub.com/authors/wendy-soliman

ALSO BY EVIE HUNTER

Revenge Thrillers

The Sting

The Trap

The Chase

The Scam

The Kill

The Alibi

The Takedown

Dirty Business

The Hopgood Hall Murder Mysteries

A Date To Die For

A Contest To Kill For

A Marriage To Murder For

A Story to Strangle For

PEAKY READERS

GANG LOYALTIES. DARK SECRETS.
BLOODY REVENGE.

A READER COMMUNITY FOR
GANGLAND CRIME THRILLER FANS!

DISCOVER PAGE-TURNING NOVELS
FROM YOUR FAVOURITE AUTHORS
AND MEET NEW FRIENDS.

JOIN OUR BOOK CLUB
FACEBOOK GROUP

BIT.LY/PEAKYREADERSFB

SIGN UP TO OUR
NEWSLETTER

BIT.LY/PEAKYREADERSNEWS

Boldwood

Boldwood Books is an award-winning fiction publishing company seeking out the best stories from around the world.

Find out more at www.boldwoodbooks.com

Join our reader community for brilliant books, competitions and offers!

Follow us
@BoldwoodBooks
@TheBoldBookClub

Sign up to our weekly deals newsletter

https://bit.ly/BoldwoodBNewsletter

Printed in Dunstable, United Kingdom